Copyright Notices

Acknowledgements

This book has been years in the making, if you count all those nights sitting in Blues clubs, soaking up the music, the lore and the ambiance. I've relied on many people for help. Here's just a few of the folks I owe a big debt of gratitude to:

First and forever to Bob Weinberg, who opened so many doors and made so many things possible. My editor and publisher, Tom Strauch, who believed in the Blues. To my parents, who always encouraged the dream.

To the members of my writers' workshop, whose comments made this book far better than I could have on my own: Martin Mundt, Andrea Dubnick, Larry Santoro, and special thanks to John Weagly: without your help, the book would never have made deadline. Also thanks to Becky Maines for outstanding copyediting, and to the Twilight Tales gang for encouragement and support.

Sincere thanks to Mark Skyer, whose comments made the Blues bits more authentic. To biographer Paul Garon, and Suzanne Flandreaux at the Center for Black Music Studies, for invaluable help in tracking down copyrights on songs written in a time when "copyright" was but a vague notion to most Blues performers. And to Bob Koester, for the Blues history lesson so long ago.

To the gang at B.L.U.E.S. on Halsted–my home away from home–Rob, Jami, Jennifers L & H, De, Big Ray, Mark, Diane, P.J., Kathy, Annie, Tom, Bill, Richard, Kristin and all the friendly faces.

And finally, to the many wonderful musicians and Chicago Blues folks: Liz Mandville Greeson and the Blue Points, Bonnie

Lee, "Chick" Rodgers, Barbara LeShoure, "Big Time" Sarah, Nellie "Tiger" Travis, Jimmy Burns and the Jimmy Burns Band, Pinetop Perkins, Billy Branch, Pistol Pete, Carlos Johnson, Chico Banks, Otis Rush, John Primer, Michael Coleman, Kid Dynamite, Giles Corey, Willie Kent, Jimmy Johnson, J.W. Williams, Linsey Alexander, Buddy Guy, Koko Taylor, Frank Pellegrino and Doc, and so many, many others.

This book is dedicated to

Barry Jens
the love of my life and supporter of my dreams.

The blues ain't nothin' but a slow achin' heart disease
Just like consumption, it kills you by degrees

—IDA COX

I.

1981
Preacherman Gets the Blues

Got the Lonesome Blues when my baby said good-bye
Got the Lonesome Blues when my baby said good-bye
If I weren't so mean, I'd sit right down and cry

"Axman, I know it's a lousy guitar, but the contract says you play the first number on the house guitar—that's the way it's gotta be."

"Woman, you don't scare me with your spook stories. You're lucky to get us in here. Me an' the boys got a new album out and a deal goin' with Gibson. Gave me a custom-made guitar; plays sweeter 'n honey. We ain't gonna drive off our audience, opening on that piece of shit. Besides, if someone from Gibson saw me playin' a Fender, they'd cancel the endorsement contract. I ain't gonna risk that money just to pacify your ghost."

The musician looked fine strutting up there on the stage in a silver silk shirt that set off his cocoa-colored skin, black creased pants and cowboy boots polished to a high shine. Axman turned his back on the white club owner and wandered across the stage, blowing through a series of fancy riffs. It was show-off stuff. Frustrated, Miss Sarah ran a hand through her tangled brown hair. The shock of white hair just over her left eye was coarser than the rest, and never stayed in place, but her daughter told her it made her look cool.

"Look, you want to sacrifice a warm-up number, or a whole set?" Miss Sarah said to his back. That turned the young musician around.

"You threatening me, girl?"

Miss Sarah met his dark gaze. "I'm not the one you have to be afraid of."

She turned and walked away.

It was twenty minutes before opening time, but Miss Sarah unlocked the door anyway. She didn't like to see anybody standing out in the rain–with good reason. She struggled to shove the massive oak slab into the corner. Warped by fire, age and rain, she didn't need to prop it open.

The club was located in Lincoln Park; one of Chicago's trendy North Side neighborhoods, filled with your professionals who worked downtown and rented high-priced apartments from an older generation of German immigrants or faceless management companies. It was just a twelve minute cab ride to the Loop, even less to Rush Street. For the most part, Chicagoans left Rush Street to the tourists, sailors and college kids. Cityfolk from the Loop northward, went to Lincoln Park–with its neighborhood pubs and overabundance of quirky restaurants–to play.

The regulars at the Lonesome Blues Pub started filing in, soggy and sloshing in their shoes. Many of them had been regulars back before the fire, when the club had been named Baby Blues. It had been a trendy, glitzy place then, with red Formica tables, that had gold glitter floating under the surface, and tubes of colored neon light that ran in racing stripes across the walls and ceiling. But that had been before the fire that had gutted the place and forced the previous owner to sell. The building's reputation as a Blues club remained, and with the fire, it had gained yet another tourist draw: the ghosts.

Only the shell of the building had survived the fire, and Miss Sarah hadn't had the money to glitz the place up. Though she was already five months pregnant, she had waded into the wreckage with mop, bucket and bleach, then bided her time till she found a neighborhood pub going out of the business. She promptly bought all the secondhand furnishings. The barstools were functional, if well-used. The sturdy wooden bar, shaped like a squatty U, and the massive, oak back-bar, with a mirror and shelves for the liquor bottles, would last a century.

The main room was long and narrow, with the front door leading into the back of the club. She'd situated the bar along the right wall, toward the back. The "bleachers," a section of raised seating fenced off by a wooden rail, sat opposite the bar. She'd hired neighborhood workmen to build a modest stage, just big enough to hold five musicians, with simple box steps leading up to it in front. The bathrooms, and a small area for the musicians to hang out, was located in an alcove behind the stage.

There was nothing fancy about the place, but it had a reputation for good music. The previous owner had passed his contacts list on to her and introduced her around to folks in the industry. After only a few shaky months, the hometown bands and the neighborhood regulars came back to the club.

Miss Sarah turned up B.B. King on the stereo, then set up the early patrons with their first round of the night.

She stocked a full bar, but there wasn't much call for it. A North Side Chicago Blues club had two kind of patrons. The young white professionals, in their fancy suits and loud ties, chugged Miller Lite straight from the bottle. And the old black men in their black felt hats, each with a single gold tooth that flashed when they smiled, ordered double shots of Wild Turkey–"in a snifter, if you please, ma'am."

"Mom, it's raining again, really hard!"

Her daughter, Sally, known around the club as Little Mustang, came bounding over to the waitress station and climbed up on a barstool. At ten years old, her nose barely reached the rail of the bar when she stood up. Her hair was the color of corn on the cob and fell in long curls. She wore blue jeans with red flowers embroidered up the sides and a red pullover with a daisy outlined in glitter on the front. The jeans were already too short on her. Sally had long legs and a gawky stride that would turn graceful as she got older. But for now, she tended to trip over her feet and outgrow her jeans faster than Miss Sarah's sewing machine could fix them.

"Hey, Li'l Mustang!" The grizzled patron winked at her over his snifter.

"Hey, yourself, Old George!"

Old George let out a laugh that was equal parts wheeze and chuckle. He sat in his "reserved" seat, two chairs back of the cash register. The cash register sat at the very center of the length of the bar. Most regulars didn't venture past that point, preferring to linger in back. They left the loud seats up front for the tourists who made it this far north, and the college kids from DePaul. The seat next to him was also on the reserved list. His crony would be in soon, and they'd begin spinning tales, keeping Miss Sarah and the regulars entertained until the music started. The two old men hadn't missed a night since the club opened, except for a three-day hospital spell a year or two back. Miss Sarah never had figured out which one had been the patient, and the old men weren't talking.

Little Mustang slurped at the soda in front of her, digging for the last few drops at the bottom of the glass.

"Sweetheart, how many times have I told you not to do that? It's rude. Why don't you put out the ashtrays and candles for me?"

"'Kay, Mom."

Miss Sarah smiled as her daughter grabbed the stacks of red plastic ashtrays and wound through the maze of tables and barstools, making a production of sliding the ashtrays across the tabletops. They slid to a stop in the very center of the table each time. Little Mustang had plenty of practice at this chore, though it seemed to take her longer to complete the task each time she did it. Not because she was loitering; she stopped to greet each of the regulars by name. She had a way with the customers, better even than Miss Sarah. Perhaps it was the precociousness of youth, but Miss Sarah suspected her daughter simply had a talent that she herself had never grasped.

Miss Sarah had bought the club while she was pregnant. So in a way, she'd started taking the baby to work with her while it was still in the womb. It hadn't seemed a bit odd to continue doing so once Sally was born and she couldn't afford a full-time sitter. She'd grown up on the knees of the Blues greats: Buddy Guy, Koko Taylor, Son Seals, Junior Wells, Lefty Dizz and a host of others. They'd played checkers with her between sets, sung her lullabies, even changed her diapers in an emergency. If the baby started fussing in the middle of a set, all the band had to do was break into a rendition of *Mustang Sally*. It calmed her down and put her to sleep every time. When the musicians weren't playing with Little Mustang, Jayhawk, the house ghost, was.

Old George slurped his whiskey. Miss Sarah was certain he did it on purpose, knowing she couldn't reprimand him. The

Felt Hats doted on Little Mustang. They kept her out of major trouble, but were never slow to encourage her to a bit of mischief.

"Git your picture yet?" Old George asked. A cackle lurked beneath the question. The club walls were rapidly filling up with framed pictures of Little Mustang posing with the guest musicians.

Miss Sarah slapped the wet dishrag onto the bar. "Nope. Don't believe I need a picture of that man on my wall."

Old George arched a crooked eyebrow. "Dat boy givin' you trouble? The spook ain't gonna like dat." He cackled out loud this time. Trouble with the ghosts made for a good show...if you were a spectator. But Miss Sarah always worried when the ghosts started acting up. Someday, somebody was going get hurt. She hoped tonight wouldn't be the night.

Miss Sarah tried to ignore the booming thunder outside as she continued her prep work, quartering limes and dumping cherries and olives into the condiment box. She picked up a bar rag and gave a halfhearted swipe at the wooden counter, taking comfort from the familiar bumps and grooves. She knew it was clean; she'd washed it thoroughly the night before.

She ducked under the bar and went to stand by Carl, who was collecting cover at the door. Carl was a senior at DePaul University with the linebacker build that set the physical standards among bouncers. This was the second night he'd filled in for Mark, the regular guy.

"It's a wicked night, Miss Sarah."

"That it is, Carl." Nervously she scanned the black, billowing clouds backlit by lightning that splintered the sky.

"Doesn't seem to be affecting business though," Carl said, handing her a stack of bills. Little Mustang joined them at the door.

As Miss Sarah left to deposit the cash in the register, Little Mustang whispered to Carl, "Mama doesn't like storms, on account of Daddy."

Carl just said, "Oh," not knowing what the little girl meant. Miss Sarah didn't talk about her dead boyfriend much. Carl was curious, but it felt sleazy to pump a ten-year-old for information.

To Miss Sarah's mind, Little Mustang was still too young to know the whole story. Don had been a computer programmer for IBM, with a fondness, but little talent, for the Blues. He never knew he had a daughter. Drunk on champagne after proposing, he'd dragged his electric guitar out in the rain to serenade her. Don was electrocuted when water seeped into the amplifier and blew several fuses. He'd been playing *Stormy Monday* when he died.

Miss Sarah picked up the PA mike near the back door, switched on the sound and said, "Showtime." She switched the mike off again and watched as the band, all but Axman, left their table near the stage and climbed the steps into the spotlight. She waited till they'd picked up their instruments, then adjusted their mikes to a height slightly different than the one they'd chosen during setup. The second guitarist and bass player strummed their instruments once or twice, to make sure they were still in tune. The drummer beat a quick rat-ta-tat-tat-boom to settle the sticks in his hand. The universal rituals of every live band. Finally, the drummer gave her a nod, indicating they were ready to be announced. Miss Sarah clicked the mike back on. In a voice deeper and more boisterous than her normal speaking tone, she said, "Welcome one and all, Blues fans, to the Lonesome Blues Pub. It's wet outside, but a good drink and a hot band will warm you right up. We've got a rare treat tonight–a band all the way from Tallulha, Mississippi, with a new album, 'Backwater Blues Gonna Get You.' Give a big welcome to Dirtwater Records' recording artist, Sonny 'Axman' Williams and the Delta Backwater Blues Band. Come on! Give it up!" she urged the crowd.

The drummer tapped the countoff with his sticks and the bass, harmonica and rhythm guitar jumped into the opening strains of *Deathbed Blues*.

A chill went down Miss Sarah's spine. She had a bad feeling about the opening number. But Felt Hats were bobbing up and down in approval.

Old George nudged his neighbor. "That boy can blow a harp!"

With a whiskey-and-menthol-aged voice, the drummer growled into the mike.

Man in black came to take my baby away
Man in black came to take my baby away
Kissed her cold lips, spirit had fled at break of day

The band played through three verses and an extended jam, warming the audience up before calling the "star" to the stage.

The drummer growled into the mike, "And now, a man so bad he's scared of hisself. Give it up one time for the Axman!" The guitarist slithered through the crowd and climbed the three steps at the front of the stage. He nodded, cooling acknowledgment of the applause.

Miss Sarah stepped to the end of the bar to give him the evil eye, a silent warning. Axman winked at her. As he reached for the house guitar, Miss Sarah let out the breath she'd been holding.

Feinting left, Axman reached right and picked up his custom-made Gibson.

"You've dug your own grave," Miss Sarah whispered.

The regulars got a firm grip on their glasses and started to mutter.

"The spook's not gonna be happy."

"Jayhawk'll teach 'im."

Miss Sarah moved to fill drink orders.

Carl met her at the counter, handing her more cash. It was standing room only now. She took the money and grimaced. "Just hope you don't have to pass it all back out."

Carl walked back to the door with Little Mustang. "What'd she mean by that?"

"Mama's afraid Jayhawk's gonna get mad. Axman knew the house rules, plus, he was rude to Mama. Jayhawk doesn't like that."

Suddenly the lights flickered.

"Lightning must have hit a circuit breaker," Carl said. The power switches were all in a cabinet behind the bar to prevent mischief or accidents.

"Nah, that's just Jayhawk warming up," the girl said.

Carl wasn't as dumb as he looked, but he wasn't following the conversation. "Who's Jayhawk?"

Little Mustang gave him a look that said, *You're an imbecile.* What she said out loud was, "Jayhawk is the ghost in the guitar."

"There's a ghost in the guitar?" Carl knew he sounded stupid, but he had to ask.

"You've heard of Billy Jay Hawkins?" she asked in a voice that clearly indicated the answer should be *Yes*.

Carl shook his head *No*.

With a sigh that spoke volumes, she put her hands on her hips and explained, "Billy Jay Hawkins, *otherwise* known as Jayhawk, was only *the* best Blues guitar player in Chicago in the '60s. And he played right here in this club–before Mama owned it. Everybody said his last night here was awesome! During the last set, the fire broke out. Everybody was rushin' to get out. He tripped over a power cord and fell off the stage. Some say he impaled himself on a mike stand. Others say it was just his guitar's whammy bar." She sounded disappointed that it might be something so tame. "Anyway, he died right there at the foot of the steps." She leaned between patrons to point to the exact spot.

Some of the Suits standing near the door snickered.

Carl checked over his shoulder. "Where'd you hear that?"

"Old George and Ratman told me," Little Mustang said.

"Does your mom know you're going around telling stories like that?"

Little Mustang gave an indignant shake of her head. "Don't have to go round tellin' it, everybody *else* knows the story."

Mark had warned him strange things went on in the place, but Carl hadn't paid much attention to the warning; he figured the regular doorman was just joshing him. Of course, Mark had looked pretty serious at the time. Carl stuck his hands in his front pockets and hunched his shoulders. "The guitar seems like a grisly souvenir. Why doesn't Miss Sarah just get rid of it?"

"Can't," Little Mustang said. "When Mama bought the club, the guitar was sitting up on the stage. You can move it, but by the next night, it's always back at the same place."

Axman looked out over the audience as his fingers ran through a standard turnaround. He could tell the crowd was restless; there was a low buzz of conversation and folks shuffling in their seats, but he knew his playing wasn't at fault. Perhaps it was the storm, or the spook stories the white woman made up to drum up business. He'd nail down the audience with the second half of the solo. He stepped up to speak into the mike. "That felt so good, think I'll do another." He glanced behind him, making sure the band caught the cue. He repositioned himself so a spotlight was shining directly on his guitar, then tilted the neck of the guitar up to a more dramatic angle, rocking the body back and forth and making a show of his fingerwork, over-emphasizing each movement. White crowds were more impressed with a solo if you made it look hard–didn't matter how hard the riff really was. He lunged forward on his right knee as he launched into a new melody line.

A shriek of feedback shot out of the bass player's amp.

Axman straightened up awkwardly and threw the bass player a look that sent the musician scrambling to adjust the speaker controls.

Little Mustang crossed her arms and leaned against the door post. "That boy sure is slow."

Carl looked around nervously, to see if any of the patrons had heard. "I don't think you ought to be calling the musicians 'boys.'"

"Well, if he acts like an idiot–"

"And," he said more forcefully, "I don't think your mom would appreciate you walking around telling ghost stories; it could be bad for business."

"Stupid musicians are bad for business."

Carl sputtered. "Little Mustang! You better watch your mouth." He felt a hand on his shoulder. It was Ratman, reaching up to calm him down.

It was hard to tell how tall Ratman had been before arthritis crippled him up, but he didn't stand taller than five foot now, from the crown of his broken felt hat to the tip of his scuffed and worn snakeskin boots.

"Li'l Mustang," he rasped at the girl, "you been practicin'?"

"Yup!" She nodded proudly. "Got the G down real good!"

"That's my girl. Run 'long now and he'p your mama, while I talk some sense inta this boy."

"Ratman, you're the best." Little Mustang gave him a quick kiss on the cheek. He returned the affection with a tobacco-stained grin.

He paused deliberately, until the young girl was well out of earshot. He stared at Carl, considering him mightily. Then he patted through his old coat pockets. Ratman's eyes lit up. He pulled his harmonica halfway out of a pocket, shook his head, put it back, and continued searching. Finally, he found the ever-present pack of Kools.

Carl sighed, quietly.

The Felt Hats had a way of taking their time, moving extra slow, that was designed to drive you half crazy. But it also made you relax. You had to; there was no rushing them.

When Ratman was good and ready, he spoke.

"Got a match there, kid?"

Carl sighed again and checked his pockets. He pulled out a pack of matches and lit the old man's smoke.

Axman knew he had them now—there was no more rustling in the crowd, no one weaving through the audience on the way to the john. He smiled slickly, stepped back to widen his stance, fretted up an octave, and prepared to blow the audience away with the sweet, singing high notes that were his trademark.

Then his strings broke; E, B and G, in quick succession.

Axman snarled an obscenity into the mike, and the band shut the song down. He stalked off the stage to a round of applause liberally laced with hooting and laughter.

The drummer leaned into the mike. "Stick and stay, folks. There's lots mo' Blues ta come."

Behind the bar, Miss Sarah quickly fired up the stereo system, slapping in the closest tape at hand.

The Devil gonna take me when I'm gone
Devil gonna get my soul when I'm gone
Been a bad man and done my woman wrong

Miss Sarah shivered. Too many dark implications in the lyrics tonight. But she wouldn't turn off Demon Jack Jenkins.

I shot a man to watch his life leak out
I shot a man to watch his life leak out
In my whole life I ain' had nothin' that I cared about

Some folks said Demon Jack had gained his musical talents by making a pact with the Devil. If there were evil spirits out tonight, it made no sense to offend them by turning off his music.

Carl was too young and inexperienced to be superstitious. "Speaker feedback, broken strings, flickering lights–those things happen at all clubs," he insisted. "You don't have to blame it on a ghost." He was having a hard time believing the stories the Felt Hats were telling him.

"'Course they do, son," Old George assured him. "Things like that happ'n all the time." He chuckled in a way that made Carl squirm.

"But it's the pattern of 'festations, that's what ya gotta watch for," Ratman told the young man.

All three men turned to look at the empty stage. At that moment, the bass player's mike stand toppled sideways into Axman's mike, which fell, dominolike, into the harp player's stand. The tangle of metal poles and wires finally fell off the stage onto the nearest table, sending customers scrambling.

Old George said, "That happens all the time, too, son. I seen it m'self, hunerds of times."

Shit! Miss Sarah thought, then immediately felt guilty; she didn't allow language like that in her bar, not with an impressionable young girl underfoot. But it just *had to be* a table of suits and chicks. She hurried over to help right the table and barstools, and massage shaky nerves.

"Little Mustang!" she yelled toward the bar. "Get six Miller Lites and three glasses!" Chicks always wanted glasses. "And a bar rag!"

"This round's on the house, folks," she told the group, as Little Mustang came over balancing the heavy tray. Miss Sarah helped her slide it on to the table so it wouldn't tip and spill the drinks. As they passed the beer bottles around, Little Mustang said in a stage whisper, "Bet Mom'll even set ya up with a round of shots if you say pretty please." The hint brought a slurred rendition of "Pretty Please!" from the group. Miss Sarah laughed, relieved. They were drunk and having a good time. The accident would be forgotten after another round of drinks. She took their order and headed for the bar.

Miss Sarah set up the shots and gave her daughter the high sign to pick up the tray. She'd let Little Mustang handle the delivery; she'd charm away any leftover shaky nerves. And if it was illegal to let a minor serve alcohol–well, Chicago cops would look the other way in return for a free beer once in a while. The cops knew it was tough for a woman and child to make their way in the world.

Only after the crisis was over, did Miss Sarah stop to chew out Jayhawk. She didn't go anywhere special to do it. He could hear her wherever she was in the bar, and the regulars were used to seeing her talk to the air. She turned her back to the crowd for a semblance of privacy. "I know you're pissed, but what say you don't kill the customers. If the club shuts down, that guitar of yours won't ever get played, now will it?" She got no response. No flicker of lights, no sudden change of music on the stereo. She'd never seen Jayhawk materialize, nor heard him speak; still, she could tell he was sulking. She sighed. It was time to see if she could negotiate with the other side in this conflict.

Carrying a tray of complimentary drinks, she stopped at the band's table. "You boys have a good sound. You *could* have a really good night here."

"Get that spook of yours under control, woman!" Axman said in a surly voice.

Miss Sarah sighed. The man was young, talented and cocky. And now he had a major record deal. It'd be years before he'd unplug his ears to a bit of advice. "He's not a pet," Miss Sarah said. "Do one number on his guitar, and he'll leave you alone. That's not asking so much. Some of the old-timers even think it's lucky. When Lefty Dizz played here, he'd do a whole set on it. Said all his gigs after that were twice as good. Came back whenever he thought his luck was changing."

The guitar player spun around on his seat and tried to push past her. "Save the ghost stories for the toorists, woman. I got fans to greet."

Miss Sarah stood her ground, blocking his exit through the narrow aisle between tables. "Suit yourself, Axman. But Freddy 'Flyin' Fingers' Wilson copped an attitude, too. Came in here talkin' trash, refused to play Jayhawk's guitar."

The drummer piped up, "He walked out of here with a bunch of bruises and a sprained wrist. Couldn't play for a week."

Axman sneered at him. "White woman got you spinnin' tales for the toorists, too. But who's signin' your checks, man? Best remember that."

Miss Sarah tugged at the white lock of hair that fell over her left eye, a nervous habit. "I don't know for sure if Jayhawk hurt Fly Wilson, or if Fly just got shook up so bad he tripped. Believe what you want...but don't think three strings and a couple mike stands are his limit."

"He gonna hurt me? 'Cause you tell him to?" Axman's words were more of a challenge than a question. The guitarist feigned a broad step forward, like he was gonna knock her over.

Miss Sarah didn't even flinch.

"He's never hurt anyone, yet. But he's got the power to." She turned and looked pointedly toward the bar, where Jayhawk was floating glasses and pouring drinks. The guitarist followed her gaze.

"Boo! All these ghost stories and it ain't even Halloween," he said. This time Axman did step forward, so close that their bodies brushed against each other.

Miss Sarah crossed her arms, but stepped aside.

"So, Jayhawk's pretty P.O.'d tonight, huh?" Carl asked the old men. A look of uncertainty had crept into his eyes.

The bouncer had wandered over to the old mens' seats at the bar. He stood so he could keep one eye on the door and still talk to them.

"Hell no, son!" Old George gave the bouncer a good-natured slap on the back. "Jayhawk's jez teasin', now. Givin' the guy *time* ta mend his ways. If the kid picks up the guitar next set, ev'r-thing'll be all right."

"And if he doesn't?" A tremor had crept into Carl's voice.

"Well then, we'll see what we does see," Ratman said, nodding to himself.

"Why, I heard one time, Old Snake Eyes Thompson–they called him Snake Eyes 'cause he had a bad wanderin' eye, ya see, so's when ya looked at him, it 'peared he 'as lookin' in two different directions 'twonce," Old George said, rubbing his gnarled hands together with gusto. "Anyways, he and his band 'as in here. They'd jez made their second record, an' they 'as actin' like big shots. Wouldn't let anyone sit in with them, wouldn't play Jayhawk's guitar, hittin' on all the women–"

"Includin' Miss Sarah," Ratman added.

"Jayhawk, he specially don't like that," Old George explained. "They 'as just making a general nuisance of 'emselves."

"Tha's 'bout right," Ratman said.

The young bouncer was perfectly caught in the old men's double-barreled storytelling.

"Well, what happened?" Carl demanded.

"They 'as killed," Old George said, matter-of-fact.

"Oh, Jayhawk toyed with them first," Ratman said. "Mike stands fallin', speakers cuttin' in 'n out, every string on stage broke: bass, lead, rhythm guitars."

"And fiddle," Old George said.

"That's right," Ratman nodded, recalling. "The strings broke, even the spares in the cases."

"Yessir!" Old George agreed. "They went to put the spares on an' they 'as no good, comin' straight out ta packet."

"Jayhawk was flashin' lights, flippin' mikes off and on, even locked one of the fellas in the john. Then..." Ratman dropped his voice to a whisper.

Carl and Old George leaned closer to hear the rest of the story. "Durin' the last set, old Jayhawk, he just up and quit. Din do nothin'. By that time, the musicians were so rattled they couldn't hardly play a lick. They jus' kept waitin' for somethin' to go wrong."

"Never did," Old George said.

"No sir," Ratman declared. "Not till they was on their way home."

"Then what happened?" Carl squeaked.

Ratman pulled out a cigarette and searched his pockets for a pack of matches. Impatient, Carl offered the man a light. His hand shook ever so slightly as he held the match.

"Why, they was killed," Ratman said finally. "Van hit a slippery patch, spun outta control and ran into a ditch."

"That's it?" Carl couldn't keep the disappointment out of his voice. "They died in a car accident?"

"That wasn't what killed 'em," Old George said, shaking his head.

"No?"

"Nah," Old George said. "Their 'quipment did it. The amps and speakers stacked in the rear of the van slid forward. Police found 'em with their skulls crushed. Old Snake Eyes' eyeballs had popped out. They was sittin' up there on the dash, pretty as you please, lookin' round."

Ratman snorted.

"Jayhawk got those boys in the end," Old George assured Carl.

"'Course, them things do happen," Ratman added.

Carl was feeling equal parts scared and foolish. But he didn't have time to think about it; the old men had already launched into their next story.

The bassist laid down a standard walking line. The drummer softly filled with his brushes on cymbal and snare. The harp blew a lonesome riff. The band in sync, the drummer called Axman to the stage. "And now, ladies and gentlemen, won't cha welcome back a man who learned to play guitar sittin' atop a tombstone in a Delta graveyard at midnight, Mr. Sonny 'Axman' Williams."

The applause was sparse, but the band didn't let on like they noticed.

"Thank you!" Axman called to the crowd, trying to hide just how thankful he was that they hadn't cleared out after the first set.

"If ya'll been outside tonight, and we know you have, then you know what we're talking about when we say...we got *The Wet Weather Blues.*"

When Miss Sarah heard the title of the song, she gave her nerves up as a lost cause and poured herself a double shot of Southern Comfort, slugged it back and poured herself another.

Old George and Ratman hadn't had this much fun since they'd hid Sugar Blue's remote mike in the tank of the women's john.

"Sing it one time!" Axman called to the band.

Rain and hail beating on my back
Can't find no shelter, now that's a fact
Rainin' so hard, that I can't see
The Wet Weather Blues is drownin' me

In the corner of his eye, Carl saw a tall, stern-looking man stride through the door. The massive oak slab slammed shut behind him.

Carl looked uncertainly between the door and the new patron. Decision made, he moved to get the money from the man since he was already inside. Ratman and Old George grabbed on to his elbows. Carl could have carried them across the whole bar, frail as they were, but he'd gotten in the habit of listening to what they said.

"Boy, don't you know *nothin'?*" Old George asked.

"Ya don' pass the collection plate to th' Preacherman," Ratman said.

There was fear in the old men's eyes and voices. Carl decided anything they were scared of, scared him, too.

Ratman felt a tug at his sleeve. It was the little one. "Li'l Mustang, git behind your Ma now, you hear?"

She nodded, solemnly, and slipped into the crowd.

The band played on.

Preacherman stood, framed by the oak door, willow-thin and unnaturally tall, a perfect replica of the old-time, backwoods parson. Round-brimmed, black felt hat, black frock coat buttoned up the front, with long black tails flapping behind. Legs too long and eyes cold as hellfire, Preacherman didn't look all human. But he did look mean.

Preacherman stood, waiting for his presence to seep out in front of him, quietly tapping on a body's shoulder, table by table, whispering in the ear, saying, *"Preacherman is here."*

The crowd parted for the newcomer. Miss Sarah got a good look at him through the corridor of bodies. The man was completely dry, despite the storm outside.

The stranger thumbed the brim of his hat at her. Miss Sarah nodded stiffly. She didn't care much for the red glint in his eye. She moved to help Carl reopen the door.

Axman felt the change in the room. He cursed the ghost and kept on playing–he'd be damned if he was gonna let a spook steal his crowd.

He didn't know the danger that came in with that thought.

Miss Sarah watched as Carl kicked a wedge under the door. No gust of wind had blown that old door shut. She turned to find the black-clad stranger standing behind her. His face was deathly pale. Miss Sarah took two steps back before nodding at the man.

His head bobbed and swayed reptilianlike. When he spoke, his voice sounded like the belly of a snake slithering over loose gravel. "I hear this club harbors a spirit."

His eyes flashed with accusation.

Axman's amp, a top of the line Twin Reverb, cut out for the third time in minutes, as he led into the intro of *Hoochie Coochie Man*. He wanted to slam his boot through the amp, but that might scuff the polish on his boot. Instead, he slammed his guitar into its stand and jumped from the stage to the barroom floor. With a silent apology to Muddy Waters, the drummer closed down the song.

Axman tried to brush past the stranger standing at the foot of the steps.

"Ahhh, sssson," Preacherman said, "perhaps it would be a convenient time for a guest to play a song or two?"

"You can sit in with the band if you want–if the damned spook will let you do anything," Axman growled over his shoulder.

"I do not think he will bother me," Preacherman said to himself.

The crowd was quiet as the stranger climbed the steps. The parson's hat and long, black tails were set off by the glare of the spot; shifting figures of shadows and light.

The drummer had a bad feeling, as he covered his mike and leaned forward to quiz the guest.

"Mama, that man's gonna play Jayhawk." Little Mustang stood on her tiptoes to peek over the bar. She hoisted herself up to sit on the beer cooler, so she could see better.

Miss Sarah decided she'd been too quick to judge the stranger. "Maybe things will quiet down a little."

Blond curls bouncing, Little Mustang shook her head and kicked her heels against the cooler. She said in a singsong voice, "I don't think so."

The Preacherman plucked a couple of chords, testing the action of the old guitar, then rambled through a series of arpeggios. The house lights flickered and dimmed, though no human hand had touched the switch.

Finally, the wandering intro led into a gritty rendition of Lightnin' Sam Hopkins' *Long Way From Home*. A smattering of applause broke out as members of the crowd recognized the song.

As the Preacherman filled out the first verse, the silver tips of his boots began to glow. He played with a delicate touch, but there was a cruelty in his movements.

Ask any musician, they'll tell you guitars have a mystical quality and seem to take on a life of their own. They become a partner in a great performance, your closest friend. Preacherman played the house guitar with a viciousness few had ever seen. Still, the playing was masterful, with an infectious rhythm that couldn't be ignored.

By the end of the number, white chicks were dancing in the aisle, the speakers hadn't cut out once, and the house guitar had never sounded so good.

Sitting at the band table, Axman was happy; somebody else had played the spook's guitar. Now he could go finish the set. He strapped on his guitar as the band brought the song to a close. The applause was enthuisastic and wild, louder and longer then any he'd received tonight. Axman felt a stab of jealousy, but shook it off. The crowd hasn't really heard yet what he could do when he was warmed up and not fighting the interference of a ghost. His next set would blow the audience away, and put this parson in his proper place. He motioned for the Preacherman to sit in with him for another number.

Preacherman nodded stiffly.

Tradition said when a guest earned that kind of reception, you gave him another solo number before taking back the bandstand, but Axman didn't care. It was the second set and he still hadn't had a chance to show his stuff. Besides, the ghost hadn't interfered with the guest once. That was more than he'd had. He gave guest's choice on the next tune to pacify the man.

There was a malicious glint in the Preacherman's eyes as he said, "Don't suppose a young punk like you even knows *Satan Came Walking*."

It was an obscure song, but Axman had made a study of Blues tunes featuring the Devil. Bands could build a myth, a reputation, around songs like that. The man had been hoping to show him up. Careful not to stand where the mike could pick him up, Axman shot back, "I reckon I can play it better'n you." He took pleasure at the surprise on the Preacherman's face.

"We'll see, son. We'll see." Preacherman nodded to the drummer to count off the song, and stepped up to take lead on the first verse.

> *Satan came walking up to my front door*
> *Satan came walking up to my front door*
> *Said, "Son, what are you waiting for?"*

Between verses, Preacherman took the first solo, fancying up the riff before he threw it to Axman. It was a standard variation, Axman had no problem echoing it. Adding a twist at the end he tossed it back, then stepped forward for his turn at the mike. But Preacherman wasn't finished, he did a more intricate variation on Axman's riff. By the time Preacherman brought the solo to a close, his fingertips were glowing red. The crowd applauded the winner of the first round of the duel.

Little Mustang was studying the red indicator lights on the amplifier behind the bar. When she was an infant, Jayhawk had kept her amused for hours making intricate patterns with the flashing lights. Tonight, the volume and tone levels were turned as high as they would go, but only four of the eight rows of lights were lit.

> *I said, "Oh Devil, you must have it wrong."*
> *Said, "Oh Devil, you must have it wrong.*
> *I ain't been on this earth very long."*

Miss Sarah had three taps running as she lined up a row of shot glasses on a tray. She used her forearm to pop all three taps off just as the glasses began to overflow.

"Mama, Jayhawk doesn't—"

Miss Sarah snapped, "Sally! Can't you see I'm busy?" Customers were lined up three rows deep trying to fight their way to the bar. "It's way past your bedtime. Go on into the office and get ready. I'll be in to tuck you in, soon as things slow down."

She'd kept a crib, now a trundle bed, in the office for the

little girl from the day the club had opened. Sally was used to the noise, and had no problem falling asleep while the music played. There was a local cab driver who loved the Blues, and made the club part of his regular territory. In return for free admission and all the coffee he could drink, he gave mother and daughter a free ride home each night. With years of practice, Miss Sarah could sleepwalk Sally out to the cab, up to the apartment and into her bed, without the girl ever fully waking up. It wasn't the ideal way for a little girl to get the sleep she needed at night—but it beat the alternatives.

"But Mama, it's *Friday*, and Jayhawk—"

"To bed, now! Jayhawk will just have to take care of himself." Miss Sarah turned to help the next impatient customer.

Little Mustang's eyes filled with tears as she watched the fifth row of lights slowly fade out. She took a last look at her mama, then slid down from the cooler and went looking for Ratman and Old George.

On stage a cymbal flared.

The Preacherman was showing off mightily, bending strings and hamming up the least little curlicue of music. Axman decided it was time to show folks who was in charge of this show. There were rules of protocol in the music world, that governed who played when, and who took the lead, and who played support, and how long each man played, and when you ended the dueling and pulled back together, as friends, to finish the song. But now, the rules had been thrown out. They launched into a no-holds-barred duel to a musical death.

Strings flashed and speakers whined. Electricity crackled through the air.

The drummer muttered a little prayer to himself, but kept playing, as he watched his spare sticks float past his head.

Ratman and Old George were in the back corner, deep in their snifters of whiskey, mumbling between themselves.

"Shoulda known the Preacherman would be out in a storm like this," Ratman worried. "Ain't seen him around these parts since Blind Boy Richards died."

"Now there 'as a man din wanna go," Old George chortled.

"Watch what you say!" Ratman snapped. "Lessun you feeling

particularly lucky, I wouldn't be insultin' spirits tonight."

"That's not Jayhawk playin'," Little Mustang said, suddenly, as she popped into sight. Only her golden curls, bright eyes and the tip of her nose appeared over the table.

The old men jumped, their whiskeys splashing.

Ratman said, "Child, you just scared a year of life offen me. And I haven' got it to spare."

"Goes double for me," Old George said. "Looky at that, don't she look just like those Kilroy faces we used to scrawl on the walls in dubya dubya two? Don' she, just? Those 'Kilroy was here' signs scared more'n a few of them Japs. Course, Kilroy had a longer nose 'n she does an' didn' have no hair–"

Ratman shook his head. "We ha'n't got time for your tall tales."

Old George rambled on.

Ratman took a good look at the girl and saw the fear leaking out of her eyes. He patted the barstool beside him. "Climb up here where we can see you."

Little Mustang pushed the barstool even closer to him, then scrambled up.

Satan said, "You lived fast and hard.
You got three bodies buried in your backyard."

The old oak door slammed shut. Again. Miss Sarah was busy at the bar. Carl fought to open it by himself this time. Despite his two hundred and fifty pounds of muscles, he was having no luck.

Miss Sarah tried for the third time to pour a shot of Jack for a customer. The shot glasses kept floating away.

"Jayhawk, I've had about enough of this foolishness," Miss Sarah told the ghost.

The Suit was getting more desperate for his drink. Miss Sarah knew he needed it for courage. But courage to stay or courage to go, she didn't know. She took a look at the fear in his face and decided her resolve could use some stiffening, too. She set two more shot glasses on the bar.

"Hold on to those," she told the Suit.

The man clutched the glasses firmly. She poured them both

a double.

"That's on the house, friend."

Killed the man that done my sweet woman wrong
'Twas just bad luck the others came along

"He's killing Jayhawk," Little Mustang told the old men, with a seriousness beyond her years.

Ratman and Old George nodded in agreement.

"Reckon so," Old George said.

"What are we gonna do?" Little Mustang prodded the conversation along.

Ratman took a long, slow look around the club.

With a hand curled by arthritis, Ratman gestured toward Carl, who was still fighting to open the door. "Ta start with," he said finally, "tell that fool ta come over here, 'for he hurts hisself."

Little Mustang went and brought the bouncer back.

Axman and the harmonica player had teamed up against Preacherman, but they were still losing the duel, badly.

When Preacherman grabbed the riff, Axman stepped back to complain to his drummer. "It's not right, embarrassin' a man on stage–front of people!"

"Some men is like that," the drummer told him. "It's nothin' you won't live through."

"Gonna send the man back to the woods till he learns some club etiquette!" the guitarist insisted.

"Steady, Axman," but he was already gone. The drummer shook his head, throwing sweat in both directions, then growled to himself, "Can't cool a temper in heat like this."

With a roundhouse step that nearly tripped both guitarists and threatened to send them tumbling off the riser, Axman reclaimed center stage. In an un-Blueslike manner, he borrowed a move from Pete Townsend and swung his arm wildly, windmill fashion, jamming out a trio of power chords.

Preacherman gave an evil grin, stepped around the young guitar player, and threw his arm up preparing for a wildmill swing of his own. For a breathless second, his arm hung in the air and the audience held its breath.

Devil said, "Come on son, it's time to go
I got other souls waitin', don't you know?"

Claws scratched across strings. Claws that had sprouted in the flicker of time it took the Preacherman's arm to fall to the strings. The searing chord blasted through the amp. Fire spewed out the speaker's mouth.

The blast blew Axman clean off the stage.

"Believe it's time we did something 'bout that man," Ratman said to his conspirators.

They watched the patrons picking themselves up from the table that had collapsed and ended the Axman's flight.

"I could turn off the power," Carl offered. "The switches are just behind the bar."

"Well, *do* it, son," Old George told him. Wheezing, the old man eased himself to the floor.

"Where do ya think you're goin'?" Ratman asked him.

"Thought I'd pull the plug tat the wall," Old George said. "I reckon a little ol' flipped switch ain't gonna stop the Preacherman none."

Ratman nodded. "Jus' don't go gettin' yerself hurt."

Little Mustang turned to her friend. "What can I do?"

"You stay here with me, li'lun. We'll be the reinforcements," he said softly.

The drummer gave a sickly smile to Old George, who'd sneaked around back of the stage. The musician couldn't do much more: demon faces had appeared on the heads of his drums. They were talking to him.

"...then we'll take your guts, dry them across rusty steam pipes and string the Preacherman's guitar with them. Then, we'll..."

"I hear ya! I hear ya!" he bawled.

The drummer was playing for his life.

Miss Sarah had no chance to see what was happening on stage. The crowd at the bar was thicker than August mosquitoes and all clammering for drinks. She was trying to anchor down the pint and rocks glasses, she'd given up on the liquor bottles. They floated in a perfect circle above her head, following her as she moved up and down the bar.

Miss Sarah wondered if Jayhawk was controlling the crowd somehow, sapping their fear away. Then decided, nah, they stayed for the same reason people chased ambulances or went to horror movies–for the thrill of it.

Miss Sarah gave him a brief nod as Carl squeezed behind her and pulled open the power box. The indicator lights on the amp were already out, though the levels should have been shooting off the scales, but he didn't have time to worry about that.

He flipped off all the switches. The music continued to blare. He flicked them all on, then off again. The lights didn't even dim.

Behind the stage, Old George had eased himself over to the power outlet and levered himself to his knees. His hand reached for the surge protector as the Preacherman spotted him.

Preacherman let out a roar, *"We're bound for the fires of hell burnin' down below!"* A bolt of lightning flashed through the club and hit the stage.

Old George was knocked out the alley door.

Carl was thrown over the bar.

A great ring of fire shot up to circle the stage.

Patrons scrambled away from the burning tongues.

A gleaming, flame-licked guitar rose slowly up out of a chasm that had erupted in the stage floor.

"Got the Me and the *Devil* Blues," Preacherman crowed. He flung the old guitar into the fire and reached to claim the demon gift.

Ratman turned to his best friend in all the world. "Li'l Mustang, you 'fraid of hellfire?"

Little Mustang shook her head *No.*

"Well then," Ratman said, and sighed, "I ain't either. Reckon it's time we showed tha' Old Devil how ta play the Blues."

Little Mustang hopped down and waited as he eased himself off the barstool. Then the little girl took the old man's hand. They walked down the aisle, as fast as Ratman's arthritis would allow.

"Sally!" Miss Sarah screamed as she saw her daughter walk into the ring of hellfire at the base of the stage. "Oh my God! Stop her!" With a sweep of her arm, she cleared the collection of bottles and empty glasses from the bar. She hitched one leg up on the cooler and hoisted her other knee onto the bar to climb over.

Carl grabbed her by the waist and pulled her back.

She turned around and slammed her fists into his chest. "Let me go! I've got to save her!"

"You can't," he said gruffly, and pulled her closer into a bear hug. "You've got to trust the old man."

"We're going to die. We're all going to die!" she wailed.

The demon band shrieked in acknowledgment.

"I've got to get to my daughter!" She began fighting again, and nearly slipped out of his grip.

"Miss Sarah, you can't. Old George said only the righteous can pass through!"

She screamed, "And Ratman's righteous?"

"Are you?"

She sobbed.

The hair on Ratman's arm sizzled and burned away. He looked down at the little girl to check on her. She'd come through the fire fine. Though her golden curls were singed, she didn't seem worried. She looked up at him, her blue eyes full of trust.

She slipped her hand out of his, then bent to search through the flames for Jayhawk's discarded guitar. Her hands lit on it and she picked it up. The white finger-guard had a long black scorch. She rubbed at it with her sleeve. Then she slung the strap over her neck and struggled the guitar into position. The instrument was almost as big as she was.

Together, Little Mustang and Ratman climbed the steps of the stage.

Preacherman was caught up in an unholy rapture as flames crawled up the tails of his coat. His guitar screamed. A hellish band—all tails, pointy ears and claws—could be seen in the flickering flames.

Unnoticed, Little Mustang plugged her guitar into an amp.

Ratman pulled an old rusty harp out of his coat pocket. Ratman whispered to the little girl, "Why don' we show this man where *we're* from?"

With a deliberateness born of too-little fingers and not enough practice, Little Mustang strummed out the opening chords of *Sweet Home Chicago*.

Through the wailing screams of the demon band, the terrified patrons at the front tables could just make out the words being sung by the unlikely duo.

Baby don't you wanna go, to that California place
Sweet home Chicago.

The front tables cheered the hometown anthem and picked up the beat.

Little Mustang gained her confidence as they moved into the verse. She'd been over this part hundreds of times. This was how Ratman and Buddy and Koko had taught her addition, subtraction and the multiplication tables–the easy ones, anyway.

Still pounding with one hand, the drummer shoved his mike in front of her. She squinted into the spotlight and wished she could wave at her mama, but she'd lose her place if she lifted her hand from the guitar. Little Mustang sang,

One an' One is Two
Two an' Two is Four
One thing is for certain
Don't want the Devil playin' here no more

Ratman let out a cackle.

Preacherman played on against their tune. But he'd lost some of his fire.

Little Mustang had a handle on the chord progressions now. She winked at the old man. Ratman lowered his harp and took a turn at the lyrics. He rasped,

Said, Four and Four is Eight
An' Eight and Two is Ten
Old evil Preacherman
Ain't gonna know where he's been

"Whatcha say, Little Mustang?"
And Little Mustang said,

Two and Two is Four
And Three and Two is Five
Ratman, Me and Jayhawk,
We're gettin' out of here alive

The crowd was with them now, clapping in time and cheering them on. The old oak door creaked open an inch, as the hellfires started to burn down.

The demons were starting to lose their grip on the drum heads. The drummer just laughed and beat the hell out of 'em. The crowd joined in on the chorus.

"Come on Baby, don't you wanna go, back—"

"Where?" Ratman prompted the crowd.

They roared the answer, *"Sweet home Chicago."*

The fiery chasm gurgled and belched, then seemed to reverse itself: instead of billowing sulfur and flame, it began to suck the denizens of Hell back home.

Preacherman began his slow descent into Hell, still clutching the gleaming guitar. The pit slurped up the last of the hellfires, then the chasm closed.

The stage was scorched but solid.

Little Mustang was still playing Jayhawk's guitar for all she was worth. She could feel the spook stirring, gaining strength.

"One more time," Little Mustang called to Ratman.

Ratman took a long look at the cheering crowd, then turned back to Little Mustang.

"I'll do it—for you," Ratman said. With a growl from the back of his throat, he sang,

Eight and Eight is Sixteen
And twice that is Thirty-two
Shore 'nough there, folks
We done give the Devil the Blues

Miss Sarah had to kick the crowd out an hour later, after a final set. Ratman played his harp, Little Mustang sang back up, and Axman played Jayhawk's guitar. Miss Sarah sat at the end of the bar with Carl and watched the show. They had to duck their heads ever, so often, as Jayhawk floated the stray glasses back to the sink.

Finally, Miss Sarah insisted they had to go home. Ratman and Old George were at the tail-end of the line, as the crowd filed out. They shrugged into their coats then stopped to say good night.

Old George shook her hand. "Miss Sarah, you sure do know how ta put on a show!"

Ratman winked. "See ya all tomorrow night."

As the group wandered into the night, Jayhawk made the lights wink back.

You may be wondering why Robert Johnson described Chicago as "that California Place." California had long been known as a land of milk and honey, a Promised Land. In the South, at that time, mechanization was eliminating the fieldhand jobs, and Blacks were being put out of work. But California was a long ways away. The *Chicago Defender*, a Black national newspaper, put out the call to Blacks living down South to come to Chicago, where there was a shortage of labor and high-paying factory jobs waited. Chicago became the new Promised Land, the new California, where dreams could come true.

II.

1989
Miss Sarah Leaves the Blues Behind

The brand new, sleek, black, Cadillac sat at the curb, muffler growling, machine and driver both eager to hit the road.

Miss Sarah stood, one patent leather pump on the sidewalk, one on the street. The skirt of her new dress waved gently in the breeze, as if it too were eager to be off. A faded suitcase sat on the sidewalk beside her. As the engine revved again, her eyes turned to the dark, handsome man who sat in the driver's seat, fingers drumming a be-bop rhythm on the steering wheel. She willed her hand to reach for the glittery silver door handle on the car–to reach toward a shiny silver future–but it was as if a ghostly pair of hands had taken hold of her shoulders. Reluctantly, her body turned around.

Behind the dusty frame window of the club stood her daughter, arms crossed, eyes scowling, tear tracks glistening on her cheeks.

A girl who never frowned once, in all the years she'd been kept up late by the music, pestered by the drunks, tormented by the ghosts.

A girl with golden curls, a new gold tooth and six pairs of snakeskin boots.

A girl who'd been bartending since she was thirteen–cops paid no never-mind to a widow woman and her child trying to make a mostly-honest life in a cold, hard world.

A girl who had nothing but a smile for musician, patron and ghost alike, but had nothing but a scowl for this handsome

Cadillac-driving man who offered a better life for mother and daughter far away from this city, far away from the memories and far away from the ghosts.

A daughter who might never speak to her mother again.

The muffler growled, the daughter scowled, the silver door handle beckoned. And Miss Sarah stood, with one foot in the gutter and one foot on the curb, and pondered what to do...

The Blues ain't nothing but a woman cryin'
She caught the one she loves most lyin'

Little Mustang, who wasn't so little anymore, had just finished fiddling with the knobs on the soundboard for the band's mike check and was ducking toward the door, when her mother called out, "Little Mustang, why don't we get a picture before it gets busy?"

The girl closed her eyes and sighed. If she'd just been a moment quicker. "Mama, it's *Mustang*, not *Little Mustang*, and there's no more room on the walls!"

"Don't be silly, there's always room for one more picture," her mother said.

But the girl spoke the truth; every inch of wall space in the club was covered with framed black and white photographs, all of them featuring Little Mustang and a guest musician. Little Mustang as a babe still in diapers, perched on the neck of Lefty Dizz's guitar, her legs dangling down over the frets. Little Mustang as a toddler, seated behind the drum kit, banging the sticks down on the cymbals behind Big Time Sarah. Little Mustang as a girl of fourteen, singing a duet with Barkin' Bill.

She'd been a cute, precocious child, popular with the musicians and patrons alike. Now just weeks away from turning eighteen, the precocious nature was turning rebellious, always pushing, testing the limits. She'd traded in her white dresses and pink bows for skin-tight black jeans, snakeskin boots and clingy silk shirts in a neon rainbow of colors.

It was all too flashy, too *ethnic*; not proper for a teenaged, white daughter of a single mother. They were all alone in this world. Miss Sarah had kept them safe by keeping her head down, her words soft and her actions demure. The world had a way of slapping down those who strutted around.

Miss Sarah's one indulgence was the pictures. She pulled her ancient camera, complete with the giant reflecting bowl for the flash, from under the counter. It'd belonged to a newspaper once; she'd bought it at a church rummage sale.

Liz Mandville Greeson, the frontwoman for the Blue Points, called from the stage, "C'mon, Little Mustang. You know your mama's not gonna let us go till we get this picture. And me an' the boys want to grab some supper before the first set."

Little Mustang rolled her eyes but trudged up the steps.

Miss Sarah shot the singer a grateful look. Liz was another white girl tryin' to make her way in the world of Blues. Perhaps ten years older than her daughter, the singer had taken Little Mustang under her wing. And while she'd been a less-than positive influence on her daughter's fashion choices– "Make it short, make it shiny and give it fringe," Liz liked to say–Miss Sarah supposed a young, red-headed Blues singer had to capitalize on what assets she could. After all, most folks expected Blues musicians to be old, black and male.

"Why don't we get you girls with your guitars?" Miss Sarah suggested, to appease her daughter. She knew Little Mustang had been trying to slip out to steal a little practice time before the club opened.

Little Mustang slung Jayhawk's guitar over her neck left-handed, so that it hung upside down, Jimi Hendrix style. She fretted through several chords. She'd learned to play two songs upside down, wrong-handed. Though privately, Miss Sarah didn't think she played them all that well, the gimmick was a crowd-pleaser. The two girls crossed their guitar necks like dueling Tommy guns and launched into the opening bars of Hendrix's *Red House*.

They quit as soon as they heard the flash pop.

"How 'bout one more, for good measure?"

Little Mustang already had her guitar in the stand. "Mama, you got your picture. Let the band go eat."

Miss Sarah stowed her camera and cast about for undone work. She spotted the whole limes on the counter and smiled; any excuse to keep Little Mustang behind. "Honey, will you cut up–" but her daughter was gone.

Miss Sarah was alone with the ghosts.

The Blues ain't nothin' but a good woman feelin' bad
Seems like good times ain't never been had

Miss Sarah brought the butcher knife down hard, slicing through the tender flesh of the lime and thudding deep into the wooden cutting board. It sent a jolt of pain through her hand; the arthritis that had crippled the women of her family for generations was kicking up more often these days. She knew better than to make such extreme movements, such strong demands on her hands. But she was angry at Little Mustang for leaving her alone, and angry that she was afraid, constantly afraid, in her own bar.

It hadn't always been like this. She knew, before she signed the final sale papers, that the club was haunted. But Jayhawk was...harmless. Helpful, even. Other ghosts had come in occasionally, ghosts of Chicago Blues musicians, mostly. Jayhawk had kept them in line and they'd been a tourist draw. Miss Sarah hadn't been fond of the ghosts, would rather her club didn't have that sort of distinction, but it had seemed innocent.

Until that night, when everything had changed. When she'd watched her daughter walk into a ring of hellfire. If Little Mustang and Ratman had lost, Jayhawk wouldn't have been the only soul forfeit.

Miss Sarah had fended off drunks and mashers and coked-up college kids. She'd stopped bikers from brawling in her bar, stood up to drug dealers who wanted to sell their junk in her club, even run off some small-time hoods who had tried to extort protection money. There wasn't a living thing that she feared.

But oh, how she feared the dead. How she feared death. Ever since she'd seen the hellfire and realized Heaven and Hell were real, she feared that when her day of judgement came, her soul would be found wanting. And most of all, she feared the hungry, greedy need she saw in the eyes of the ghosts. She knew with all her heart that their sole purpose on earth was to steal the life of the living. And if sometimes they came into the club just to have a beer and relax, that only meant they were taking some time off from the project.

She didn't fear Jayhawk. But she feared that he could no longer protect her and her daughter. He'd never quite recovered from his battle with the Preacherman, never gotten his strength back. He seemed to get weaker with each passing year, as if he was fading.

As Jayhawk lost his strength, Little Mustang gained power. Her presence, even just the sound of her voice, could control the ghosts. It was an unconscious power. Her daughter never had to exert her will. She never had to fight them, never realized they were a threat. So, she could not understand her mother's fear. And Miss Sarah could never bring herself to tell Little Mustang that the ghosts behaved very differently when she wasn't here.

Miss Sarah had been afraid to be alone in the club, afraid of what the ghosts would do when her daughter wasn't there, for years. Eight years.

It hadn't been an issue when Little Mustang was younger. Miss Sarah wouldn't let the girl roam the streets or sit home alone; so the girl was always at the club. Now that she was older, she wanted to explore the world, wanted to spend her nights off with friends, wanted to come in late when she didn't have to work the early shift. More and more, Miss Sarah was alone with the ghosts. She didn't want to shackle her daughter to the club. But the torments they devised grew worse each day.

Tendrils of white mist crawled up the basement stairs like a severed hand. One finger reaching for a tenuous hold, the others scrambling up behind. As it reached the top step it paused, resting, before it scrabbled across the open floor, an army of white whisps snaking through the air.

Miss Sarah felt the mist wrapping cold fingers around her ankle, trying to climb higher up her calf. She let out a sob, then pushed her hand to her mouth and bit down on her fist. Crying only encouraged them. She'd make no sound.

Though the sun wouldn't go down for another hour yet, the windows darkened like a storm had squatted down and hovered outside. Miss Sarah hit the light switches, but the bulbs only flickered like little candle flames.

A wind moved through the bar, though Miss Sarah knew no door or window was open. It wailed and cried and sang of death.

It whipped at her face, and at her bare arms. A second sob escaped, and she heard an evil voice cackle at the victory. But she didn't have to listen to the wind's song. Fear buckled her knees; using the wooden bar as a crutch, she hobbled to the tape player. The mist muffled the uneven click of her one-inch heels.

Sitting atop the stereo was a homemade tape, Little Mustang's new demo, the first song: *Blue Monday* in jump style. The lively swing music and her daughter's voice would chase these demons away.

The mist thickened, it had climbed as high as her waist now, and threatened to flow over the bar.

Her hands fumbled with the plastic case and she nearly dropped the tape; it was slippery, as if it or her hands had been dunked in oil. She juggled it to the player, savagely poked at the button that released the hungry mouth, slotted the tape in and slammed the tape tray closed. It took two jabs to hit the play button, but when she did, she let out a sigh too close to tears and sank down into herself, waiting, huddled, for the music to drive the evil away.

She waited there *(too long!)* in silence. The music didn't come. She looked up with desperation clouding over her eyes; the *power* light was on. She cranked the volume as loud as it would go. Nothing. Then she heard it, the whir of fast forward. She jabbed at the stop button, punched play once more. Still the machine whirred on. Faster now, impossibly fast. She feared the tape would break. The whirring grew to a roar in her ears. Without warning it stopped, the silence filled with dread, as if all the evil, Miss Sarah, and the club itself held their breath.

A plaintive wail, a lone guitar with tinny strings, her daughter's voice, but reaching across decades, as if trapped in some earlier, more awful time.

> *I said, "Hell, Houndog!*
> *What'd you shoot me for?*
> *I never done nothin' to you"*
> *He said, "I got the Crazy Whiskey Blues."*
>
> *Blood was pourin' from my side*
> *Held up my hand to stop the fight*
> *He fired again and blew my finger*
> *Clear into the night*

Faces formed in the silvery mist and each let out a hideous laugh. Miss Sarah batted at the images that hung in the air, her fingers tearing through mock flesh and bone. A crowd of apparitions formed around her, pressing her in an ever-tightening circle. Isolating her, trying to obscure her vision of the rest of the bar. What mischief was afoot? She ripped through the curtain of floating faces—still laughing, always laughing, her arms windmilling in a frenzy, breath caught in her throat, until the mist seemed to break, to part like a curtain before her.

Her daughter cried...

I guess sometimes we all get
The Crazy Whiskey Blues
When they come down and clutch your heart
There ain't nothin' you can do

There was a man at the other end of the bar; a light-skinned black man with big ears. His ears were the only big thing about him. He was no taller than she, and frail. Not old, just skin and bones. And those ears! They stuck out from his head like the open doors of a '47 Packard.

That was all years ago
I still got the lead in my side
Since he shot my finger off
I never could play guitar right

He was behind the bar, reaching toward the top shelf for the good whiskey. With bottle in hand, he turned to face eight women lined up at the bar. Each perched on a barstool, proud as peacocks, like they owned the place. Each tapping a shot glass in a primitive drum beat on the bar, garish nails clicking on each glass. Perfect nails in screaming colors on soft, unwrinkled hands. Low-cut shiny dresses. Nails tapping. Glasses drumming. That man, grinning big and bigger, as he poured out her best whiskey without measure into each glass. Poured each to overflowing and cackled. And the good whiskey spilling over the sides, running down the women's chins as they slurped at it, drank it down and drummed for more.

I wander from town to town
Playing for whiskey and dimes
Late at night I get
The Crazy Whiskey Blues sometimes

The anger flared like kindling soaked in kerosene, the flaming anger drove back the darkness and gave her strength. She charged, like a woman done wrong too long, down the aisle, shrieking at the ghosts all the way, "Get out of my club! You take those hussies and those floppy ears and get the hell out!"

She snatched the bottle out of the man's hands, and his grin hung there crooked on his face, like it'd been broken off.

The man looked real, looked *solid* anyhow. She could see the muscles working in his neck as he started to speak.

"You got any money? You gonna pay for that whiskey?" She snatched a shot glass away from one of the women who was raising it to her lips. *(How dare she drink that!)* The whiskey sloshed out and splattered down the woman's shiny yellow dress.

"I hope that stains permanent!" (The women looked solid, but they didn't look real.) "You march your frilly, painted ass right out of here!" (The dresses and the nails screamed with color, but their *skin*, their arms and faces and hands, was black and white. Not shades of brown, black and white, like an old TV program, or a picture out of a history book.)

That realization seemed to suck the air right out of Miss Sarah's lungs, seemed to smother the righteous fire burning in her belly.

Her daughter wailed...

I guess sometimes we all get
The Crazy Whiskey Blues
When they come down and clutch your heart
There ain't nothin' you can do

Gang that brought Sonny Boy Williamson down
Musta been drinkin' whiskey that night
They put an ice pick through his heart
Took his money and his life

Miss Sarah turned to the women, and their faces seemed to

grow longer; their teeth grew sharper and they were smiling, evil smiles: all pointed teeth and flashing eyes and nastiness.

"Sweet Charley always did love the ladies," the woman in the green dress hissed. "And the ladies loved him. Devil knows why, as ugly as he is."

> *Charley Patton's wife had 'em*
> *Crazy Whiskey Blues, I hear*
> *When she took a knife and slit his throat*
> *Clear from ear to ear*

And Charley (Charley Patton?), was still stuttering, an apology, an explanation. Another woman, in a green shiny dress and red painted nails filed to pointed-claw sharpness, slipped up behind him. She flipped her arm above her head, and Miss Sarah saw a straight-edged razor gleam. It hung in the air for a sweet-silver moment before it came arcing down and tore through the soft loose skin of his throat.

The gash curved upward below each ear. And still the man was smiling, dark red lips stretched back in a grin and a wide crimson smile gaping, slobbering blood, at his throat.

The razor arced up high in the air again, like the pendulum of a grandfather clock, poised for another deadly swing. Miss Sarah threw out a hand—afraid the woman was going to sever the man's head from his body—as if her hand, her will, had any power against these spirits. The sharp-edged blade flashed again, sliced through the soft webbing between thumb and finger of Miss Sarah's hand. Without slowing, it snapped muscle, tendon and flesh at the back of the man's neck.

The body tumbled forward on top of Miss Sarah; the dead weight bearing her down, the blood slicking her face and arms. A scream, all jagged edges, tore loose from her throat.

And her daughter cried...

> *I guess sometimes we all get*
> *The Crazy Whiskey Blues*
> *When they come down and clutch your heart*
> *There ain't nothin' you can do*

> *When they come down and clutch your heart...*

Mustang rounded the corner, still two blocks away. From there, the entrance of the club looked like a Hollywood premier: all lit up in red and white flashing lights. She knew her mother wouldn't splurge on a beacon light–though Mustang had pushed to rent just such equipment the night B.B. King and Koko Taylor had agreed to do a live "rehearsal gig" at the club. Mama had said no, they couldn't afford such frivolous luxuries. Perhaps she'd been right–they couldn't have squeezed another body into the club that night; the crowd had been so dense the ghosts had hung from the rafters. But Mustang was convinced that the beacon light would have proclaimed it an event, and that folks might remember the club as a place where events happened. But Mama had no feel, no flare, for show business. She wanted Lonesome Blues to be nothing more than a neighborhood bar. But a business had to aspire to greater things if it hoped to meet the ever-escalating cost of rent for North Side real estate.

As Little Mustang drew closer, she could make out an ambulance...parked directly in front of the club. She broke into a run, slowed by high-heeled boots on broken sidewalk pavement, and too-tight leather pants.

She was breathless by the time she reached the edges of the crowd. "What happened?"

A tall, dark, olive-skinned man stepped in front of her, his arms spread wide to block her way. His hair was slicked back with gel, his suit was flashy but cheaply made. "This is no place for a young girl." Without slowing, Mustang gripped his wrist, pushed up and ducked under his arm, deliberately kicking the large sales case *(What was in there, a vacuum cleaner?)* sitting next to him as she went by. Through the milling bodies, she'd glimpsed the pale face of the woman lying on the stretcher. The grips reversed as Mustang tried to push deeper through the crowd; she found the man now held her wrist in a tight grasp. "You don't need to be seeing that, and they don't need you in the way."

Mustang gestured with her free hand and snarled at him, "That's my club, and that's my mother. Who the hell are you to tell me my business?"

His smile was sardonic, his voice condescending. "You're too young to be in that club, much less own it. I knew who you were by the way you were panicking. Just let the medics finish bandaging your mother up first; you don't need to see all that blood."

"I wasn't panicking," Little Mustang said indignantly. "I've seen blood; it's red and runny and a bitch to wash out of your clothes. Now let me go!" She jerked her arm free and elbowed her way through the crowd, jabbing harder than was necessary to clear a path. She jolted to a stop next to the stretcher.

It hadn't been false bravado, but seeing her mama like this, looking so sickly and frail, was a shock–not because Little Mustang was afraid of a little blood. There was no blood to be seen, though a small bandage was wrapped around her mama's hand and most of her body was obscured by a heavy blanket.

Mama's brown hair looked faded against the white sheet of the stretcher; the shock of white hair that fell just over her eye seemed to have grown wider. Arthritis had already started to claim her hands: they looked like withered wings clutching the blanket. But most disturbing was the paleness of her mama's face; it looked like all the blood had leaked out her body.

But Mama had fainted before. More than once Mustang had seen her looking paler than a ghost. You didn't get used to it, exactly, but you learned not to panic when it happened. More disturbing than her color was the trembling, as she tried to raise up and talk. A young medic, he couldn't be more than a year or two older than Mustang, laid a hand on Mama's shoulder and coaxed her back down. Mama was in shock. Mustang knew all about that and how to treat it. She'd passed both the basic and advanced emergency first aid units in health class just last month. She was even certified by the Red Cross to give CPR.

She grabbed the arm of the young medic. Before the startled young man could get out the words "Who ar–" Little Mustang answered, "Her daughter. The only family she has. What's wrong with her?"

He put an arm out. Mustang bristled, but he wasn't trying to block her way. Instead, he ushered her closer to the gurney. Mustang knelt next to her mother, took her hand. "Mama, how you doing?"

Her mother mumbled something, but Mustang couldn't make it out.

The medic said, "She's not too bad, really. Small cut on her hand. It'll probably take a couple of stitches. We're more worried about the shock and disorientation. She's lost some blood, but we're kinda confused about how much. The cut's small, couldn't have bled that fast."

Mustang looked at him, eyes wide with anger and disbelief, "Let me see if I've got this right: There's an ambulance here, but a Band-aid, a blanket and a bit of quiet was all she needed?"

"Shock's a tricky thing. You can't be completely certain about these things, but if she'd been wrapped in a blanket right away, she'd probably be out of shock by now. Hard to say though, depends on what caused it–could be blood loss, or some people just have sensitive constitutions. The slightest injury, a twisted ankle, can send them into it. Cases like that, a warm blanket and some quiet will cure it. 'Course, that doesn't speak to her disorientation."

"That could have been caused by all the ruckus of the ambulance and the crowd," Mustang insisted.

"I shouldn't' be saying this, but..." He gave a sharp, silent nod. "The ambulance thing can really shake people up, sometimes make a borderline case worse."

"So who called the ambulance?"

The medic hooked his thumb toward the stranger.

The stranger had been waiting for an excuse to butt into the conversation. "When I hear a pretty woman scream in terror!" (Little Mustang wondered how he could tell a woman was pretty just from the sound of her scream.) "...and I find her passed out on the floor in a puddle of blood!" (Now who was talking about blood in front of her delicate little ears?) "...I don't just walk away!"

Mustang said, "Mister, nobody asked you to walk away. Only to use a little common sense before calling an ambulance. You don't use a cannon to kill a fly, and you don't call a surgeon to put a Band-aid on a little cut. We have a full first-aid kit in the office; complete with bandages, disinfectant and smelling salts. An ambulance was overkill."

"You don't treat that kind of blood with a Band-aid!"

"She only needs two stitches!"

The medic cut in, "There *was* a pretty good-sized puddle of blood on the floor in there, a lot of it soaked into your mother's dress, but it doesn't seem to be hers. Her blood pressure's too high to have lost that much. We were kind of wondering if there might have been another victim, but there's no sign of one...except for that extra blood."

The stranger chided the medic, "Do you really think this conversation is appropriate for a girl her age?"

Mustang and the medic stared at the man for a long moment, then turned to face each other, ignoring his outburst.

"Is there any way you can clear the riff-raff out? All this confusion can't be good for my mother."

The medic shrugged. "We don't have the manpower to enforce it. Besides, he'd probably get to stay; he's the closest thing we have to a witness. So far, your mom hasn't been able to tell us much. It's still a bit of a mystery."

He turned back to his patient; checked her pulse and her pupils. "How you doing, Sarah? Can you tell us any more about what happened?"

She fluttered her hands as she answered weakly, "I told you already...cut myself."

Mustang nodded to herself grimly; she had a pretty good idea of what had happened. Not who, exactly, but a general idea of what. "I don't suppose you believe in ghosts?"

The medic let out a short burst of laughter, though it didn't sound like he was mocking her. "I've heard the stories about this place. You really think it's haunted?"

She shrugged. "It'd explain the extra blood–ghosts do tricks like that."

"S'pose it would, but it's not my call. Tell you the truth, we were just debating whether we ought to call the police. We're supposed to call 'em in whenever a scene looks suspicious."

Not the police! She was years under age, nothing in the bar was up to code and there were just too many things that couldn't be explained. The local beat cop had always looked the other way, but if there was an official investigation...Little Mustang tried to keep her face blank and her voice calm as she said, "That's not really necessary, is it?"

"Well..."

She could see he was wavering. She turned on the puppy dog eyes, and said in a playful voice, "If there'd been someone else, my Mama, or her *rescuer*, would have saw him and said something."

"We found a kitchen knife in there, and some fresh cut limes." He was trying to convince himself. "The wound looks consistent with something self-inflicted by accident. You know, the knife slips while she's chopping, that sort of thing. But there's all that blood..."

Mustang turned to her mother, praying silently that she was coherent enough to bluff. They'd had plenty of practice explaining away the ghosts. "Mama, there wasn't anyone else in the bar, was there? You didn't carve up some stranger and hide him in the cooler again, did you?" Little Mustang forced out a frilly laugh.

Miss Sarah coughed out a sound that might have passed for laughter. "Noooo. Just me, the limes and a carving knife." (She'd been listening!) The effort exhausted her, though, and her breathing became more ragged.

Either the testimony or the condition of his patient seemed to settle the matter. The medic said, "If I can convince my partner, we'll skip the cops. But, we're gonna have to take her in." He shot a look at the stranger–glad to blame the news on someone else. "The cut's nothing. She probably didn't need an ambulance. But the shock...We should have left before this, but she asked us to wait, see if we couldn't get it under control here."

"Can't you wait a little longer?" Mustang pleaded. "She seems like she's getting better, to me."

The medic spread his hands. "She's just not stabilizing. For her own safety, we need to take her in."

Little Mustang nodded reluctantly.

A snide voice said, "Seems to me you're awfully casual about your mother's well-being."

She whirled and stomped toward the stranger until they were nose to nose, or would have been, if Little Mustang had been a foot taller. "And you're awfully casual with my mama's money–unless you intend to pay that ambulance bill! I appreciate you rushing to my mama's rescue, but what say you back off and let *family* handle this now?"

He crossed his arms across his chest in the classic male *I'm getting fed up with your nonsense* pose. "Where was this *family* when she needed help?"

Little Mustang wasn't intimidated; this stranger was only the most recent in a long line of men who'd thought that mother and daughter needed a man's guiding hand when times got tough. "You may have noticed–as you were getting ready to pitch my mother on a product she don't need," Mustang kicked the sales case, "that my mama's a grown woman, and I'm near to–"

The stranger snorted. Their faces were so close Mustang could feel the expulsion of moist air. She swiped the sleeve of her jacket across her cheek.

"That means I can occasionally walk to the grocery, or the store around the corner, without either of us need'n to call in a babysitter for the other one. We don't need your help, or anything you might be selling, 'round here!"

An old black man in a battered felt hat and a faded suit jacket ambled his way through the crowd as fast as his arthritis would let him.

He surveyed the man and girl locked in mortal combat–mortal if looks could kill–then pushed his hat back and shook his head. The two stood scowling at each other, eyes locked, trying to stare the other down. He crept closer. Ratman took a deep breath, hunched his shoulders, then jabbed his arm in betwixt the two, his hand scraping the man's stomach and girl's ribs as it pushed through. They fell apart, then whirled on their attacker, stopping short when they realized it was a frail old man.

"Now that I got your attentions, let me say a piece." He turned to the man. "Son, youse a stranger here. An' Miss Sarah an' Li'l Mustang have done a fine job of taking care of one t'another for more years than you can count. I reckon the two a them can take it from here."

Mustang stepped to the old man's side and gave the stranger a triumphant glare. But the old man wasn't going to let her off that easy. He turned to her. "Seems to me you might be talkin' to yore Mama rather than arguin' with this here fella."

Little Mustang nodded meekly and pushed through the crowd to return to her mother's side. From the corner of her eye she could see Ratman giving the stranger a piece of his mind. She'd liked to have heard it, but seeing it'd do.

Her mama reached a shaky hand out, and Little Mustang knelt and took it in her own. In a quivering voice Miss Sarah said, "Guess I'm going to the emergency room. I been trying to talk them out of it, but the ghosts keep interrupting." Her eyes drifted left and Mustang saw fear cloud her mother's face, as if she could see something that wasn't there. Something awful.

Tears welled up in Mustang's eyes, but she held them back. "Mama, I'm so sorry. I shouldn't have left you alone. Should have waited for Big Ray to get in. I thought...I thought you and Jayhawk would be all right for a little while..."

Miss Sarah gripped her daughter's hand tighter and leaned forward. "I shoulda been. It's not your fault, Little Mustang. I shoulda been." Miss Sarah fell back.

Her voice was weaker when she spoke again. "A girl your age shouldn't have to baby-sit her mother."

"Mama..." Little Mustang didn't know how to say it. "You be all right if I stayed an'...?"

There was pride in her mother's eyes. It almost made Mustang cry. Her mama's pride should have borne Mustang up, but instead, it made her feel little. Too young to do it, carry the load all alone. She didn't want to leave her mother's side. Wanted her mama to beg her to stay.

Instead, her mama said, "Ratman and Old George will watch over you. And Big Ray. Let one of them bartend if it looks like police are gonna come by. Liz is popular, be a big night."

"But Mama..."

"You'll do fine."

"You call when they're ready to let you go." Little Mustang couldn't keep the panic out of her voice now. "I'll send Dee over to pick you up."

"Get Big Ray to walk you to the bus stop. Don't be walkin' alone that time of night."

The medic laid a hand on Mustang's shoulder. "Time to go," he said gently.

Reluctantly, she let go of her mama's hand as they lifted the gurney into the ambulance. She heard her mother call out, "Run on now, Little Mustang. Gonna be a big night. You'll do fine."

Mustang watched them lift the stretcher into the ambulance and close the doors. Then she squared her shoulders and turned toward the club. She could do this.

The stranger was still lurking in the crowd. He stepped in front of her, blocking her way again. "Aren't you going with her?" he demanded.

Who was this man to pass judgment on her! The job ahead of her was tough enough without his interference. With more confidence than she felt, she said, "Someone has to run the club.

We got a crowd lined up waiting to get in."

"A daughter's place is beside her mother, especially at a time like this."

"Closing the club isn't going to pay that ambulance bill, and we haven't got health insurance."

The stranger blanched. *Good, maybe he'd finally run out of his self-righteous pomp.* "Naturally I assumed...I'll do what I can—"

Little Mustang's voice was hard and grown-up as she said, "You've assumed too much, and done more than enough. Any more help from you and we'll be bankrupt."

"If there's anything—"

"Mister, just stay the hell out of my club."

The Blues ain't nothin' but a woman who's told ya so Why them men gotta act so low?

Big Ray had arrived at some point during the commotion and taken his post at the door. Somehow, he'd managed to coax many of the gapers into the club. Little Mustang had a good memory for faces and names; most of these folks were strangers. Apparently, an ambulance was even better than a beacon light for drawing a crowd. Little Mustang waited for the bouncer to collect the cover from the latest group of people, then slipped in the door behind them.

Big Ray greeted her with a sly smile. "Wassup, Little Mustang? We flyin' solo tonight?"

"Looks like it. If the cops don't shut us down. They look the other way when I waitress, but they've warned me off bartending several times. If they get word that Mama isn't here..."

"Don't cha worry, we got it covered. And if we can't talk 'em out of it, well...be the most excitement these North Siders have had in a good long while."

Little Mustang gave an affectionate tug on his beaded braids. "Ain't that the truth."

Some of the South Side clubs had...*lively* reputations. She never got tired of hearing the stories Big Ray, Ratman and Old George told about them. Mustang didn't often get to go to the South Side clubs. For one thing, Lonesome Blues Pub was open seven nights a week, and it didn't make much sense to pay someone to work for you in your own club, so you could go listen to Blues somewhere else. Second problem was, she was still under age, and the other clubs didn't have the same kind of "arrangement" with their local beat cops. The arrangement was, if Little Mustang swore on a stack of Bibles she wouldn't drink a drop of liquor until she was a day past twenty-one, she could waitress in the club and the local cop would look the other way. In exchange, the Lonesome Blues Pub made a generous donation to the Policemen's Widows and Orphans Fund each Christmas.

Little Mustang busied herself behind the bar serving patrons. The musicians were gathered in the alcove behind the band, but Liz came out to the main room when she saw Mustang was short-handed. "Sorry to hear about Miss Sarah. She gonna be all right?"

Mustang popped the taps off on two beers before she answered. "Yeah, she's just a little shook up. Gonna rest tonight, but she'll be back tomorrow." At least, Little Mustang hoped so.

A college boy elbowed up to the bar, interrupting the conversation. "Let me have two Buds and a Lite."

Mustang put the last two drafts on the tray of drinks in front of her, finishing the order for table three.

"Want me to drop this off?" Liz asked.

"I'd appreciate it."

"Got cash coming?"

"Nah, they're running a tab." She smiled her thanks at the singer, then turned to the college boy.

When Dee, the waitress arrived, she immediately slipped behind the counter. "Hey Little Mustang! Need me to cover the bar a while?"

Mustang nodded. "I'm going to sneak off to the office and see if I can scare up some more help. I know this was supposed to be your easy night, but can you take the front? I should be able to cover the back from the bar, if I can't find a second waitress. Oh, and could you pick up my mama–"

"Big Ray filled me in. Knowing hospitals, they'll hold her several hours. Crowd will have thinned down before she's ready to go, anyhow. Shouldn't be a problem."

Mustang did a quick survey of the room. There was a steady trickle of folks coming in the door; paying cover, stopping at the bar for a drink, then finding a table. Things seemed to be running smoothly, for the moment anyway. She'd better grab the phone while she could. With luck, she'd catch Jami, who lived just a ten-minute bus ride away. She ducked under the bar and started for the office, then stopped. It was too quiet. That's what she'd forgotten. "Dee, can you turn some music on?"

Dee walked over to the stereo. "Looks like your mom was listening to your demo. Want me to play that?"

Mustang blushed. "No way. Maybe after the last set; drive people off. Give me that thing."

Dee tossed the cassette to her.

She caught it one-handed, then headed for the office. First she'd make a phone call, then she'd settle another matter with a certain ghost.

The Blues ain't nothin' but an achy heart disease
No break from sadness, 'cept in death's release

The stranger was puffing slightly as he finished the ten-block walk to the parking lot. Parking was expensive in this neighborhood, and while he wasn't hard up, you had to watch your pennies if you wanted to spend your dollars. He slid behind the wheel of his black Cadillac, but didn't start the car. He did his best thinking here behind the wheel, before the motor was turned on, before he hit the road. His daddy had always told him, "Never put the wheels in motion till you got your destination firmly in mind."

And his mind was locked in a fearsome debate. Should he head back to the hotel, or go visit that pretty lady in the hospital? That daughter of hers was something. A handful or two more than a single mother ought to have to bear.

The old man had called her "Little Mustang." The name fit her to a T: she was as willful as a wild horse. Or as willful as he imagined a wild horse might be. Someday he'd make it to that dude ranch for a vacation. Ride the horses, see the mountains, bed down under a blanket of stars.

It was a pleasant dream, but the pleasant dream only made him think of that pretty lady even more. How awful, how scary it must be for a woman alone in a hospital. His own mother had wasted away in a bug-ridden, rat-infested, state-run hospital. He'd not been able to visit her much, those last years of her life. He'd been out on the road selling stuff, any product he could get his hands on, to help pay his mother's hospital bills. He'd left the pretty lady in a lurch by calling that ambulance, never once thinking she might not have insurance. He shoulda thunk. He'd only gotten medical insurance himself when he joined up with this new company. Maybe if sales went well while he was in the territory, he could chip in a little something toward the bill.

Meanwhile, least he could do was go visit the pretty lady. Keep her company.

The Blues ain't nothin' but
a woman want to jump in the river and drown
They may find her body, but her heart'll never be found

Miss Sarah lay in a hospital room she couldn't afford, and alternated between worrying about money and worrying about the ghosts. It was all going so very wrong.

She remembered the early days, when she first bought the club. The fire had gutted the place, but left it structurally sound. It'd taken a heap of cleaning, gallons of paint and months of airing out, but it had all seemed fun, romantic somehow. Crazy is what it was.

There she was: pregnant, her fiancé dead, neither her parents or in-laws-to-be willing to have anything to do with her. She'd bought the club in memory of Don, the man who'd knocked her up (though he didn't know it). Damned fool was standing in the rain, playing *Stormy Monday* when he died–and how could you tell that to anybody without hearing them snicker?

She and Don had had big plans and a nice nest egg saved up. They had a little house in the suburbs picked out, and had plotted exactly when Sarah could quit her job without it causing a hardship with the bills. But all the plans and dreams had disappeared into thin air. Since they weren't married and Don didn't have a will, his parents saw no reason to acknowledge either Sarah, or their grandchild. Nor did they see any need to provide any financial support for their son's progeny. Miss Sarah had sent those would-be in-laws pictures of Little Mustang each Christmas–not because she was looking for handouts, but because she thought a girl ought to have grandparents. The letters were always returned unopened.

So, she'd turned to the ghost in the club. Jayhawk. He never physically materialized like the other ghosts. Miss Sarah didn't know why. His body had been impaled on a mike stand, some said his own guitar's whammy bar, as he fell off the stage, rushing for the door after the fire broke out. Maybe his body had gotten all burned up, and he didn't want folks to see it that way. He never spoke, either, but you could tell when he was around; there was a cold, heavy cloud lurking in the air

He seemed to "sleep," if that's what ghosts did, in a beat up, old, black and white Fender guitar that sat on the stage. Supposedly, it was the one that had killed him. Sarah wasn't sure she believed that.

As far as Miss Sarah knew, he'd never left the club. Maybe he was trapped there. But where had he been this evening?

That floppy-eared man, and those witches with him, were not the work of Jayhawk, of that she was sure. Jayhawk had always protected her and Little Mustang. Watched over the club, watched over them, like a husband.

Jayhawk wasn't the ghost of Don, but somehow, the two had sort of merged in her mind. Jayhawk clearly loved Little Mustang like a father, and had been a more dependable baby-sitter than the string of college girls she'd hired. Finally she'd put the crib in the office of the club. Jayhawk played lullabies through the stereo to lull the baby to sleep. But elsewhere in the club he'd broadcast other music for baby status reports. *Wade in the Water* meant Little Mustang needed a diaper change. *Good Bootie and BBQ* meant she was hungry, and Roy Orbison's *Crying* meant she was unhappy and Jayhawk didn't have a good guess why.

Jayhawk could even feed Little Mustang a bottle, if Miss Sarah was particularly busy. It was odd to see the bottle suspended over the crib, just hanging in midair, but it was always at the right angle so the baby didn't suck air as she was trying to feed. Air made for an upset tummy in a baby; it was something most new fathers didn't know, but Jayhawk held the bottle like an old pro. Miss Sarah figured he must have had children when he was alive. Even as a ghost, he made a pretty good stepdad for her child. And if she came to think of him as Little Mustang's father, as if he were her dead fiancé, instead of Don? Well, who could blame her? It's not like his ghost had ever shown an interest. Ghosts from all over the city visited the club; some nights there were more ghosts than live folks in the bar. But Don–Blues fan that he was, her fiancé, father to her child–had never once materialized in the Lonesome Blues Pub.

Mustang flipped the cassette over and over in her hand as she talked on the phone. It took some coaxing to get Jami to agree to come in. She'd been on her way out for a date.

"Oh, hel--ck. All right," Jami agreed, finally. "But I'm gonna invite him to the bar, so I'd appreciate it if you didn't go tattling to your mom that I had a boyfriend hanging around."

Little Mustang took a deep breath and let it out before she spoke. She didn't tattle on the waitresses, ever. At least, not since she was ten or twelve years old. But she couldn't ask the woman to work on her day off, then snap at her just because they were both feeling grumpy. She said, "Not a problem. We'll comp him at the door, and I'll be happy to buy him a couple of drinks."

"You'll buy him more than that."

"Whatever. I appreciate you coming in at the last minute."

Mustang let the waitress grump a little more. Only half-listening, the cassette caught her eye. The plastic window showed that the tape had run nearly to the end. Mustang had rewound it before she put it on the tape deck and her mama couldn't have listened to it that far through; she'd only been alone for half an hour.

Mama didn't fool with the tape player while she was working, just put something on and let it play in the background.

Mama wouldn't have messed with the tape, but someone else might have...

She hung up with Jami, then barked, "Jayhawk!"

She slid the tape into the boom box on the desk then stood back, hands on hips, and waited. An unseen finger hit the rewind button, stopped it, then pressed play.

Mustang cringed at the audio quality, her own playing, the

roughness of her voice. But this wasn't the time for a music critique. Jayhawk was telling her what happened.

> *Charley Patton's wife had 'em*
> *Crazy Whiskey Blues, I hear*
> *When she took a knife and slit his throat*
> *Clear from ear to ear*

"Oh hell!" Little Mustang swore, then looked around guiltily. She wasn't allowed to curse. No one but Jayhawk was listening, so she didn't bother to sweeten her words. "God dammit, that's just a myth!" Patton had eight wives, and supposedly hundreds of lovers. (But she suspected that was just bragging.) Legend said a wife slit his throat and killed him, but in reality, he'd had his throat cut in a bar fight. It hadn't killed him, but it did change the quality of his singing voice. He'd died years later of a heart condition, in a hospital bed, his eighth wife at his side. He was only forty-three. Or maybe forty-seven. No one was quite sure when he'd been born. Point was, he died young.

Little Mustang had sung the myth because that's what the Blues was about. The myth was more true than reality. If it wasn't true, it oughta be. Apparently the ghosts had acted out the myth–for a private audience of one.

Mustang snarled at Jayhawk, "Where the hell were you when this was going on? You've done a lot for us, but Mama and I been good to you, too. You know how much business having a ghost has cost us? You think the other ghosts would be hangin' 'round here if we didn't tolerate you? You know how many musicians bitch and moan about having to play your piece-of-shit guitar? It won't even hold a tune no more! And that's the musicians who are still willing to play here!" In the back of her mind, she was glad she'd remembered to have Dee turn on the stereo; it'd be bad for business if the customers heard her screaming at a ghost.

"We got a list a page long of musicians who won't play here no more on account of your pranks. Sweet Baby Brown crosses to the other side of the street rather than walk by the place!" In retrospect, having the timid singer perform at the club Halloween night had probably been a bad idea. But Little Mustang wasn't in charge of the schedule...yet.

"Dammit, you're supposed to be keeping an eye on the club!

Keepin' an eye on Mama! It's 'bout time you started pullin' your weight around here. If you can't keep the other ghosts in line, there's gonna be hell to pay. You deliver a message to Mr. Charley Patton and his wives—they aren't welcome in this club no more. And I'll tell ya one more thing, if things don't get better fast, Mama's gonna close the club—then who the hell do ya think's gonna play your guitar?"

Jayhawk dimmed the lights, held them low, so the room seemed to be lit by a single flickering candle. The darkness caught Mustang by surprise. She was so angry she wanted to break something—records, chairs, necks, something, and she wanted to hang on to that anger. But she knew what he was trying to tell her. He wasn't a particularly powerful ghost. Not anymore.

He couldn't keep the evil, mischievous spirits out, not when Mama threw open the door to 'em with her fear. Little Mustang took a deep breath and let it out in a whispery sigh. The ghosts fed on fear, and her mama was a walking banquet. She couldn't blame Jayhawk for the spirits taking advantage, not when Mama made it so easy.

Her mother had invited clerics from a dozen faiths out to bless the place, witches to sweep the place with sage and smoke. She'd held seances and consulted psychics. Read a library full of books on how to banish the spirits of the dead. She'd even talked a priest into doing a secret exorcism. The one thing she couldn't do was the one thing that would work: Let go of the fear.

Her mama was full to the brim with fear, and over-flowing. Not just of the ghosts, but life itself.

And there wasn't a damned thing Little Mustang could do about it.

She heard the music begin in the other room, realized it was time to get back.

She pulled the office door closed behind her, making sure the lock clicked; then she ducked under the drawbridge of the bar. As soon as Little Mustang was situated, Dee hit the main floor to collect drink orders. If the dirty glasses lined up on the bar and around the sink were any indication, the crowd was thirsty. The band was rocking and there were already two couples up and dancing—it was still early for that. There was no real dance floor, just a small clearing in front of the stage. Dancing didn't generally seem like a good idea to the crowd until they were well-lubricated—usually long about the end of the second set.

Liz gave her a nod from the stand and stepped up to the mike.

I've been crying since the day that I was born
Tears are the only jewels I've ever worn
Life made me an offer that I can't refuse
I'm serving a life sentence of the Blues

That was Miss Sarah's life wrapped up in a lyric. Her own, too, Little Mustang supposed. But she wasn't looking for a parole.

Blues ain't nothing but
a woman 'fraid to take 'nother chance
but Lord knows, I've had no luck in romance

The doctor said Sarah wouldn't be in the hospital long, a few hours at most, but they didn't have room for her to take up a bay in the emergency room all that time. They'd put her in a daybed room that they used for short-term observation of patients. A nurse had brought Miss Sarah a radio. The music was playing quietly when the stranger knocked hesitantly on the frame of the open door. A bouquet of flowers peeked from behind his back.

"Feelin' up to some company?"

Miss Sarah waved him in. He waited till she struggled into a sitting position, then, with a grand flourish, presented the flowers.

"Daisies and carnations! They're beautiful. Thank you. But you shouldn't have."

He waved her off. "It's the least I could do."

She laughed, "You rescued me! I should be bringing you flowers as a thank you." A thought struck her. "How'd you get in here? I'm officially still in the emergency room, they don't let you have visitors there."

He blushed and stammered, "I uh, well I figured that'd be the case, so I told them I was your brother. I thought you might want some company."

"That was kind of you." She didn't know what else to say; an awkward silence fell between them.

As a bartender, Miss Sarah had had a lot of experience talking to strangers. She'd learned it wasn't so much what you said, but that you said it. The flowers had caught her fancy and she let them bring a memory to her lips. "I love fresh flowers. They always made my mama sad; she hated to think they were going to wither and die. But my grandmother had a big garden of flowers. Used to be a vegetable garden till the arthritis took her hands. After that, she just flung out handfuls of wildflower seeds each spring. Her yard was a riot of color by summertime. Couldn't hardly get through it, but it was beautiful."

The man had taken a chair while she was talking. He was sitting forward, formal still, but, she thought, more comfortable than a moment ago.

"Do you grow flowers in your yard?"

"No," she admitted, and wondered if he could hear the hint of sadness in her voice. She'd always wanted a big backyard where she could fling out seeds by the bucketful. But the apartment building where they lived didn't have a patch of ground that wasn't paved in cement. "No, and I'm hardly home during daylight hours, so I couldn't enjoy them anyway. But..."

"But what?"

The man's voice was warm with a hint of devilishness. And wasn't he just the handsomest thing! Good lord, she suddenly felt shy, like a tongue-tied schoolgirl.

"You couldn't have noticed in all the commotion, the flowers clinging to the brick wall on the side of the club? Morning glories, climbing vines. They're good in the city. I planted those. So pretty, the petals blue and white. Such delicate flowers, but such sturdy vines. The flowers are only open for a few hours each morning. Most days, they've gone to sleep by the time I arrive. But even closed, they're beautiful, and just knowing they bloom fresh every morning is a cheering thought..." Her words trailed off, the thought come to an end. When he didn't say anything, she grasped for another one.

"Little Mustang says we ought to pull them down and put up a promotion board to advertise the upcoming bands, drum up some business for the club. I know she's right, but I can't bring myself to tear down the flowers."

"The city needs a touch of nature–" *Finally he spoke!* "–a lot more than it needs another advertisement. And that's coming from a salesman!" He laughed.

It was an easy laugh–maybe just a tad too loud, but not forced; as if it was something he did often and didn't care who heard him. Miss Sarah looked to the door, wondered if the nurse would come and hush them. She decided she didn't care if the nurse came.

"Is that classical music you're listening to?" There was a touch of mockery in his voice.

Suddenly, she felt up to the challenge. "You don't think a Blues woman can enjoy classical music?"

"Is that what you are, a Blues woman?"

"I run a Blues club. Some would say that'd make me. But what I really am is a small town girl who grew up and got lost in the big city, never did find her way home."

"Where's that small town girl from?"

He was leaning back in his chair now, slouching comfortably, one leg crossed over the other with his foot resting lazily on his knee.

She said shyly, "Grand Detour, Illinois."

"What?"

"A tiny little town called Grand Detour, Illinois; you've never heard of it."

"Sure I have, it's north of here, near...near Rockford, isn't it?"

It was a good bluff. She laughed, "Sure it is, if you call an hour and fourteen minutes nearby. That's how long it took us to get to the 'big city.' And it's due west of here, not far from Dixon; I know you've heard of that.

"Boyhood home of Ronald Reagan," he said.

"But there's no reason you should have heard of Grand Detour."

"I'm a salesman and that's in my territory, or near to it. I wouldn't have thought you could name a town in northern Illinois I didn't know. You've caught me with my pants down."

Suddenly they were both blushing at his double-entendre naughtiness. *He was flirting!* She was flirting back. It'd been a lifetime and half since she'd felt this way. His eyes were wide and his face was open, as if this wasn't just small talk, that he really did care where she might be from.

"Grand Detour has a grand total of two hundred and twenty-four residents. They send a city worker out to paint the sign every time the hospital calls with a new birth."

He laughed at that. She'd hoped he would; she liked his laugh. "They never."

"I swear they did. Don't know if they still do it. There may be no call to. Not many births there, now. The kids don't stay. No job prospects, I guess."

"Would you go back?"

"Not sure they'd want me; fallen woman from the big city. Might be a bad influence on the young'uns that still lived there."

Big Ray's growl swirled through the club. "Give it up once again, for Miss Liz Mandville Greeson and the Blue Points! As they make their way to the stage for the third and final time tonight...C'mon, you can do better than that!" The applause grew louder with the bouncer's encouragement.

Mustang hoisted herself up backwards onto the beer cooler to sit a while. She'd earned a rest. She'd personally seen to it that every person in the bar had a drink and all the dirty dishes were drying in the sink. But she'd done it. They'd kept a crowd all night, and she'd kept up on the drink orders, kept the cash in order and properly recorded, and in general, kept things running just as smooth as if her mama were here. Her self-congratulations were interrupted as she heard Liz introducing the next tune.

"...wanna send this song out to my good friend, Little Mustang, your bartender tonight and a special young lady who's got a birthday comin' up in a few weeks." That brought the requisite cheers from the crowd. "This number's off my first album, *Look at Me*. It's called 'Someday You'll Win.' Let's go, boys!"

As the drummer clicked off the bouncy, up-tempo beat, Little Mustang grinned. It was one of her favorite songs.

Well my mama went crazy, and my daddy left
So there I was, all by myself
Well things was bad and things went wrong
But in the back of my mind I heard this song

Well don't give up and don't give in
You're a natural born good woman
Some day you'll win
Hold on a little longer, you're only getting stronger
And everyday the sun, comes up again

The couple sitting at the back bar tossed down a generous tip and waved good-bye. Little Mustang waved back. They'd been there from the beginning of the evening, drank a steady two drinks per set, had made cheerful bar talk and tipped well. She hoped they'd be back. But she didn't mind them leaving just then, 'cause there were two old black men who'd been huddled in a back corner too long, waiting for spaces at the bar to open up.

Old George rushed his stubby legs forward to claim the seats before someone else could move in. Ratman and his arthritis took it slow and easy on the amble up to the bar. He took a breather before he inched himself onto the barstool; still, he was wheezing slightly as he spoke, "Guess you'll forgive an old man for breakin' up that sidewalk tussle when you were winning."

Mustang grinned. "Couldn't stay mad at you more'n about two minutes, ya old coot." Though they were fifty or sixty years older than her (Little Mustang couldn't tell for sure, and they weren't talking), these two felt-hatted veterans of the Blues were her best friends in all the world.

"Thazz good. Why Don't cha pour a coupla thirsty old men a drink before we turn to dust?"

Mustang leaned back and reached an arm above her head to snag two miniature snifters from the hanging rack of glasses. A twist to the right put the cognac bottle in reach. She set the glasses on the counter and poured a double measure into each, then lifted her glass of Diet Coke up to toast them.

"Here's to flyin' solo!" Ratman said, as they clinked their glasses together. "You near as good at this as Miss Sarah." Little Mustang flushed at the praise. She'd been thinking it secretly, but it was good to hear someone else say it.

Old George chimed in, "And here's to a birthday comin' up."

A look of confusion came across Ratman's face, but it looked fake. "Somebody gots a birthday? Who'd that be?"

Old George cackled, "A certain somtabody who's gettin' too big for her britches, that's who."

"All right..." Mustang drawled. "Ya'll are comin' to the party, in a couple weeks, aren't ya?"

Old George sputtered, "Now, has we missed a one of yore birthday parties, girl, in all the years we knowed ya? Hellfire, we been comin' to make a to-do about you since before you could bemember! And yore school plays, and yore band concerts—and let me tell ya the sacrifice my ears made for that!—gradgeation cer'monies, got my toe stepped on by a fat lady cheerin' for her Brian—" Old George was on a roll, but Ratman cut him off.

"What he's tryin' ta say is, we'll be there. But there's one little hitch. We's a bit stuck on what to get a girl that ain't a child no more, but's a far distance from bein' a woman yet."

"Not so far," Little Mustang growled at him.

"Far 'nuff," Ratman insisted.

Old George knocked on the counter twice. "We had two ideas."

"Been arguin' 'bout it for months."

"Finally 'cided we'd let you decide betwixt 'em." Both men nodded their felt hats in unison, looked at her expectantly.

Mustang said, "Sounds all right to me. But I gotta know what they are before I can decide...don't I?"

Old George chuckled and said to his partner in crime, "Might be fun to make her choose without knowin' what they were, like that game show, where's they used ta have to pick between curt'in number one and what was behind the door on the left."

"Nahrr," Ratman growled. Then he amended, "Maybe t'another year. This one's special. Eighteen and all. Gift's gotta be special. Sumptin she really wants."

"Ohhh, ahright. Takes the fun out of it though," Old George grumbled.

"Here tis," Ratman said to Little Mustang. His face was serious, his voice was urgent. Mustang felt a quiver in her stomach. For all their joking, this was a serious business to the two old men. She'd better give the decision careful thought.

"We gots enough money to either buy ya a new, an' a little-better, guitar than that beat up, old starter you been playin' around with..."

Mustang's heart flipped.

"We kinda had our eye on one a them Fender Mustangs.

They's a mite smaller 'n the regular ones–jez perfect for a young woman with small hands, such as yourself. They's got a good Bluesy sound to 'em, and it bein' named the same as you, it kinda seemed appropriate."

"...or," Old George said, "we can make an appointment with a dentist an' get ya a gold cap for one of yore teeth. Cain't be a proper Blues woman without a gold teeth." Both men grinned then, showing off their own gold teeth, flickering in their candlelit smiles.

Little Mustang felt like the breath had been sucked out of her lungs. This was big stuff. Rite of passage stuff.

Just then, Jami bustled up and hoisted a tray laden with dirty pint glasses onto the bar. "Little Mustang, is there some reason Jayhawk isn't bussing tables tonight? Slow nights, I wouldn't mind clearing tables, got nothin' to do. But tonight, when we're slammed, THAT'S when he decides to take the night off. Did he go to the hospital with Miss Sarah?" She looked puzzled, then added, "Can he leave the club?"

"Girl's right," Ratman said, glancing around like he could spot the ghost. "Haven't seen nor heard a sign of the house spook all night. Not many other ghosts here tonight, neither."

Mustang snarled, "They had their fun earlier this afternoon. Cleared out 'cause they knew I was pissed off."

Old George snapped, "Watch yore mouth. You know Miss Sarah don't approve of that kind of talk."

Ratman said, "but I think Jami's right–Jayhawk ain't able to leave the club."

"Maybe he's layin' low. I chewed on him pretty hard a while ago, for what happened this afternoon," Mustang admitted.

"He wahrn't no part of that!" Old George insisted.

"What happened anyway?" Jami asked.

"He didn't stop it," Mustang insisted. She felt guilty for having yelled at Jayhawk, and was worried she might have gone too far with the ghost, but she wasn't going to tell these guys that. He was probably just off sulking. The waitresses would just have to bus their own tables for a night. Waitresses at other clubs had to do it all the time.

"Wherever he is, I hope he comes back soon," Jami said.

Little Mustang hoped so, too.

Miss Sarah was having so much fun talking to this handsome man that she was almost disappointed when the emergency room doctor came in, checked her pulse, her pupils and her temperature, declared her free to go home, then bustled out again.

"Free at last, free at last," the handsome man boomed. Miss Sarah shushed him, then giggled.

"I suppose most folks are sleeping along the ward, but I'm glad you won't have to sleep here," he said.

The nurse came in with the release forms. Miss Sarah signed them with a flourish. As she returned the pen and papers she said, "I need to call my daughter, but the phone in this room isn't working. Is there one I can use at the desk?"

The man interrupted before the nurse could reply. "There's no need for that. My car's right outside and I'm already here. It'd be silly for you sit in the lobby waiting for a ride. I can have you home in no time."

Miss Sarah was dearly tempted, not just because she didn't want to wait for who knew how long, till Dee could get away. A ride would mean they could talk a little longer, and Miss Sarah was enjoying talking to this man. "Well..." she said, looking at her watch. "It's still the busy time at the club, and Little Mustang's never run things by herself before. It seems a double burden to call and take away one of the experienced staff members."

"So you'd be doing your daughter a favor by accepting a ride from me."

She'd only just met this man, but in all her years as a bartender, dealing with hundreds, maybe thousands, of folks who strolled in off the street, she'd become a pretty good judge of character. Her instincts were telling her that this was a good man, a man she could come to trust very quickly. "For my daughter's sake then," she agreed. "I'll wait and call her when things slow down there."

Saint Mary's church tower had just chimed one-thirty as Little Mustang said good night to the last customers–Ratman and Old George, of course.

Old George asked, "Sure ya don't needs us to help out with closin', what with the spook stayin' gone, an' all?" His words were ever so slightly slurred, and Little Mustang could tell by his tone he was hoping she'd say no to a tired old man.

Ratman added, more sincerely, "We could carry glasses to the counter. Not sure I's could lift the barstools up top the tables, but I could wield a washrag, sweep if you need me to. Handle some of the chores Jayhawk us'ally does. And I can walk ya to the bus. Girl your age shouldn't be walkin' alone this time a night."

Like this frail, arthritic old man was gonna protect her from someone who wanted trouble! But Little Mustang wouldn't insult her friend. "I think we've got things in order, but I thank you kindly for the offer. Big Ray will see me to the bus stop."

The old man chided the bouncer, "Ya wait till she's on that bus now, you hear?" Big Ray nodded his assurance, then held the door wide as they shuffled toward it.

Just before the worn-down heel of his snakeskin boots cleared the threshold, Ratman turned back. Big Ray quietly sighed.

"Girl-child." Ratman grinned so big, Mustang could have sworn she could see his back molars. "Ya done good tonight. Real good." Without waiting for an answer, he slipped out the door.

Big Ray locked the door behind them, then slumped against the door with another sigh. "Busy night, but things went smooth, sure 'nuff..."

He sat a moment, then roused himself. "Sittin' here's not gonna get that beer up from the cellar, though." He bent forward and let the momentum bring him back to his feet.

Little Mustang took pity on him. "That'll wait till mornin'. We all put in a day and a half tonight."

"And who's gonna carry 'em t'morrow? A little Bit like you? Up those stairs?"

"Done it before," Mustang said.

"That's all you and your mama need, get your back out before you even legal–"

"Mama!" Little Mustang shrieked. "How could I have forgotten about Mama?"

Dee looked up from the table she was washing, her face shifting from guilt to worry. "Wasn't she supposed to call?"

"Maybe we couldn't hear the phone?" Mustang said, her voice rising higher.

"Nuh-uh," Big Ray assured her, "I kept an extension near me all night–knew she'd be callin'."

"The hospital." Little Mustang pulled out the card the attendant had given her.

The three clustered around the phone as the line rang once, twice, three times. Finally, a voice on the other end. Little Mustang's voice quivered as she spoke into the receiver. "My mama was brought there in an ambulance, 'bout nine o'clock tonight..." She gave the receptionist the necessary details, then waited, fidgeting with a straw; after she dropped it, an ashtray. Finally she said, "Are you sure? Could you check– Okay, thank you." She hung up and turned to the anxious faces.

"She was released two hours ago. Said she left with a man who claimed to be her brother."

Blues ain't nothin' but a restless worried mind
Walk the floor nights, shadows right behind

Dee drove Little Mustang home, despite the fact it took her twenty minutes in the wrong direction from her own house. It would have taken twice that time on the bus, and still Little Mustang shifted in her seat, fidgeted with the seatbelt and failed entirely to keep up her side of a conversation. She was thankful when Dee gave up, turned on the radio and stopped worrying about the speed limit. She wished again that she and Mama could rent one of the apartments over the bar. But they couldn't afford a two-bedroom apartment anywhere in that neighborhood, not even on twice their pay.

When Dee pulled up to the curb of the three-story brownstone, Mustang had the door open and was out of the car before it rolled to a stop. She hadn't even said "thank you," but there'd be time for that tomorrow. She fumbled the key into the front door lock, then took the hall stairs two at a time, up to the third landing. More fumbling with keys on the two apartment-door locks, and finally, she burst into their home. "Mama?" she called too loudly. She didn't care if she woke the neighbors up.

A nightlight glowed from the outlet near the stove, lighting a dim path from the front door through the living room, into the kitchen and past the bookshelves filled with photo albums. But the hall on the far side of the living room, which led to the bedrooms, was wrapped in shadows. Mustang reached for a living room lamp. Light flooded the room, but it didn't chase away her fears. She'd tried calling home from the bar, but there'd been no answer.

Because of the late work hours, they turned the phone off while they slept and sometimes they forgot to turn it back on. Mustang checked–the ringer was on.

There was no sign that her mother was home, except that Mustang was certain they hadn't left the nightlight burning when they left that morning.

"Mama?" she called again. The bathroom door was closed–she slammed it open but found it dark and empty. Down the hall she went, calling her mother's name. The door to her mother's bedroom was closed, but Mustang didn't bother to knock. The hall light reached narrow fingers into the room, Mustang could make out a shape perhaps two?, in the bed. She hit the light switch.

The light blinded Miss Sarah momentarily. *That girl never remembered to give a warning before turning on a bright light in a dark room!* She struggled to sit up and shake the cobwebs from her mind. She glanced groggily toward the nightstand, saw the clock and her bottle of sleeping pills. "You're home early, did everything go all right? Give me a moment to wake up..." She realized she was still hugging the pillow to her chest. *The inspiration for that wonderful dream?* She tossed the pillow to the side of the bed and yawned. "I'll make cocoa...you can tell me all about the night." She swung her legs over the side of the bed. "And I can tell you about that nice man."

Perhaps she wouldn't tell Little Mustang everything. Some things a mother didn't share with a daughter. "We had the grandest time talking. He–" Finally she felt the chilling silence from the doorway, saw the stricken look on her daughter's face.

"Honey, what's wrong?"

Little Mustang whispered, "You were supposed to call."

It was the whisper, more than the accusation in the words, that chilled Miss Sarah. "They released me early, during the club's busy time, and he was already there. He brought me home and visited a while. I figured I'd call..." Her words trailed off as she realized what she'd done. "I'm sorry, honey, I was going to wait and call after things slowed down. The crowd always thins out just after midnight. But I guess I took my sleeping pill too early and drifted off." Had her daughter grown two inches while she wasn't looking, or was that just the rigid backbone making her look taller? The betrayed look on her face that made her look older?

Miss Sarah laughed, shakily. "I am sorry, honey. But it's not like you've never missed a curfew or forgot to call."

"When?" Little Mustang demanded. "When was the last time I forgot to call? When was the last time I was out with my friends, rather than working beside you at the bar?"

The shot hit its mark. Miss Sarah had to admit Little Mustang's rebelliousness didn't stretch to staying out too late–except when she was working. And when had the girl last had a day off? A week ago? No, she'd done the door on her day off, because Big Ray had a gig in Waukegan. Two weeks ago she'd filled in for a sick waitress... Was it any wonder the girl's only friends were musicians, retired musicians and drunks? "Honey, I–"

"You were with him? That stranger? That salesman. You were having such a good time talking to him that you couldn't remember that your underaged daughter was working in the club for you, worrying about you all night? You were having so much fun you couldn't be bothered to let me know you were home safe? Couldn't take thirty seconds out from your thrilling conversation with him to phone me?"

Little Mustang looked at the mussed-up bed, the bed that normally was so neat the other side didn't even get untucked overnight. Shadows grew around her face; her voice grew softer yet; bitterness dripped from each word. "Or maybe when you went to bed early you weren't alone, and you just didn't want my tender little ears hearing all that heavy breathing."

Miss Sarah leapt from her bed. Her knees were still shaky and her balance was off, but that didn't stop her from slapping Little Mustang so hard it left a full print of her hand burning on the girl's cheek. "I'm *still* your mother! You can't talk to me that way!

You worked hard? Well goodie for you. You worried about me? I've done the same for you, every day for eighteen years. And what I do with a man is none of your business. Now go to bed."

Little Mustang turned without a word, then suddenly bolted down the hallway and slammed the door to her room.

Miss Sarah heard the lock click.

"Dammit!" She would not feel guilty about spending time with that handsome man. He'd made her feel happy, made her feel like a lady. For the first time in years.

Blues ain't nothin' but a sweet talkin' man
Next mornin' all's left is footprints in the sand

Ratman lit up the first smoke of the morning with shaky hands, had to set the lighter and cigarette down 'fore he was through, while he weathered a coughing spell. A sip of lukewarm coffee calmed his scratchy throat. 'Course, "morning" was a relative thing. The light shooting like a dagger through his kitchen window said it was closer to noon than sunrise. But he'd worked late last night, bartending at the Lonesome Blues Pub. Three days now, and Miss Sarah still hadn't screwed up the courage to go back in and face the ghosts. And the one ghost Miss Sarah thought of as a friend was still missing. "Girl musta said sumtin' fierce to that spook to drive him off. Surely hope he come back, or that girl and her mama gonna have a terr'ble heartache." Ratman was mumbling to himself, trying to get his throat working before company came.

Sad-eyed Sarah...that woman hadn't knowed more than a minute a happiness at a time, in all the years he'd knowed her. She and the girl ought to close up the club for a week, take themselves a vacation, somewhere outside the city. But those two weren't talkin' to each other. Weekend was coming up, and the girl wanted to pretend there weren't a thing wrong–that she ran the club all by her seventeen-year-old-self all the time. 'Course, the ordering wasn't done–they'd run out of Miller Lite long about second set tonight, the books were behind, the paychecks weren't writ, and it was nearly time to print the schedule for next month with most of the dates still empty. The girl knew how to help with all the chores around the club, and she worked harder than anyone he knew except her mama, but that didn't mean she was ready to run things.

He gulped down the coffee. Had to wake up fast; he'd have company soon.

That girl was smart as a whip–should go on to college and make something of herself. She said she was gonna work a year, save up some money toward tuition. But he knew that guitar was singing a siren song to her, and she had talent, and a stage presence, sure enough. She'd been naggin' her mama to book her in as one of the regular acts. She didn't have enough songs yet for a full night. Not yet. Barely had enough for half a night–she was counting on guest musicians sitting in. And they would. But her band wasn't good enough to back her up on her own songs yet. No way they could back up a parade of guests. And practice wasn't gonna fix the problems with the bass player. She'd have to work up the courage to fire him and find a replacement. That meant auditions, and lots of rehearsals, to teach the new guy all the songs they did know. And they *had* to get a new name for the band. Ratman shook his head.

The young had energy; the old had wisdom. Too bad a body couldn't have both. He winced as he shifted in his chair. Little Mustang had done the dishes for both ends of the bar last night, so he wouldn't have to bend low over that bar sink. But there was enough bending and stretching and lifting to get beers out of the cooler, glasses from the racks and bottles from the top shelf to flare up his arthritis. He didn't know how much longer he could fill in. He was subbin' for two. The club couldn't survive if both Miss Sarah and the spook stayed gone for many days longer.

"I got too old for this shit years ago."

She'd be along soon...

There she was, tap-tap-tapping at his door, that dimestore guitar slung over her shoulder. He waved her in. Her hair was still wet; she musta gone from shower to clothes and out the door in three jumps.

"Girl, you spendin' time at home at all these days?"

"I sleep there," Little Mustang said shortly. She perked up. "Gotta new song I want you to hear. Chord progressions aren't too tough, I think the band could pick it up in one, mebbe two rehearsals. You ready to hear it?"

"Customarily, you might say hello and visit a spell before gettin' to the favor. But I can see youse all fired up 'bout this one. Like usual." He nodded toward the kitchen counter. "Get an old man another cup of coffee 'fore you start the concert."

She grabbed his cup on her way to the counter, sloshed coffee into the faded green mug, slid it across the table directly into his waiting hands.

"You want a soda or sumtin?"

She shrugged. "Maybe after the song."

"Well, play it then, girl. Don't keep me waitin'."

She seated herself on a rusted metal chair, settled the guitar on her lap, strummed it twice, adjusted the tuning on three strings, strummed again, cleared her throat, then for a brief second, sat motionless.

Ratman dearly loved that pregnant pause just 'fore a song got started; the silence seemed deep as the old Mississippi, overflowing with promise and wonder. The girl strummed the first chord, then her voice chimed in clear and clean. It'd take another ten years in a smoke-filled club 'fore she'd developed a Blues voice, but this was sweet and lonesome, all at once. She played a lazy, slow-footed tune, filled with heartache and weariness; the sort of melancholy you got at closing time in a gin joint on the seedy side of town.

Sittin' here thinkin'
And sittin' here drinkin'
Wonderin' if it's time to say we're through
Drinkin' my mind off of you

Sittin' here sighin'
And sittin' here lyin'
Telling myself you can change too
Just Drinking my mind off of you

Sittin' here buyin'
And sittin' here flyin'
Dreaming I can find somebody new
I'm Drinking my mind off of you

Bartender ignore these tears
They've been distilling for years
Love will do that sometimes
So pour me a double
I'll give you no trouble
I'm just drowning my heart in the Blues

Sittin' here cryin'
And sittin' here dyin'
Cause I know I can't leave you
Drinkin' my mind off of you

So pour me a double
I'll give you no trouble
I'm just drinkin' my mind off of you

The last chord faded into a melancholy silence.

Ratman growled, cleared his throat, spoke again. "Shouldnta girl your age be writin' bad love poetry?"

Little Mustang snorted. "I ain't never been in love."

"What about that Billie Wilkins in—"

"That was seventh grade!"

"Or that Charles-sumptin on the junior varsity football team?"

Little Mustang shuddered. "That was just a crush."

"Well how 'bout that young man took you to prom?"

"A bout of temporary insanity, I assure you. Now what did you think of the song!"

He grumbled. "It be too old for you. Young'un your age ought not be so jaded. You ain't never been lovesick yet." He sat silent. She sat waiting, eyes anxious—eager and afraid at the same time.

"Too old for you," he scolded.

"But damn good," he grudgingly admitted. "Good enough to be recorded by a name."

Her smile lit up the gray room like a blazing star. It was a smile that could inspire young men to heroic deeds, and could send old men into battle feeling young again.

His heart twisted with the depth of feeling he had for this little slip of a girl. If he could change one thing in all his life, he wouldn't reclaim his music career cut too short, wouldn't get rid of the arthritis that left his body more twisted than the devil's backbone, wouldn't erase even one of the misdeeds of his past; he'd ask for more years to watch over this girl.

She was chattering like a magpie. He swallowed hard and frowned in concentration, trying to catch the thread of her words.

"...it'd be best if it had a piano arrangement and a standup bass. Maybe a little saxophone real quiet behind, not too hot. 'Course, the band ain't got a piano, standup bass or saxophone. But someday, when I go in the studio to record it, that's what I'll use."

Ratman wondered again how this little bit of a girl was gonna be able to run a club, get a band started, a recording career goin' and take care of a mother that was scared of her own shadow–all on her lonesome. He could help some, but even with help, the burden was awfully big for such slender shoulders. She was smilin' so bright from his praise, and from having writ a song so fine, he didn't have the heart to raise the questions. His name was Ratman, not Rainy Day. He wouldn't be the one to put her dream out–he suspected things were building up to do that, and soon, without any help from him.

Mustang crossed the fingers of her left hand behind her back as she slid the key into the lock on the front door of the club. One of two wishes had come true today–Ratman had liked her song. Even suggested she send it off to a record label, though there weren't many singers who didn't write their own songs anymore. Almost had to record it yourself and try and get airplay before a big act would consider doing the tune. But Ratman said they still bought some, and this was a classic heartbreak drinking song. Those never went out of style, though the melody she'd written was slower than most of the stuff on the radio these days. Still, Ratman liking the song had been her first wish. And with a little luck, maybe her second wish would come true: when she pushed open the door Jayhawk would be back in the club waiting to greet her.

She put her shoulder up against the heavy oak door, so warped from the fire nineteen years ago that she could barely open it. Mama said she'd always meant to replace the door, but it still did what a door was supposed to do, and there always seemed to be other things to spend the money on. Leaning against it, Little Mustang could still smell the faint odor of smoke seeping from the wood, imagined she could see the flames, feel the heat of the fire, hear the screams of the people shoving against the door, trying to get out. Sometimes she thought the ghosts from that night were trapped in this big oak door, forever doomed to relive that terrible night. Mama said the odor was long since gone, and that Little Mustang just had a vivid, morbid imagination. But Little Mustang was certain that what she heard and smelled and felt and sometimes even saw, was what had really happened that night.

And yet, the door gave her comfort. Made her feel safe and protected, surrounded by spirits of the past. The spirits were watching out for her, keeping her company. She'd pushed Mama to make a lot of changes to the club, to remodel, make things slicker, more contemporary, but she'd never encourage Mama to get rid of this warped old door. She knew she'd never feel as safe with one of those flimsy pressed-wood jobs she'd seen in the hardware store.

Besides, this one gave her exercise. Little Mustang put her shoulder to the door again, backed off so she could bend both knees for more leverage, then heaved. The humidity was high today, which meant the wood had expanded, making it harder than usual to open, but finally, it gave an inch, and with another shove, it slowly gave way.

She stepped deep into the waiting darkness, letting her eyes adjust to the gloom. She always went into the dark to greet Jayhawk before she turned on the lights, in the eternal hope that one day she might see his faint wispy image.

"Jayhawk? Are you here?" she whispered.

She had often wondered why the other ghosts could materialize but he couldn't. When she was fourteen, her English class had taken a field trip to the Chicago Public Library downtown. She'd spent the entire visit in the special collections room, sifting through the old Blues history documents. And there, amid the old concert posters, newspaper clippings and faded contracts, she'd found a picture of him. He had black wavy hair with a spit curl that rested on a deeply lined forehead. He wore a silver sharkskin suit and a black silk shirt. He was looking away from the camera. The photo wasn't a publicity still from the record label; it was a picture from the private collection of a local photographer. He'd caught the musician in a quiet moment. It was the only picture she'd ever found of him. She thought he looked sad.

She had taken it from the library. Slipped it between the pages of her notebook when the librarian wasn't looking. Not even her mama knew she had it. It was the only thing she had ever stolen. She kept it in an envelope taped to the bottom of her jewelry box. She took it out and looked at it when she was alone and lonely. She'd had it out a lot over the last three days, talking to it, pleading for him to come back.

"Jayhawk?" Her voice cracked as she whispered into the darkness again. She balled her hands into fists, jabbing her stubby nails into the soft flesh of her palms, the pain driving away the tears of desperation. "Jayhawk, please come back. I'm sorry I yelled at you. It wasn't right, wasn't proper, for me to blame you for what the other ghosts did. You've always watched out for me and Mama, always helped out in the bar and never got enough thanks for it. You've taken care of me all my life, and Mama...she's not too good, right now. The fear's all knotted up inside her, and there's that stranger twisting her thoughts... Jayhawk, I couldn't bear it if you left me, too."

She stood tensely in the silence, straining to hear something. A song start on the stereo, an ashtray scuttling on the counter. Anything that might indicate he'd come back home.

When no sound came, the tears spilled out.

**Blues ain't nothin' but an aching soul
Where hope oughta be is just a black hole**

Miss Sarah walked up Halsted Street, the psychic on one side of her, the handsome man on the other. Though her bodyguards were beside her, she dawdled. She was in no hurry to go back inside Lonesome Blues. If even Jayhawk had been driven away by the evil spirits, how could anyone expect her to go back in there and face them?

But Jami had called this morning, early. Well before any of

them usually got up. Little Mustang was already gone. The only sign of her was the water splashed about by the shower and her wet towel on the floor. Jami had begged Miss Sarah to come back–said Little Mustang was doing a good job, but she was, after all, still a child. The club needed its owner back. Needed a manager to set things in order. And if she didn't come back soon, Jami said, there were rumblings in the staff about quitting, en masse. She knew Little Mustang would never forgive her if she let that happen.

Miss Sarah had big dreams, dreams that had been buried for a long time, so long she thought they were dead. The handsome stranger had changed all that, rekindled those dreams. But she couldn't spring them on Little Mustang all at once. The Lonesome Blues Pub was the only home the girl had ever known. Miss Sarah's mother and sister had said–before they stopped talking to her–that it wasn't a proper place to bring up a child. Maybe they'd been right. They'd said she needed to find herself a husband; any good man with a job would do, that she didn't have the right to be choosy when she had an illegitimate baby to care for. All she needed was a man who didn't drink, didn't hit, had a job, and would bring the whole paycheck home. She'd bucked them on that one; thought there ought to be some love in a household. A stepfather ought to mean more, be more, than just a paycheck. But maybe they'd been right. It wasn't healthy for a young girl to be so familiar with, so emotionally attached to a bar, some drunks and a passel of ghosts. She couldn't just rip it all away from her. Her daughter would have to be weaned, and soon.

"...Ms. Sarah?"

She jumped at the gentle touch on her elbow. Wildly, she looked around, and found herself standing in the middle of the sidewalk, still half a block from the club, the two of them staring at her with grave concern on their faces.

She laughed nervously. "I'm sorry. I got lost in my thoughts."

"That's only to be expected," Ariana, the psychic, said. "I know this is a difficult, scary thing we're about to do. But I do think it's best if we pick up the pace just a bit. The preparations and confrontation inside the bar may take some time, and we want to be able to complete it all before sundown."

Miss Sarah glanced at the sky. The sun was overhead, but somehow the afternoon seemed suddenly darker. "Yes, we should hurry along."

The others let her set the pace. The sound of her sensible heels clicking on the sidewalk was purposeful and reassuring. She paused once more, just outside the club, to admire her morning glories. They'd arrived early enough that the flowers were still open.

"They're truly beautiful," the handsome man said, reaching gently to stroke the soft skin of a petal.

Miss Sarah remembered how he had stroked her cheek that way. "If I could, I'd take a bouquet of these into the club each day."

"Why don't we, then?" said the psychic. "Living things, plants, animals and flowers, can drive back the dead."

"They're morning glories." The name didn't seem to register on the psychic's face; a city girl obviously. Miss Sarah explained, "The flowers only open for a brief time each day. As soon as you pick them, the flowers close."

"Oh." The psychic shivered. "That's too much like death. That might strengthen the ghosts rather than weaken them. Bad idea. Are you sure you want them growing on the building? Such a morbid flower?"

"It's not a morbid flower," Miss Sarah said indignantly. "It's a hopeful flower. It blooms new every day. It's like rebirth. A new spring every morning. It's a hopeful flower."

The psychic waved her hands. "Whatever. I guess if that's what they symbolize to you, then they aren't doing any harm. Shall we go in?"

Miss Sarah swallowed hard, then nodded. But she needn't have gotten so nervous. She hadn't realized the entrance procedure would take so long. The handsome man's arm went around her shoulders as they stepped back and watched the strange ritual begin.

Mistress Ariana, a psychic adviser and spiritual guidance counselor, senior witch in the highly-respected Two Stupid Witches consulting firm, had come highly recommended by the New Age Merchants Association. Mistress Ariana certainly looked the part. A tiny, elfin woman, with long black hair and piercing blue eyes, she wore a black velvet bustier with red velvet inlays that pushed her breasts up to an alarming height, and a flowing skirt of black lace. The outfit was completed by black combat boots. She was currently spinning in circles, her hair and skirt billowing out around her.

She explained in a breathless voice that ebbed and flowed as she turned, "You should spin clockwise at least three times before entering. Me, I like to do more, to be on the safe side. The spinning confuses the spirits so they can't follow you in."

"Um, will that be an entrance requirement for all our customers?" The voice that came from the doorway was filled with irony, and not a little hostility. It was a grown-up voice, but it came from Little Mustang's lips. She was leaning against the door jamb, arms crossed, one boot kicked over the other with the heel propped up in the air.

For a brief second, Miss Sarah resented her daughter with an intensity that nearly choked her. How could her daughter be so comfortable here, and yet she—who had opened this club, saved this structure—was persecuted by the spirits within? Why had they embraced Little Mustang and turned so viciously on her? *This is my club!* Then the anger was gone, replaced by sadness. It wasn't her club anymore. Maybe it never had been.

Ariana had stopped spinning and was now staggering in wobbly circles from the vertigo. She laughed a tinkly laugh. It sounded like glass breaking. "You must be the daughter. You wouldn't have to require the customers to do it, though if you could get some of the regulars to, it would help. But, the aggressive, negative-energy spirits appear to have mainly focused on your mom, and she tells me that new ones keep popping up that don't seem to be local. So, we want to stop any roaming revenants from attaching to her as she passes through the world. The club seems to act as a psychic focus, a spiritual amplifier, as it were. Relatively weak, pesky spirits can attach to your mom at any time, then when they ride into the club with her, their power is magnified and they can start doing nasty things. We still have to get the ones already in there booted out," she hiked up her skirt and kicked her combat boot into the air, "but first we want to make sure she doesn't bring any new ones in to exacerbate the problem."

She turned to Miss Sarah. "Now you spin, three times, clockwise, always clockwise!"

Miss Sarah felt like a fool with her daughter watching and the handsome man looking on, but she held her chin high and did it anyway.

"Next, rap three times on the left door jamb before you pass under the archway." Ariana rapped to show them how, then stepped through the door, squeezing past Little Mustang, and turned to face them.

Miss Sarah met her daughter's eyes uncertainly, knocked three times and stepped past. Still Little Mustang didn't move. The two women were small enough to squeeze past her.

Mistress Ariana motioned to the man. "Come on, you can do it, too."

Under the teenager's withering gaze, the man turned in a half-hearted circle, rapped firmly on the door jamb, then stepped up and stopped. He couldn't squeeze past, and it was obvious Little Mustang wasn't going to move.

If it had been just the two of them, he'd have bumped her out of the way, but somehow he didn't think Miss Sarah would stand for that, even though she and the headstrong girl weren't speaking. Still, he was unwilling to back down.

Little Mustang whispered in a voice so low her mother couldn't hear, *"I thought I told you to stay out of my club."*

His eyes flashed with anger. *"I believe if I called the cops and the courthouse, we'd find your mother's name on the club deed, and a police captain who'd be very interested to know a juvenile delinquent, dressed like jail-bait, was working illegally at a bar. Your mother invited me. Step aside."*

Mustang sneered at the threat. *"You turn me in, they'll bust my mother, and that'd put a damper on your romantic plans, wouldn't it, Romeo? Or did you already get everything you were after?"* She twisted away and slipped into the bar before he could answer.

Little Mustang climbed on a barstool, propped her elbows on the bar and settled in to watch the show.

Mistress Ariana flitted back and forth, exploring all the nooks and crannies. Miss Sarah watched her wide-eyed, while darting furtive glances around the room. Even with all the company, she was still afraid.

"There's so many dark, spooky corners in here!" Ariana exclaimed.

Little Mustang wondered what else she'd expected from a

pub. Maybe fern bars could get away with recessed track lighting and torch lights nestled in amongst the greenery, but a Blues club was supposed to be dark and smoky, with no pretensions.

"What's this scorch mark around the stage? It's putting off really bad vibes!"

"That would be the ring of hellfire," Miss Sarah said stiffly.

"You never had it cleaned? No wonder–"

"Oh, we cleaned it. Bleach. Lye. Acid. Had it sanded down and revarnished. Nothing worked. Finally, I had all the boards replaced."

The psychic's mouth dropped open. "And it–"

"Came back," Miss Sarah said.

"That's one powerful etheric stain. Still," the psychic said chirpily, "we've got the cosmic equivalent to bleach and enzymes. We'll clean the place up." She tramped to the open floor space in front of the stage. "Give me a moment. Before we get started, I want to open myself up to the psychic vibrations of the room." She closed her eyes, and stretched her arms out in front of her, palms up, and tilted her face skyward. Then, with slow baby-steps, she turned in a circle. When she'd made a full revolution, her eyes popped open. "This room is just filled with negative energy! It's got to be swept from top to bottom!"

"Want me to fetch the broom?" Little Mustang asked drolly.

"Sally!" Little Mustang knew her mama was really pissed– she'd used the hated given name.

"I was just trying to help." She shrugged, as if to say she was innocent.

Mistress Ariana gave the glass-breaking laugh again. "It's a natural mistake. But your janitor has done a fine job."

Little Mustang wondered if Mistress Airhead realized that the "janitor" was sitting at the bar.

"The sweeping we're going to do today is with sage and lavender smoke. We're sweeping out evil spirits, bad memories, ill feelings, any leftover anger from bar fights, the sadness from broken hearts, just any kind of lingering negative energy. I'll need you to open all the windows in the place so that when we sweep, it all flies out the windows and dissipates, rather than getting caught in a corner where it'll just get spread out through the room again."

"The windows don't open," Little Mustang informed her.

"Haven't since we owned the place."

"Oh." The information seemed to leave the psychic at a loss. "Is there a back door?"

"Uh, yeah. Fire code requires one."

"So let's open both the front and back doors as wide as we can, and we'll just be careful to sweep toward them."

The stranger moved toward the entrance. Mustang had almost forgotten he was in the room. He put his shoulder to the door; the warped wood screeched and groaned as it was forced open, wider than Mustang ever remembered seeing it. Miss Sarah moved to help him, though he didn't seem to need any assistance.

Little Mustang thought, if there was a chance, however slim, that this charade would help Mama conquer her fears, she'd go along with it. She slid off the barstool and clomped her way toward the back door. It was just as warped as the front, but she noticed no one was leaping to help her.

Mistress Ariana dug into a carpetbag and started pulling out objects, lining them up on the bar. There was a bundle of twigs bound together in pink twine, nearly a dozen white pillar candles, two cascading strings of bells, sprigs of dried and fresh herbs, five large vials of clear liquid and a can of household oil.

"Ms. Sarah, place the candles anyplace in the bar where the spirits have disturbed or attacked you."

Miss Sarah looked at the row of candles, then scanned the room. "We're going to need more candles."

There was a trace of fear in Mistress Ariana's expression. She laughed nervously. "Just put them where the worst incidents have occurred, then."

"Whatever you say." Miss Sarah took a candle in each hand and set off to place them, heading first to where the ghost of Charley Patton had been decapitated.

Reluctantly, Little Mustang stepped forward and asked the psychic, "What can I do?"

Her mama turned and gave her a grateful nod.

Mistress Ariana handed her the oil can. "I noticed both the doors squeaked when we opened them. Why don't you oil all the hinges?"

"Um, why?"

"Squeaky hinges are a big old invitation to ghosts and troublesome spirits. It advertises the fact that the place is wide open and they can come on in and party."

"'Kay." Little Mustang headed toward the front door. She kneeled to squeeze a bit of oil on the bottom hinge. She waited to let the first drops soak in, then squeezed out more to coat the area. When she stood back up, she found the stranger looming over her.

"Want some help with the top hinge?"

He wasn't mocking or challenging or shining her on. Mustang groaned inwardly. (He's trying to connect with me...for Mama's sake.) Sure enough, when she stole a glance, her mother was watching them with a pathetically hopeful look on her face. Little Mustang was willing to go through with this psychic banishing nonsense if it would help her mama cope with the ghosts, but she'd be damned if she was gonna make it easier for this stranger to put the moves on her mother. "I don't need your help."

He stepped back and crossed his arms.

She marched to the bar and dragged a barstool to the door the legs squealing in protest as they scraped across the floor. Even with her back turned, she could feel her mother's disappointment. She climbed on the chair, squirted a liberal dose of oil over the upper hinge, then jumped flat-footed to the ground, and dragged the chair back to the bar. The stranger stalked off. *Maybe he can help Mama light the candles; a delicate thing like her ought not be fooling with fire.*

Mistress Ariana had been watching the charade. She jammed her fists on her hips and whined, "I'm sensing a lot of negative energy here, and it's not just coming from the dead. You living folk need to resolve your differences and be at peace with one another."

"Let me guess," Little Mustang said, "evil spirits can sense disharmony and are drawn to that."

"Like flies to honey!" the psychic exclaimed.

"Oh, God."

"Little Mustang, watch your language!"

Little Mustang sighed dramatically. "Mama, this is a family matter. He's got no reason to be here. You're makin' moonie eyes at him when you're supposed to be facing the ghosts. He's nothing but a distraction. If you're not gonna concentrate on the task at hand, you three can clear out and I'll start setting up for tonight. Weekend night, gonna be busy. I've got work to do."

Her mama's face had turned red and her cheeks were puffed out like she was about to explode. "How dare you!"

Little Mustang braced for another slap, but Mistress Ariana stepped between them before Miss Sarah could close the distance. "I'm sorry," she said in a firm, yet apologetic tone, "but your daughter's right. Your energies aren't focused. Your heart is with the man, and that keeps dragging your mind away from the task at hand. The spirits are strong here. We can't fight them if you aren't focused on the battle."

Miss Sarah stood there, her mouth hanging open and her eyes filling with tears. Little Mustang felt a pang of guilt, followed swiftly by anger. Mama hadn't known this man but a few days—why should she need him to walk into their club? For eighteen years they hadn't needed anyone but each other, Jayhawk, and occasionally a bit of advice from Ratman. Now, just 'cause they were going through a tough patch with the ghosts, she was letting a stranger in to ruin all they'd built for themselves.

All three women stared at the man: he was met with faces of sorrow, apology and anger. The three emotions built a wall too tall to climb.

He raised his hands in surrender, then turned to Miss Sarah. "I'll be right outside."

"Psychic said we'd be a while," Little Mustang reminded him.

Giving no sign he'd heard her, he said to Miss Sarah, "I'll wait. However long it takes, I'll wait."

They hung sprigs of dried basil and fresh rosemary over the door jambs and window sills, and strings of bells from the door knobs.

Mistress Ariana said, "The bells will scare the spirits away, the basil and rosemary will protect you. The candles are white; their light will purify the spots that are stained with the darkness. As the candles burn down, so will the power of the evil spirits. As it dissipates, we'll sweep it away." She lit the bound twigs, and a flame shot in the air. She let it burn, turning the bundle this way and that till the fire had spread evenly over all the stems in the bunch. Then with a great puff, she blew the flame out, leaving the herbs smouldering. A column of smoke climbed to the ceiling.

Little Mustang said, "That's going to set the smoke alarms off."

"Take the batteries out, for now," Miss Sarah said curtly.

Mistress Ariana waved the wand of herbs like a child holding a sparkler. As she marched around the room, climbing on chairs to touch it to the four ceiling corners, dragging it down the seam where the walls met, weaving it in and out among the legs of the barstools, the smoke trailed behind her like a comet's tail. Then, wand in mouth, she was crawling on hands and knees down the walkway behind the bar. She even waved it around the basin drains and among the water pipes and supplies under the sink, though Little Mustang didn't think it was a good idea to put fire near the cleaning chemicals.

If nothing else, thought Little Mustang, *it's covered up the odors of stale tobacco and beer.*

As she swept, the psychic implored the ghosts and gods, "Goddesses of the light, shine into this darkness and protect the women who work here. Cast your protective light like a mantle about their shoulders. Cast out the evil spirits and guide them home; let them bother this place, this woman, no more." Then she circled Miss Sarah, waving the smoking wand around her, in circles around her hips, up and down the length of her legs and torso, around and above her head, until she was wrapped in a smoky cocoon.

Then the psychic climbed on a barstool and clicked each of the ceiling fans on high, reversing the direction of the spin to push the air down and out, rather than drawing the smoke up to the ceiling. In no time, the air currents had carried the smoke out the doors. Mistress Ariana said, "Now that we've got all the bad stuff out for the moment, let's lay a protective spell down to keep it out."

She returned to the bar, pulled an empty quart jar from her bag, and opened the large vials of clear liquid. As she dumped each of the vials into the larger jar, she chanted, "Take, as a base, a measure of white vinegar to clean all it touches. And with the Goddess's hand to guide us; mix water taken from a river flowing over rocks, water taken from a well deep and true, rain water pure and sweet drawn as the drops still fall, and water from a ditch dug deep. Let the waters run together, to meet the water of the body of the woman in need..."

She broke off chanting and said to Miss Sarah, "I need some of your spit or your urine. Preferably both."

Miss Sarah looked aghast. "My ur–"

The psychic shrugged apologetically. "Spit will do." She held out the jar.

"You want me–"

Mistress Ariana nodded eagerly and held the jar up higher. Miss Sarah leaned over it, and with a distasteful look on her face, made a spitting sound. Mistress Ariana peered in at the contents. "I don't think we actually got anything. This really is the important bit. Try again, please?" Miss Sarah puckered her cheeks, made a slurping noise then leaned over the jar again. There was a visible plop in the mixture. Miss Sarah quickly turned away.

Little Mustang bit the sides of her cheeks to keep from laughing.

Mistress Ariana swirled the contents again, then poured the mixture into a large bronze ball on a chain. The thing looked like a cross between an oversize tea infuser and a censer stolen from a Catholic funeral. But there were only holes bored into the top; the liquid was stored in the bowl beneath. She held the censer in her right hand and took up a candle in her left, then retraced her path through the room, shaking drops of water out as she intoned, "May the gods of protection turn to me. May the goddess of white light come to my side. Let the angry hearts of these spirits be calmed. Let their grief be appeased. Set forth well-being for the living, and guide the dead back to their graves. Let the revenants and spirits return no more to this place."

Mustang wondered if the spell would be undone as soon as they cleaned everything with Lysol and bleach. She knew perfectly well that's what Mama would do. The thought of having her spit scattered all over the bar would be more unacceptable than the ghosts.

Mistress Ariana jumped down from the top of the bar, set the censer on the counter, dried her hands on the front of her skirt, then smiled at them brightly. "That should do it. I'd let the candles burn all the way down; that will strengthen the spell. I know this is a Blues club; the devil's music and all. But do you think tonight your musician could open with a gospel song or maybe an old spiritual, to help set the spell?"

Miss Sarah glanced at Little Mustang, the question in her eyes.

Little Mustang shook her head in disgust: *She doesn't even know the schedule!* She answered, "That shouldn't be a problem. Jimmy Burns is playing tonight. I'm sure he'd kick things off with *People Get Ready* if we asked."

Ariana clapped her hands, "That's the one about the gospel train picking up righteous souls? That'd be perfect! Better than perfect! It should transport any souls still lingering here, home to their resting place." She began packing up her supplies. When everything was tucked back into the carpetbag she said, "Well, that just leaves the bill. I get the candles at discount and I'll give them to you at cost. I had to mail-order the river water, because it doesn't stay potent for long."

Little Mustang protested, "We have a river right here in the city."

"Yeah, but they reversed the flow of it about a hundred years ago. Now it works just like an upside-down tarot card–it does the exact opposite of what a forward-flowing river does. If I'd used Chicago river water, the ghosts would be flocking here in even greater numbers than they are now." She dug into her bag and pulled out a slightly crumpled piece of paper. "I've got an itemized bill here. All together it comes to one hundred and twenty-five dollars. I can take cash, check or MasterCard."

"How much?" Little Mustang couldn't believe her ears. Miss Sarah shot her daughter a look, then retrieved her purse from the bar and pulled out her checkbook and a pen. "That will be fine," she said, as Mustang muttered, "Yeah, but the Des Plaines river is just..."

Miss Sarah had just finished writing out the check when a howling wind blew through the club. It didn't come through the door or windows; it was stirred up by something inside the room. The gust was as powerful as a tropical storm, but its targets were selective. The stack of loose receipts laying on the cooler didn't even rustle; but the candle next to them was extinguished. A whip-thin gust of wind circled through the room blowing out the other candle flames. Then a wall of wind knocked the women against the bar and slammed the doors shut.

Unbidden, a favorite line from an old movie came to Little Mustang: *Don't shoot him, it'll just make him mad.*

Darkness dropped down over the windows like nightshades,

blanketing the room in twilight.

A tearing sound pierced the air. Little Mustang whirled.

It was just Miss Sarah, ripping the check into little pieces; her hands were trembling as she let them float to the floor.

Little Mustang nodded in approval. "Now what?"

Miss Sarah didn't answer; didn't seem to hear her.

Mistress Ariana hiccupped, then flapped her hands at them. "Sorry, I always–hiccup–when I'm scared." The wind whipped around them, dragging her words away.

Little Mustang groaned. "That's encouraging." She clutched the edge of the bar, trying to keep her feet under her in the gale.

The psychic clung to a barstool and fought as the wind tried to pull it away. "I don't understand what went wrong. (hic!) That banish spell is one of the most powerful I could (hic!) find. It's adapted from an old Mesopotamian ritual."

The wind shrieked in response. Little Mustang clamped her hands over her ears.

Dark shadows seemed to climb the walls, ten feet tall and growing. The silhouettes moved with menace, as if preparing for a violent showdown. Like an old western, where the gang of outlaws meets up in the street and stride into town.

Little Mustang shouted at the psychic, "You better get my mother out of here. I'll see if I can calm these guys down."

Mistress Ariana nodded, then shouted, "Where is she?"

Little Mustang scanned the room. The club had filled with heavy shadows; she could barely see two feet in front of her. "Mama? Where are you?" There was no answer. She turned to Mistress Ariana. "Check the front section, I'll look over the back." Pulling herself along, one handhold at a time, she worked her way down the bar against the wind; searching more by feel than sight. Down the length of the bar, across the main floor, around the corner of the stage. Faintly, she heard the psychic call out, "I don't see her." A tangle of barstools flew through the air and crashed into the stage. Little Mustang paused beneath a table to catch her breath. That was when she heard it: a low-pitched wail.

Little Mustang crawled toward the sound. She bumped into the bar, then felt her way around the corner to the aisle behind it. The sound was growing louder. It was even blacker back here. She groped in the darkness. Her hand touched flesh; her mother's wrist. She clamped onto it and inched forward.

Miss Sarah had wedged herself into one of the storage areas under the bar, between two cases of liquor. She was curled in a ball, her hands wrapped over her head. She rocked back and forth in time to her keening. Little Mustang wrapped her arms around her, covering her body with her own. "It's gonna be all right, Mama. It's going to be all right." Her mother didn't seem to realize Little Mustang was there.

Mustang heard the sound of smashing glass; beer mugs, bottles, the mirror maybe. The wind whipped in a cyclone around them, cutting at their hands and faces. Mustang put her hand to her cheek; it came away with blood. The wind was carrying shards of broken glass.

"Mama, we gotta get out of here." She pulled the woman to her feet, wrapped an arm around her waist and started toward the door. Still her mama wailed a low, wordless moan.

A thick mist seeped into the whirlpool of wind. Faces and figures began to form. These weren't the ethereal bodies of the musicians who came to hear the Blues each night. They weren't the ghosts Little Mustang had played with as a child. Where other children had imaginary friends, Little Mustang had had playmates that were invisible, but real. And dead. Little Mustang had discovered young that she could see ghosts when others couldn't. She'd quickly learned not to talk about the ghosts to live folks, not even Mama.

These spooks, though, were something different. Had the psychic botched the spell and accidentally summoned them? They were creatures out of the blackest nightmare: moldering bodies, with the flesh hanging in tatters and broken bones jutting out at jagged angles. Worms crawled from the orifices of their skulls and their sunken, hollow eyes glowed with a cold blue flame. Where hands should have been were cloven hooves and sharp-taloned claws.

What if these were the ghosts her mother saw? What if Mama saw one kind of ghost, and she saw another? Little Mustang's stomach churned. She was to blame. It wasn't Mama's fear; it was the wide-open trust she herself had in the spooks. She'd welcomed the ghosts, never realizing there might be more than one kind.

The copper tang of terror filled her mouth as she stepped in front of Mama to shield her. Little Mustang tried to speak, only a croak came out. She cleared her throat, braced her knocking knees and tried again. In a voice far too trembly and not nearly as loud as she intended, she said, "Get out. You're not welcome here any more."

A disembodied face swam out of the mist and hovered nose to nose with her. Little Mustang screeched at it, "GET OUT OF MY BAR!" Hands grew where only a head had been. They grabbed Little Mustang by the lapels, lifted her off the ground, and hurled her across the room.

Miss Sarah heard her daughter hit the wall with a sickening thunk. Before she could run to the rescue, the apparition stretched out an arm an impossible length; across the room and over the bar. It grabbed a bottle–one of the fruit-flavored vodkas–and broke it across the edge of the counter. The sharp scent of raspberry wafted through the room. The spirit whipped the jagged-edged bottle toward Miss Sarah's face.

"KNOCK THAT SHIT OFF, OR I'LL KICK YOUR ASSES FROM HERE ALL THE WAY BACK TO HELL–BY WAY OF CLEVELAND!" A deep, womanly voice boomed across the room, so loud it made the liquor bottles rattle. The apparition seemed to implode. As it popped out of existence, the broken bottle dropped to the floor and shattered. It was as if the howling wind had been pouring from a faucet, and someone had turned the nozzle off. The sudden silence was deafening. The mist dissipated; soaking into the floor, and the very air itself. A sudden scent of perfume filled the air.

The lights flickered on.

They heard the man yelling and pounding on the front door. Invisible hands threw open the oak slab. The man burst in, blustery and wild. "I've been banging on the door for five–"

With a frightened *meep!*, Mistress Ariana swiped her bag from the counter, dashed for the exit and slammed headlong into the man, knocking him to the ground. She stomped on his hand in her scramble to get out. He yelled, but she didn't slow down or look back.

The man sat up, clutching the fingers of his left hand, and thundered, "What the hell has been going on in here?"

Miss Sarah's eyes moved in an intricate pattern between the

four figures like a connect-the-dots puzzle in a child's book: from the man, to the exit where the psychic had so recently been, to her daughter standing in the middle of the floor dazed and slack-jawed...and back to the ghost.

Little Mustang was spellbound. Standing before her was the greatest Blues guitar player of all time. The woman was wearing a sleeveless, slinky, leopard-skin dress, so short the hem of a lacy black slip peeked out beneath it. The dress was belted by a long chain of silver dollars that clanked when she walked. She had a matching bracelet of four coins, and drop earrings made from three shiny silver dimes. And strapped to her back, with a belt of leopard skin that exactly matched her dress, was a top-of-the-line, steel-bodied National guitar. It was Memphis Minnie, the woman who had routinely beat Muddy Waters, Tampa Red and Big Bill Broonzy in live musical duels all over the South Side of Chicago. She was right here in the Lonesome Blues Pub.

She looked more solid than most ghosts. You could still see through her, but only faintly. And the colors were faded, though most ghosts couldn't do colors at all.

A barstool slid behind Mustang. She collapsed onto it. "Mama?" she said, without once taking her eyes off the woman before her. "Jayhawk's back, and I think he brought a friend."

Her mother whimpered, "Just what we need, another ghost."

The ghost laughed at that, revealing a mouth crammed full of gold-capped teeth. It wasn't all that special to see a single gold tooth: most of the musicians and the Felt Hats had them. Some even had silver caps with a star or heart-shaped design cut out of the front. And once, a national act had come in sporting a front tooth with an inlaid diamond. But never had Little Mustang seen a full mouth done up in gold.

Memphis Minnie strode across the room. Little Mustang could have sworn she heard the high heels clomping on the floorboards, even though the ghost's feet seemed to hover a good inch above the floor.

"Now doll, I ain't just any ghost. And Jayhawk traveled all the way to Memphis to ask my aid. Been a while since I been back here, so I didn't much mind." She looked around. "Not a bad club ya got here. This'n's cleaner 'n most. Ya got no dance floor to speak of. Wouldn'ta had no business without room ta dance, in my day. 'Course, 'tweren't no North Side clubs atall, back then."

Little Mustang stuttered, "C-c-can, um, can I have your autograph?"

"Little Mustang!" her mama scolded.

Memphis Minnie just laughed. "Chile, Jayhawk done tole me all about you. Said you play a fair bit of guitar–we'll see 'bout dat. I'll sign your diary, we'll play a tune or two, and set and jaw a bit. Later. Ri' now, your mama and I got bidness to tend to." She nodded toward the man, who was still standing goggle-eyed. Little Mustang would have bet the farm he was goggling because he was seeing a ghost, and not because it was Memphis Minnie, only the greatest Blues woman of all time. "Why doncha have your daddy there run you on home for now?"

"He's *not* my father!"

Memphis Minnie said, "Don't make no never mind; he's a man, and menfolk always got cars. He c'n getcha home."

Little Mustang stood up on wobbly knees, but continued to stare.

"Go on now, girl. Git."

"looked just like the 1930 Vocalion publicity picture!" Little Mustang finished breathlessly.

Ratman protested, "I never seen a picture of her in leopard skin."

"I didn't mean the dress. I've never seen that one before, either. But her face, her hair, her *guitar.*"

Little Mustang must have been under the ghost's spell to get into the stranger's car, but she hadn't been so dazed that she let him drive her home. He'd have wanted to come in and wait for Mama. So, she'd insisted he drive her to Ratman's house instead. As she hoped, Ratman's invite to the man had been so stilted that the stranger had said an awkward "no thanks" and gone away.

"What do you think I should play for her? I was thinking I could play one of my originals. She wrote at least two hundred songs while she was alive, I figured she can tell me if mine are any good. I could do *Drinkin' Again* or *Crazy Whiskey Blues*–that sort of sounds like some of her songs, but she always drank gin, do ya think she'd like a song about whiskey even though she drank gin? Or do you think I ought to play one of her songs? Maybe *Nothing in Rambling* or maybe she'd be offended if I did her stuff. I could–"

"Little Mustang!" Ratman roared.

She stopped talking and looked on, worried, as he paused for a coughing spell.

When it was over, he finished his sentence. "Girl-child, I know you is excited to meet your all-time favorite heroine righ'tere in the flesh...well, spirit. An' I wanna hear ever word 'bout it. But let an old man's ears have a little rest whys you take a breath now an' 'gain."

She dropped her head sheepishly. "I'm sorry. I know I've been running long at the mouth."

Ratman smiled indulgently; she was parroting back a phrase he'd used to say a long time ago, only in the direst of cases, when an old man had needed a little quiet from a chattering magpie of a girl. But that was back when she didn't stand higher than his knee. He was certain he hadn't used it in half a dozen years.

"We'll pick out the perfect song, I promise," he said solemnly.

That didn't lift the look of shame from her face.

"Wha' t'you worryin' over?"

"I'm talking on and on, and I didn't even tell you the most important bit."

"Let's see, ya covered wha' she said, wha' she was wearin', how old she looked, the hairstyle she 'as sportin' an' which guitar she 'as carrying." He winked at her. "What's left?"

She blushed. "It's not about her, at all. It's Jayhawk– he's back."

"Great glory to God in the morning!" Ratman jumped to his feet, in slow motion, but fast by his standards. He pushed his chair back and did a shuffling soft-shoe.

Little Mustang laughed. "Sit down, you old fool. Before you hurt yourself."

After Miss Sarah hammered out a deal with the ghost, she went home to change and eat just a bite of dinner. To her disappointment, neither Little Mustang nor her handsome man had been there to greet her, though she'd secretly hoped that maybe both of them would be. Too soon to ask so much. But she wouldn't dwell on that now. Take your successes where you can find them; they'd been few enough of late.

Memphis Minnie had agreed to clear out the evil spirits, revenants, poltergeists and more rambunctious of the apparitions. And she had agreed to do whatever it took to keep them out–even if that meant Minnie had to move her haunting grounds to Chicago full-time. In return, Miss Sarah had agreed to stop all the psychic and exorcism stuff. The ghost had said, "You was just rilin' them up. There ain't but a handful a preachers what can do a proper ex'rcism. Takes a powerful kinda brimstone-and-hellfire belief, and they ain't preachin' that kind a faith much these days."

There was leftover meatloaf and potatoes in the fridge. She warmed those and ate them quickly; without a dinner companion, there was no reason to linger. Besides, she wanted to get back to the club early. She rinsed her dishes and set them in the sink, then headed out.

Miss Sarah stepped up to the door of Lonesome Blues a good hour before the rest of the staff were scheduled to arrive. Blues clubs didn't keep the same hours as most bars. On weeknights, the doors opened to the public at eight in the evening. The music started at nine-thirty and ended at one-fifteen. By one-thirty the audience was cleared out. They were open later on weekends.

Miss Sarah had come early to do the setup, to take care of all the little chores the staff usually helped with, before they arrived. It was just a token gesture, to let them know she appreciated how they'd all filled in, in her absence. And tonight, sometime, she'd make up with Little Mustang. The girl's birthday was just a week away. She'd do it up big: find another present beyond what was already wrapped and hidden in the closet. Their budget couldn't really afford it, especially not with the hospital and ambulance bills on the way; but a girl only turned eighteen once, and Little Mustang had been carrying a woman's load of work and responsibility.

Not just this week; longer than Miss Sarah had realized. Little Mustang had always been by her side working. When other children were fussing about having to do chores at all, Little

Mustang had been fussing that she wasn't allowed to do more in the club. It'd taken Miss Sarah by surprise when she realized that, by all rights, she ought to have named Little Mustang a partner in the business long ago. For a moment, she considered making that the bonus birthday gift...Except she feared the City wouldn't look the other way anymore if they flaunted the girl's underage presence.

If things went as Miss Sarah hoped, she could present Little Mustang with a check, instead. They didn't own the land the club was on, but she could sell the business. The lease was transferable and good for another ten years. With that money, Little Mustang would be able to enroll in college right away. If she was frugal, she wouldn't even have to work part-time, and could concentrate on her studies. Miss Sarah wasn't sure what she'd do with her share of the money yet, but she had a few ideas. She slotted her key into the lock.

Miss Sarah heard rustling in the dark, but, she told herself firmly, *Memphis Minnie is taking care of the rogue ghosts now;* she had nothing to worry about. She reached for the light switch. As the light flooded the room...

Wild applause broke out.

Standing there in a row, like a scruffy honor guard, stood every member of the staff, even the ones who weren't scheduled to work tonight, and all the regulars, too. They clapped and cheered until she thought she'd sink right through the floor from embarrassment. There were even six or eight ghosts standing at the end of the line.

For She's a Jolly Good Woman suddenly blared through the stereo. That was more than she could stand. "Jayhawk, turn that off!" The ghost accommodated the request by changing the song to Donna Summer's *She Works Hard for the Money.*

The honor guard broke up and she found herself surrounded, trying to respond to a dozen people at once, congratulating her and telling her they were glad she was back. It was like a grand homecoming, though she'd only been away a few days.

Not only was the night's setup done, the place had been spruced up. A banner of red shiny fringe lined the timbers around the riser section and the foot and ceiling of the stage.

Little blue lights had been snaked between the rows of liquor bottles; the mirror behind the bar reflected the soft blue glow. Everything seemed to sparkle; even the glass in the picture frames and the metal legs of the barstools seemed to shine brighter. She wondered if the crew had gone on a cleaning binge, or if it was just the fact that the evil spirits had been driven away.

Dee and Jami had a row of shots lined up along the bar, a rainbow of liquid colors. The clear ones were probably tequila or gin. The golden brown were whiskey. The basics for the old-timers. The brighter colors were the more adventurous concoctions for the younger generation. The orange ones were vodka and OJ concentrate. The red ones were probably cranberry and Absolut. The yellow ones, lemon drops. The blue was rum and blue Curaçao. And the single black one with bubbles was Diet Coke. Miss Sarah smiled as she saw Little Mustang reach for that glass.

They crowded the bar, jostling elbows as they picked out a drink. Then the motley crew turned to face Miss Sarah and raised their glasses in the air. Miss Sarah wasn't a heavy drinker; hadn't done a shot in years. But maybe just one. She selected an orange drink and lifted it to match their toast. With shouts of "Welcome Back!" they tipped their heads, gulped the drinks and slammed the shot glasses down on the bar. There was more than one person left sputtering. But there was laughter, too. And for the first time in a decade, Miss Sarah felt like she had a family here, in this beat-up old Blues club.

**Oh the Blues ain't nothin' but a woman can't see her man
He ain't never around when she got time on her hands**

There was a reason waitresses usually dated musicians, Miss Sarah thought wryly, though when her girls asked her advice on the matter, she generally counseled against it. Musicians didn't have a regular paycheck, didn't have insurance and tended to quit their day jobs if they got one good music gig. But, they did work the same hours. She was at the club six, and sometimes seven nights a week, and after her unscheduled vacation, she wouldn't have a day off anytime soon.

She and that handsome man had been trying to see each other as often as they could, but their schedules kept getting in the way. He was dayside, she was nights. He worked nine to six, she worked seven to two. That gave them one hour a day, and afternoons on the weekends. It wasn't much time to get to know each other. Sometimes he came to the bar during the first set. If things were slow, she could talk to him between pouring drinks. But it was difficult to carry on a conversation over the loud music. And it didn't look good to the girls; she'd discouraged their boyfriends from hanging out while they were working.

Still, management should have some perks–she'd take what time they could steal. They'd made a game of their dinner hour, finding unusual places to go; always near the club, so the travel time didn't cut into their "date." Today, they were meeting at the Lincoln Park Conservatory, a greenhouse for tropical plants and domestic flowers. She stood on the sidewalk outside, admiring the flower beds that stretched through the park, as she waited for him. She glanced at her watch; five after. She hoped he'd get there soon, so they didn't have to hurry through their meal. She saw his head bob up behind a family pushing a baby stroller. He waved when he spotted her.

"Hello, Pretty Lady!"

"Hello, handsome man!"

"Are you hungry?" He held open a brown paper bag for inspection. The heavenly scent of Italian beef and green peppers floated out of the bag. She dipped her hand in and stole a french fry. It was still hot. He must have found a sandwich shop nearby.

"Hey! No fair!" he said, slapping at her hand.

She grinned and took a bite. It was golden and crispy with just a tang of salt. Perfect!

They went in, quickly found a bench under an exotic fern, and spread their meal out. The sandwiches were messy; they were only good if dipped into the bowls of beef broth with each bite. They giggled through the meal; grabbing for the same french fries and trying to eat the sandwiches without splattering each other.

When they'd finished, they wadded the papers up and stuffed them back into the paper bag. Miss Sarah reapplied her lipstick while he went looking for a garbage can.

She stood up as he returned. "Walk a while?" she asked,

holding out her hand.

Hand in hand, they strolled the winding paths, ducking under the leaves and fronds that hung over the path.

"How did you become a traveling salesman?" she asked.

"I've always been good at talking to strangers," he said. "Just love to meet new people, roam the country, see new places. See what's the same and what's different from town to town."

"No family at home, missing you?"

"My dad's back there, still lives in the city, in the house his grandparents bought. Neighborhood's changed a lot since then, but he won't leave. I've got two sisters in the suburbs, and half a dozen nieces and nephews."

"Ever get tired of the road, think about settling down?"

"Sure," he said, and laughed. "Every time I hit road construction in the summer, and every time I wind up stuck in a blizzard in winter—which happens at least twice every January. But I'll settle down one of these days. I'm a family man, at heart."

"I'm sorry you got off to such a rocky start with my daughter."

He shook his head. "It's mostly my fault. I thought she might be scared and need some looking after when you were injured. Most girls her age would have been scared by the ambulance and blood and the thought of their mother going to the hospital. She's not like most girls."

It was Miss Sarah's turn to laugh. "No, she's not. She's pretty fearless. She went through some tough situations when she was young. But she was scared the other night, just the same."

"She didn't show it."

"She never had much use for tears, even as a child. She learned young, watching the musicians, that no matter what was going on behind the scenes—if you'd been evicted from your apartment that afternoon, if your boyfriend broke up with you, or your mother just died—no matter what, you put a smile on your face to meet the audience."

"She's not like most girls her age," he said again.

"No. She started playing harmonica when she was four, switched to guitar when she was seven. She can tell you the history of every Blues musician who ever played in Chicago—but she doesn't have a clue who New Kids on the Block are."

"But you do?"

"I still read *Rolling Stone*," she said with a twinkle in her eye.

They stopped near a reflecting pool filled with water lilies and giant koi fish. "Let's sit here a while," he suggested. They settled on the low stone wall. A speckled orange fish came to the surface and blew bubbles at Miss Sarah. "He's begging for food."

Sarah splashed her fingers in the water; the fish swam closer to investigate. "I'm sorry, Mr. Fish, I don't have any food for you. But you're a fat old thing. I don't believe you're starving."

"A cool head in a crisis–I admire that. But I wonder, did she learn that from the musicians, or from you? Seems to me, you're all the role model a girl could need."

Miss Sarah squeezed his hand gratefully. "I wish that were true, but I've been so weak and scared. Lately it seems like she's the grownup and I'm the scared little girl."

He pulled her close and hugged her. "You are many things, Sarah, but I wouldn't say weak is one of them." He drew back and studied her. "Your daughter ever do drugs, get in any trouble?"

She was shocked by the question. "Little Mustang!? Never!"

"So, as a single mother, in a time when that wasn't really accepted or supported, you raised a daughter, kept her out of the street gangs, away from the drugs, made her focus on school so she got a high school diploma and may even go on to college, and taught her a work ethic and practical business skills, in the process. At the same time, you started a small business, kept it going for eighteen years–most clubs and restaurants fail in the first year–ran it single-handed, and held your own in a competitive industry." He spread his hands wide. "Show me the weakness in that."

Miss Sarah's mouth fell open. "But the ghosts...I've been so afraid..."

He took her by the shoulders and turned her to face him. "Sarah, kids tell ghost stories round a campfire to scare each other. Most folks wouldn't spend one night in a haunted house if you paid them. Ghosts are scary. That's not weakness–it's just common sense."

Sarah turned away and trailed her fingers in the water, studying her reflection in the ripples. The white shock of hair had tumbled out of place again. She smoothed it back into place with wet fingertips.

"It doesn't scare my daughter," she said finally.

"Forgive me, but the young are fools and fools go where angels fear to tread."

"Is that what you think I am?"

"An angel? Yes. My angel."

"I think my halo slipped," she whispered.

"Let me fix that for you..."

The kiss was warm and moist and filled with the promise of more tender things to come.

The Blues ain't nothin' but a low down heartache
Hurt so bad, it's bound to break

What on earth was he gonna do about that girl? The man shook his head somberly as he aimed his Cadillac northeast along Highway 29. It was a three-hour drive back to Chicago. He got up two hours early every morning so he could drive out to the target area and still put in a full day of sales calls, pitching the new Hoovaluxe vacuum cleaner. But he found himself pointing the nose of the Cadillac back toward Chicago a little earlier each day. Too long to be commuting twice each day; he ought to move his base of operations into the territory he was trying to cover. But what could he do? He was falling, hard and fast, for that sad-eyed woman. Those eyes didn't look so sad when they were looking into his.

It was crazy—he'd known her only two weeks and yet...he was certain this was a woman he could make a life with.

Corporate headquarters had called again. Wanted to know why he was still hanging around Chicago, neglecting the rest of his territory. Chicago wasn't home; Detroit was. Headquarters had an opening in their main office. A job that would let him drive to work and back each night for two weeks, without having to stop for gas. His supervisor had already agreed to write a letter recommending him for the position.

That was putting pressure on him to decide. If he was gonna stay a salesman, traveling the territory, he could simply route his trips through Chicago, stop off and see Sarah, court her proper. But an office job would tie him to his desk. There'd be long hours for the first year or two; wouldn't be the time or energy for weekend jaunts.

His heart was sure of the woman. He could make a life with her, buy a house–with the raise from his new job she might not even have to work. They could start a family; it was late for her, but not too late.

Standing in the way was that girl. Not quite old enough to be on her own–at least according to her mother, and yet, too old to blend in to a new family. An only, unruly, wild child. A child that didn't like him, not one little bit.

Her birthday party was two days away. His pretty lady had invited him–against her daughter's wishes, he was sure. Sarah said the girl had agreed. Maybe the girl was feeling generous, though he couldn't detect a generous bone in her body. But she'd gotten what she wanted; she'd dragged her mother back into the club against her will. Made her face the ghosts. Foolishness, that's all it was. A person ought to be afraid of ghosts. The girl's affinity toward them, friendship with them, was unnatural. A sign of a disturbed mind.

She was playing with dark powers she didn't understand. He wondered if she dabbled in the black arts. If somehow, she'd cast a spell or accidentally summoned a demon, if maybe that was what had attacked Miss Sarah in the club that night. A guilty conscience would account for the girl's hostility. He didn't put it past her to try and summon more ghosts, the spirits of famous musicians, to draw a bigger crowd to the club. Mother and daughter claimed that the "house" ghost had brought that profane woman's spirit to the club, but he wasn't so sure. Just look how the wild child fawned over it, following the tattered tail of the spook like a lost puppy.

That girl was in the thrall of ghosts.

A pile of discarded clothes lay on Little Mustang's bed that she'd tried on and rejected as not quite the right thing for the party. Now she was modeling a tight red mini dress, with a hem three inches shorter than she'd ever worn, in front of her closet mirror. Mama would not approve, but it wasn't Mama's birthday. She clipped the price tag off the sleeve, then belted the dress with a scarf of gold lamé and dug out a dozen gold-tinted bangle bracelets and matching drop earrings from her jewelry box. A pair of black hose was next. A black velvet beret with a gold brooch and black stiletto heels completed the outfit. She'd have to pack more demure clothes for this evening. Mama would never let her waitress in this outfit.

She carried her tackle box full of makeup into the bathroom and set it on the sink. Mustang combed her fingers through her newly dyed hair, lifting a section at a time to check that the roots were even. She spread the hand towel over the edge of the basin to protect her dress, then leaned forward until her face was only inches from the mirror and began applying her makeup.

Most of the waitresses had offered to fill in for her, so she didn't have to work on her birthday, but she'd said no thanks. The musicians and regulars would be dropping by all night to wish her a happy birthday. If she was working, they'd be less likely to try and slip her a "birthday drink." Most of her high school classmates had been drinking since they were freshmen. At first, they'd crowded around to be her friend, certain she'd be able to get them into the bar, no fake ID needed. When they found out she wasn't going to be the inside track for an underage drink, and that she didn't drink herself, ever, they'd dumped her. She didn't mind the dumping: she'd had little in common with her classmates, other than a few cool kids in the high school band. While her classmates were buying Madonna posters and CDs by U2 and REM, she was hanging out with the greatest Blues musicians in the country—alive or dead. Her classmates had never even heard of them.

Still, the older she got, the harder it was to say no to the drinking and peer pressure—not from her classmates, from her friends at the club. Not drinking reminded them she was young.

She patted her cheek gently, to see if the base was dry. It was still damp, so she set aside the blush and dug out her eyeliner.

She was bummed out about one thing: the stranger was coming to her party. It wasn't fair—the birthday girl ought to be able to decide who got invited. But Mama had insisted, then pleaded, yelled at her, then cried, over inviting that stranger to the party. "Don't I deserve to have one friend there?" Like she wasn't friends with the staff, the musicians and the regulars.

Then Mama had decided she was against having the party at

the club and declared they were going to have it at the apartment instead. She complained they spent too much time at the bar, and a teenager ought to spend more time in a healthier environment. Little Mustang had insisted, then pleaded, yelled at her, then cried, that the party had to be at the club. She had a guest list of thirty just of musicians, regulars and staff. The apartment only held a dozen people comfortably, and Mama had gone and invited a bunch of her high school classmates; "I figured you'd want to be around people your own age." Mustang didn't want to spend time with her former classmates and she sure didn't want to be in close quarters with that stranger. Finally they'd reached a compromise: the stranger for the club.

If Mama wanted to add a dozen people she thought Little Mustang oughta be friends with, then fine. Mustang would take their presents and let them eat her cake, but it'd be done at the club, where she could spend time with the folks and ghosts she really wanted to be with.

She finished painting her lids in a swirl of glittery colors, then added six layers of mascara. Bright red lipstick finished the look.

Little Mustang wiggled her hips and posed seductively in front of the mirror. A sexy woman stared back. She grinned at her own reflection. "Mama's gonna have a cow when she sees *this*."

The Blues ain't nothin' but an aching heart
A man and your mama tearing you apart

Miss Sarah had gone to the club early to prepare for the party. She set the bags full of decorations, photo albums and party favors down on the sidewalk and shifted the sheet cake to one arm. Before she could dig the keys out of her purse, the door swung open.

"Thanks, Jayhawk. Much appreciated."

The ghost lifted the cake out of her arms. She watched it float toward the bar, then hover there, uncertainly.

"Oh...let's do the cake down at the stage end of the bar. And we'll do the presents back here. Do you want to take the cake out of the box and put the candles on?" She dug into one of the bags until she found the candles, then slid the boxes in quick succession down the bar. The cake wasn't as pretty as it might have been. But when the order was chocolate cake with milk chocolate frosting, the decorating options were limited. She'd had the bakery scroll a guitar and some music notes on top in tinted vanilla frosting–but the design couldn't be too complex, or Little Mustang would complain the vanilla frosting covered up the chocolate taste. The girl was so mature in some ways, and yet so childish in others. Perhaps that was just the way of eighteen-year-olds, to fluctuate uncontrollably between childhood and maturity.

Miss Sarah saw movement out of the corner of her eye–Memphis Minnie was on stage, bent over her guitar. Soft music drifted through the room. Miss Sarah eyed the ghost while she divided party favors and bowls of snacks among the tables and busied herself with the dozens of little party chores. She resolved to speak to the ghost, and started for the stage. Halfway there, her nerve failed and she turned back. Casting about for something else to do, her eyes lit on the rolls of streamers.

The question burned in her mind. She hadn't had the nerve to ask it when they first met, or since. She didn't want to upset the delicate balance they'd achieved. Memphis Minnie was so mercurial. Sarah dealt with volatile personalities all the time. A musician with sudden stage fright was as bad as a sad drunk. You could predict what people would do. A firm look and a stern voice could settle most rowdies down. And if that didn't work, there was always a bouncer nearby. But you couldn't just give the sign to Big Ray and have him take the ghost's arm and escort him out the door. You couldn't control them, and when they got angry, they had no self-control. There was just no limit to the danger and damage they could do.

And yet, the question gnawed at her. She worried the thought around in her mind, unable to leave it alone. If she could just understand, she might know what to do.

As she hung the streamers from pillar to ceiling beam and back again, she caught herself turning, so she could always face the ghost. She blew a breath out. "This is ridiculous, just do it, Sarah." She set the things down and marched toward the ghost.

Memphis Minnie looked up from her playing and watched her come.

Miss Sarah stopped a few feet short of the stage. The silence stretched out as she tried to think of a diplomatic way to ask the question. When the ghost raised an eyebrow in amusement, she plunged in. "I'm afraid I don't know your history, or your song catalog, as well as my daughter does."

Memphis Minnie laughed. "You's 'fraid of a whole hell of a lot of things, honey, and that child know more about me than I c'n remember. But you didn' come over here to conversate 'bout some damned-old songs folks has long forgot. You's got a question on yo' mind."

This ghost didn't seem to be able to speak a sentence without cursing, but Little Mustang insisted that was part of the woman's legend.

"My manners bother you," Memphis Minnie said, though she didn't seem sorry about it. "I fought many a man in my day—jealous women, too. Used a knife, a gun, a broken bottle, chairs. Whatever was at hand. Kept a jackknife tucked in my garter. Came in handy more'n once. Was a rough an' tumble world in those days. A woman who stole a music crown better be able to fight off stage to keep it. An uppity black woman, that couldn't fight, had to endure awful things...if she lived at all."

"There must have been safer places to work. Why choose such a dangerous job?"

Memphis Minnie roared, "Hell honey, I enjoyed it!"

She looked Miss Sarah over with a knowing gaze. "That ain' what you wanted to ask me."

"You wrote *Nothing in Rambling?*"

Memphis Minnie nodded. "Song did damned well by me."

Miss Sarah huffed in exasperation. "Then why do you do it?"

Memphis Minnie shook her head, confused by the question. Her features blurred together, as if the ghostly image couldn't keep up with the actual motion.

The sight made Miss Sarah feel queasy, like motion sickness or vertigo. She closed her eyes until the nausea had passed.

"You askin' why I write songs?"

"No! Why do you *ramble?* Why are you here?"

Memphis Minnie's body tensed. Her voice was guarded, full of accusation. "Thought you was glad I was here. Thought I was doin' you an' the handsome man a damned favor."

Miss Sarah felt her stomach twist. Had Memphis Minnie decided to claim the handsome man as a fee for her protection?

The musician had a reputation as a man-eater. As she saw the ghost making moonie eyes toward the bar where birthday candles were floating through the air, it dawned on Miss Sarah–the ghost was talking about Jayhawk. Miss Sarah had never seen a picture of Jayhawk, had never given much thought to what he might look like. She'd sort of assumed that nobody, not even the other ghosts, could see him. As long as she and Memphis Minnie had their eyes on different men, that was all right.

Memphis Minnie was looking at her now, with sharp eyes that seemed to glow. "You want me gone, I'll go. No skin off my nose." She held up a hand, and they both looked straight through it. "Ain't got no skin to be scratched."

Miss Sarah said quickly, "I didn't mean it that way. I don't want you to go...not you particularly." She tried to explain, "I want to know why the ghosts ramble. Why don't they stay put, or go on to Heaven...I want to know why they come *here.*"

Memphis Minnie sat forward, her legs spread wide, elbows resting on her knees. It wasn't a ladylike way to sit, but at least she had on a longer dress today, with a flared skirt that came down to her calves, so she wasn't flashing anybody. Miss Sarah had noticed that the musician seemed to enjoy showing off her frilly underclothes.

"You's touchin' on some powerful questions with that one. Don't be fooled, death don't make you all knowin'. Don't get no book of rules or sudden burst of knowl'dge in yer head. Mostly, you's wanderin' around in the dark after you's dead, lot like in life. Not ev'rone. Maybe some go on to Heaven or Hell, or stay sleepin' in their grave. But those that ramble? I 'spect they's the same ones that rambled in life. Ev'r see a musician stay put for long?"

She looked around the club, but her eyes seemed to see something beyond the club walls. "I lived in this city for more'n twenty years. But I wasn't here a week or two 'fore I got the urge to travel down the road a piece to Helena, or St. Louis, or back to visit family in Memphis. I was on the road pretty much near all the time. Shouldn' be a surprise I get itchy to travel after I'm dead."

"Why couldn't you settle down? Couldn't you find the right man? Didn't you make enough money?"

The ghost laughed, and mist puffed out of her mouth like smoke rings. "I had me several husbands, some legal, some not.

And I had me plenty of money in my day, though the record comp'ny stole most of it, an' I was hard off at the end. M' sister Daisy looked out for me, and some of the young'un musicians might bring some food by, ask to cook 'em up a good meal. Weren't that they couldn' cook–theyz just bein' kindly, knew Son Joe an' I wouldn'ta et that day, otherwise. But I had a heap a money in my day and all the men I wanted..." Her voice drifted off, as her memory carried her to happier times.

Miss Sarah was jealous. Her own memory had no happier times to carry her mind to. There were moments perhaps: when her daughter said her first word, the first time her baby climbed the rickety steps to the stage to play. Well, not the first time–that'd been a nightmare! But after that, when she was invited up to play her first guest solo. Little Mustang's high school graduation. There'd been moments. But they were scattered memories, there were no happier times.

The ghost's words interrupted Miss Sarah's sad thoughts. "Mebbe one reason you see so many Blues ghosts wanderin', is 'cause a shameful number of us don't have a marker on our graves. Nothin' to weight us down to that patch of earth."

"You don't..."

Memphis Minnie shook her head. Miss Sarah closed her eyes again.

"I was the best guitar player of my time. The highest paid Blues woman. I wrote and recorded me two hundred songs, and had hit records with a lot of 'em. Even Big Bill Broonzy said I played like a man. Meant it as a compliment. He'da said more, but he was still sore I beat him in the duels. I beat him more'n once, too. He stold a bottle a whiskey from me one time. I'd beat him in a competition; crowd was judgin' and they loved me to death. Carried me through the hall on their shoulders–though 'fore it all started, they was worried tha' the contest was rigged on accounta there weren't no way a woman could beat a man at guitar. They didn't pay us no money to entertain the crowd all night. Only the winner got anything, and that just a bottle a whiskey and a bottle a gin. Leastways he didn't steal my gin...

"But there ain't no headstone on my grave. Nor on a lot of others. And half thems that do, just got a plywood marker. Shameful, what it is. We gave so much laughter and good times to folks when they was poor, earned so much money for the record companies. Folks write history books 'bout us and make docoment'ries, musicians still playin' our songs in the clubs. But ain't a one of 'em can be bothered to put our names over our grave. Ain't no wonder we ramble and stir trouble up."

It'd been hot on the ride over–Mustang had worn her denim duster that came down almost to her ankles and kept it buttoned up the whole time, so she wouldn't be harassed about her dress on the bus. But it was worth it. She got off far enough down the block that she couldn't be seen through the windows of the club. There she paused to make last-minute adjustments. She powdered the oil from her face, retouched her lipstick and unbuttoned her jacket. Then with a jaunty air, she strolled down the sidewalk to make her big entrance.

She was met with wolf whistles and applause as she stepped into the club. That, and a look of horror on her mama's face. She turned to her admirers.

Big Ray was sitting on a barstool near the door. He flipped his head back and forth, sending his beaded braids bouncing. He drawled, "Look at you. All grown up and looking good enough to eat." Then he gave a growl.

Mustang got a funny feeling in the pit of her stomach, but she wouldn't let him rattle her cool. She threw her arms around his neck and gave him a big kiss, then flounced off to greet the rest of the crowd.

"Hey, Little Mustang!" Ratman and Old George called out in unison.

"Guys, please. I'm eighteen, now. It's just Mustang."

"Well Just Mustang, ya got a kiss for an old geezer, or you too growed up for that, too?" Old George asked.

Kisses and hugs followed. Liz joined her and they squealed and exclaimed at each other's outfits. Tonight the diva was decked out from the tip of her cowboy hat to the toes of her high-heeled boots in leopard skin. The shirt, of course, had black fringe.

They had been gathered at the bar, bending over a family photo album dated *1976 #1*. A tall stack of albums sat beside them.

Little Mustang whined, "Not the baby pictures. Mama, there are pictures of me all over the club. You didn't need to bring more from home."

Miss Sarah said, "I only brought a few. I thought they might like to look at some they hadn't seen before."

Liz glanced at the stack of albums; her eyebrows shot up when she realized *1976 #3* and *#7* were next in the pile. "How many albums do you have?"

"No more than any other mother, I'm sure," Miss Sarah insisted.

Little Mustang didn't mind tattling this time. "Nine shelves, one and a half bookcases."

Liz gawped.

Mustang mimicked her mama, "But no more than any other mother, I'm sure."

Before her mama could retort, a gaggle of teenagers surrounded Mustang. She greeted her band members first, introducing them around to the kids who'd been in high school marching band with her.

Her classmates were full of questions about the club, what kind of music her new band played and what she'd been doing since they'd graduated. They boasted of their music scholarships to various colleges and complained about their summer jobs.

Finally, the group started to break up, heading for the tables where pop and potato chips waited. Her mother moved in for a quiet moment. Little Mustang steeled herself for the comment she knew was coming about the dress, but Mama just pulled her close and hugged her and whispered in her ear, "Happy birthday, Little Mustang Sally. Eighteen! Some say you're a woman now, but you'll always be my little girl." Then she gave her another hug, tighter this time. There was a sparkle of tears in her mama's eyes as they drew apart.

Miss Sarah cleared her throat, then called out to the crowd, "Let's get a group picture with the birthday girl! Everybody onto the stage."

There were moans and groans, but others were already climbing the steps, eager to see what the view was like from the musician's side of the stage. It took most of five minutes to get the crowd posed as Miss Sarah wanted them; the tall ones in back and the short ones in front, layered down the steps and along the foot of the stage, with Little Mustang right in the center. "Perfect. Everybody hold it right there." She picked up the camera and centered the shot. "Everybody say 'More ice cream, please.'" She waited for the chorus, then snapped the shot. "Not so fast," she said to those already trying to escape. "Let's get one more, just for good measure."

There were spots in Little Mustang's eyes as she wove her way through the crowd to the bar. She greeted the ghosts, who were lurking on the fringes of the crowd. She wasn't sure if her school friends could see them, so she spoke quietly, knowing the ghosts could hear her. There were Memphis Minnie and Jayhawk, of course. But there were others who seldom visited the club, who'd come because it was her birthday. Willie Dixon, a burly man, even bigger around than the standup bass he played. A producer, songwriter and musician, he'd had a guiding hand in the creation of the Chicago Blues sound. Earl Hooker, second cousin to the more famous John Lee Hooker, and a slide guitarist who influenced Jimi Hendrix and Buddy Guy. Sonny Boy Williamson I, a brilliant harmonica player who never got over the fact that a younger musician stole his name and went on to much greater fame. Howlin' Wolf, King of the Chicago West Side Blues. His half-sister was married to Sonny Boy Williamson II, but Sonny Boy I didn't hold that against Wolf—at least, not after they were dead. And Alberta Hunter, an early Chicago songstress who was infamous for her run-ins with the mob, her lesbian tendencies and the fact that she was the first black musician to be backed up by an all-white band.

As she finished paying her respects to the ghosts, Little Mustang saw the stranger arrive. She was glad he hadn't been there for the group picture. She took a deep breath. She wasn't going to let him spoil her night. She dived into the crowd, stopping at each table to chatter happily with her friends.

The musicians began banging on the door, hours earlier than they'd usually arrive. They'd agreed to play a couple short sets for the afternoon party, before the doors opened for the night. But first, all the equipment had to be hauled in. There was such a pile of amps, instrument cases and boxes with electrical cords piled at the foot of the stage, it looked like moving day. It was that way every night.

The guests drifted toward the back of the bar, to give the musicians room to work and to escape the noise of the drum kit being set up.

"Is it present time now?" Little Mustang asked hopefully.

Miss Sarah laughed. "I guess it is."

Little Mustang felt a childish glee as she looked at the small mountain of tinsel and colored paper. She seated herself on a barstool in a slow, ladylike manner, so she wouldn't flash anybody (and give Mama an excuse to criticize the dress). The teenagers crowded around as Dee refilled soft drinks and Jami passed her presents. Little Mustang plucked the gold bow off the first package and ripped into the balloon-bouquet paper.

When the last of the paper and bows had been cleared away, the pile of presents included song books and CDs, guitar strings, T-shirts, and a denim jacket with the club logo that had been autographed by about a hundred local musicians. Bubble bath and perfume, flashy jewelry, glittery eyeshadow and bright colored nail polish. All the things a woman in the Blues might need.

When the last present had been passed around, the crowd wandered away again, to find seats near the stage before the music started.

A small group was left clustered around the corner of the bar: Little Mustang, Miss Sarah, the stranger, Big Ray, Jami, Dee and Liz. And two, old, felt-hatted men, sporting grins that were about to burst. Ratman shuffled up and gave her a hug. Little Mustang was careful not to hug him too hard; his arthritis had been acting up again. Then Old George elbowed his way in for his turn.

"Soooooo," Ratman stretched the word out until he was certain he'd caught everyone's attention, "has ya decided?"

"Decided what?" Miss Sarah asked. Little Mustang studied her mama's face, to see if she was part of the act, or really didn't know.

"Has ya decided which gift you want?" Old George prompted.

Big Ray asked, "What were the choices? With you two cookin' it up, has to be good."

Old George spoke first. "The girl-child, who ain't so much a child no more, gets to decide between a brand new, medium good—none of those Les Paul models—guitar." There was a gasp in the crowd. Good guitars, even medium good guitars, were expensive, particularly for a couple of retired old Bluesmen.

"Orrrrrrr," Ratman said with a flourish, "a gold cap on her front tooth."

There were a few chuckles, then applause. From everyone but Mama; Mustang saw her shoot a helpless, imploring look at the stranger, and anger boiled up inside. If there was something to be said about the gift, then it was Mama's place to say it. The stranger had no cause to speak here.

But that didn't stop him. His voice boomed from the back of the crowd. "That may be a good stunt for a Blues musician," –the way he said 'musician' made it plain he thought they were near-to the most vile things on earth– "but it isn't proper for a young girl. A young, *white* girl."

Liz gasped.

Jayhawk flashed the club lights ominously. Little Mustang doubted the stranger recognized it for the warning it was. The ghost was ticked off.

The stranger met their stares. "I don't want to sound like a bigot, but some customs belong to one race or another, and while it may be fine within its social group, it isn't proper outside of those boundaries. Miss Sarah tells me the girl–"

He won't even say my name, Mustang thought.

"–will be going to college in the fall. Soon, with luck, she'll have job interviews. A gold tooth certainly won't make the right impression with an interviewer." His tone suggested he had his doubts about how she'd do, gold tooth or no.

In a deceptively mild voice, Ratman said, "That assumes the interviewer will be white."

The stranger answered, "Like it or not, they usually are."

Somebody snarled.

The liquor bottles on the shelf rattled; but Chicago wasn't over a fault line and there weren't any big trucks lumbering by. Mustang whispered, *"Jayhawk, we can handle this. Don't make it worse."* The rattling continued for a petulant moment, then stopped.

Little Mustang turned to her mama, silently begging her to step in, to tell the stranger he was out of line, and couldn't talk to their friends that way.

Finally, her mama spoke. But it wasn't what Little Mustang wanted to hear.

Miss Sarah took a step closer to the the stranger and said, "We may not like it, but that doesn't change the way of the world."

Friendships could be broken here tonight. Little Mustang wasn't the only one who had expected Miss Sarah to come to her friends' defense. The racist comments had shocked the group. And if what the stranger said was true—that only made things worse.

Miss Sarah plowed on, desperation in her voice. "I've heard you say that so-n-so had gone and forgotten what color he was. Carla, that redhead who always wears the caftan in here—I've heard you two laughing behind her back, and some of the musicians do worse than that! Old George, you said yourself, she'd trespassed over the color line."

The old man bristled with anger. "Dontchew go blamin' this on me, woman!"

Miss Sarah put her hand on his arm; he jerked it away. She said, "I know when it comes to Little Mustang, you're all color blind and always have been—"

Old George thundered, "Comes from us havin' a righteous hand in her upbringin'!"

Miss Sarah pleaded, "Then you should want what's best for her. You may be color blind, but out there, in the rest of the world, they're not. And she can't stay hidden in here forever."

Ratman cleared his throat. The group hushed to hear his response. With a shaking hand, he lifted his cigarette to his lips, took a drag and let it out. When he spoke, it was a whisper—but a whisper filled with sharp edges. "They's a member of this family that's real good at hidin'—but Little Mustang...she ain't it."

No one spoke.

The silence grew heavier.

Little Mustang felt her throat close up and her stomach twist in a cramp as she watched the only family she'd ever known being torn apart. She looked back and forth between the two camps: a cold determination in her mama's eyes, anger and betrayal in the others'. She was desperate to do something, to fix things back the way they were before, or at least get everyone to pretend it'd never happened. But as she looked from one sullen face to the next, she knew that wasn't within her power.

Last week, she'd made up her mind to choose the guitar. Hers was beat all to pieces and hadn't been much good when it was new. She'd been secretly saving up for a new guitar for the last six months. She'd had her eye on a blond, acoustic/electric, steel-stringed Takamine, with a rosewood fretboard, built-in volume and tone slider controls, and setting-sun rosettes carved into the soundboard, though she'd been giving the Fender Mustang some thought.

But last week, she'd ridden the bus over to the hospital and paid the money toward the bill. She'd gone directly to the business office, so Mama wouldn't try to stop her. She hadn't been noble; she knew what they'd have to do without until those bills were paid.

Little Mustang pushed past Jami and Dee. She stood at the edge of the clearing that separated the two camps; it felt like she was standing at the edge of chasm. She caught her mother's eye and silently dared her to say something now. She announced, "My old guitar's just fine, thank you very much."

"Then a gold tooth it is," Old George chortled, showing off his own gold-sparked grin.

Ratman turned to her and spoke quietly, "You sure 'bout this?" She nodded.

Old George cackled with glee. "Maybe for your twentieth, we'll get a li'l diamond inlayed inta it, like Jelly Roll Morton."

The stranger started in, *"Your mother—"*

Little Mustang slammed her hand down on the bar, sending shockwaves through her arm that left it tingling with pain. "This is none of your damned business! My mother has a voice of her own. If she has a problem with this, she can say so herself. You are NOT my father, and you NEVER will be! You can—"

Big Ray slipped behind her and grabbed her into a bear hug. He stood so tall that his arms wrapped down over her shoulders and crossed in front of her, trapping her in his embrace. He pressed his cheek against the side of her head; she could smell the spicy-sweet cologne he always wore.

The bouncer could roar loud enough to be heard across the room over the loudest electric band, but he also had a whisper that could snake through its listeners without disturbing the other patrons. His words reached only the ears of the small group. "I don't mean to break up a good family fight just as it gets goin', but the *paid* entertainment was wonderin' if the birthday girl and her band would do 'em the honor of playin' the first song?"

The question left them all off-balance, as they realized everyone in the room had turned to watch them.

Little Mustang shook loose of Big Ray's arms. The adrenaline and anger were coursing through her body so fast and furious she couldn't bear to stand still. She glared at the stranger–despite her mama's excuses, this was his fault. Little Mustang truly, madly, deeply wanted a "do-over" so she could blow out the candles on her cake again. This time, she'd wish that the stranger drop dead.

In a voice crackling with energy she said, "Love to. Thought they'd never ask. We were done here, anyway. My guitar tuned?"

"Ain't it always?" Big Ray drawled. He offered her his arm. She took it and let him escort her down the aisle at a maddeningly-slow pace.

The singer for the night's band introduced her. "Won't you welcome to the stand the woman of honor, the woman of the hour, sweet eighteen, she breaks hearts and she can sing! Let's hear it for the birthday girl! Mustang Sally and her band, the Wyld Palominos!"

The applause (or was it just her own heartbeat?) thundered in her ears as she climbed the steps of the stage.

She lifted her battered old guitar from the stand and slipped the strap over her head. Her bandmates were already in their places. They'd planned and rehearsed their guest number days ago; a rowdy, fast-paced singalong. But it didn't seem right. Not now. Not after what had just gone down. She turned to them for a quick whispered conference. She made sure the drummer remembered the right tempo, squared her shoulders, then turned back to face the crowd.

She took a deep breath and stared out across the audience, seeing the faces one by one, making eye contact with each of them. It was a moment of truth, even if she wasn't sure what the truth was.

She took her guitar off, swung the instrument back into the stand, and reached for Jayhawk's guitar. A smattering of applause broke out. She knew Jayhawk wouldn't hold her to the house rule, that'd be up to the other band. But somehow, it felt right

Then she nodded at the table full of ghosts that had settled directly in front of her, an empty table the crowd had unconsciously avoided.

Finally, Little Mustang gave the signal for the song to begin. Her voice caught in her throat and she didn't know if she'd be able to sing.

But when she parted her lips, it was there, delicate and mournful.

My heroes are all dead and gone
Buried some sixty years ago
They wandered from town to town
Playin' their music on the road

Blues men from the Delta
Women who sang in the Medicine Shows
They played the only kind of song
My heart has ever known

Miss Sarah huddled in the embrace of her handsome man's arm, and watched her daughter through a film of tears. Her daughter belonged up on that stage. Belonged here in this club. And yet, she deserved so much more than this. The club had been a safe haven in which to raise the girl, but now, it hung like a manacle on her daughter's ankle, dragging her down, keeping her from seeing all the promise the future held.

The handsome man hugged her against his chest. She turned her head so her cheek rested against his heart. In one ear she heard the soft, comforting *thump-thump*, calling to her. In the other ear she heard her daughter's triumph, her daughter's heartfelt tribute to all that she loved, all that she could love.

The words were whispered so softly she thought she might have imagined them. *"Come away with me."* Was this another trick of the ghosts? *"Sad-eyed Sarah, come away with me. The girl's grown now, and I can chase the sadness from your eyes."* She tilted her head up, saw the handsome man's lips moving. Heard the siren song of his words and the silent pleading of his eyes.

"I..." The enormity of his words, of all that they implied, made her tongue stutter, then still. Her heart seemed to shudder inside her chest, not knowing whether to sing with joy at the thought of spending the rest of her life with this man, or to break in two from grief, knowing her daughter would never welcome this man into her life.

He stared deep into her eyes, and she thought he could see clear down to her soul. *"I know what I'm asking. I know what position this puts you in. But think about it. Please think about it."* Then he slipped away, out the door and into the darkness.

In Memphis they caught the Illinois Central
You know they were Chicago-bound
Others hitchhiked all the way
To the big city town

Polished their tunes on Maxwell Street
Met friends at Tampa Red's
They always found a place to play
Sometimes they went without a bed

Mustang stepped back from the mike and began to play a slow, haunting solo on Jayhawk's guitar. It was full of tears and weariness and a heart broken long ago. They were feelings too old for her, and she knew they weren't her own. And yet, they belonged to her, like memories and stories passed down from one generation to another.

She knew there were choices being made here tonight. Paths—chosen by instinct—that couldn't easily be retraced. Alliances formed. Friendships broken, families shattered. And yet, she belonged to more than one family. She'd found one in this club, in the ghosts, in this music, that gave her what an aunt, a cousin and a grandmother would not. The feeling that she belonged.

You know a lot of them died in a poor way
Chased by demons and hellhounds
Knifed by lovers, shot by thieves
Left to bleed on the cold, hard ground

Most went young to their graves
But the music still plays on
As long as their records survive
Their legends live on in a song

Miss Sarah crept slowly to Ratman's side. She stood there awkwardly, watching his back, bent by arthritis, stiffen as she approached. Watched his eyes, keeping vigil over her daughter. As Little Mustang and the band navigated a particularly tricky section of the song that he'd been coaching them on, she saw his face soften with a smile of pride.

A terrible guilt washed over her; she was ashamed that pride in her daughter's accomplishments could no longer fill the black, cold void that was growing in her heart. Her own mother's words, which had burned like acid through her ears that awful *day they'd last spoken, sounded in her head, "You're a terrible mother. No surprise–you were a spoiled, selfish child. The only thing that's changed is, you grew taller, older and got yourself knocked up."* Miss Sarah whispered the litany along with her mama, *"I'm a terrible, terrible mother."*

Ratman seemed to sense a change in her. He turned. "Miss Sarah?"

She folded her hands tightly in front of her as if she were praying. Her fingers turned a bloodless white from squeezing so hard. When she was certain she could speak without her voice trembling, she said, "How could you do this? You love her. I know you do. How can you let her settle for this?"

Ratman took a breath so deep the air must have swept through his toes before it rushed back out again. He nodded his head slowly, as if listening to an argument only he could hear. Then he looked at her, craning his bent neck up so he could meet her eyes. "I love that child like she was my own. Your man's wrong, this ain't a black an' white thang. It's too late now to be givin' this girl a daddy. I'd help; nothin' I'd like more than to graft that broken branch onto a strong, sturdy tree. But she's put down her own roots. Ain' no way in this old world that man an' that girl gonna make peace. Puts you in a powerful sorrow position. I can't fix that. But I can be there for the girl." He turned away, as if he too had been faced with a difficult choice, and had made his decision.

My heroes are all dead and gone
Buried some sixty years ago
Wandered from town to town
Playin' their music on the road

Blues men from the Delta
Women who sang in the Medicine Shows
They played the only kind of song
My heart has ever known

Blues ain't nothin' but love beaten down
Ya know that's my heart crawlin' on the ground

Miss Sarah had shooed the staff out early, on the heels of the very last customer—not Ratman or Old George tonight. They'd left early, when the kids did. Nothing more had been said. Not even "good night." Little Mustang had gone with the other kids, off club-hopping, she suspected. Though none were old enough to drink, the kids knew which clubs carded and which didn't. She hoped they wouldn't get in trouble.

Perhaps she was just being naive, but she hoped Little Mustang was down at the lakefront instead. Mother and daughter walked there often, after the club had closed and they'd finished cleaning up. Sometimes they'd sit on the rocks and talk until the first red rays of dawn streaked across the lake.

Wherever she was, Miss Sarah was glad her daughter had gone. After she'd come down from the stage, Little Mustang's every movement had been fast and sharp, as if she might break a bone or snap a tendon just picking up and setting down a glass.

Miss Sarah had been sad when her handsome man slipped away, but she'd been relieved, too. She had hoped his absence might defuse the tension in the room. But things had gone too far, and the ghosts hadn't liked what had been said about blacks, whites and Little Mustang's future.

Miss Sarah moved around the room slowly, collecting glasses, emptying ashtrays. Memphis Minnie sat with a bottle of gin, six glasses, and a table full of ghosts, regaling them with stories. No sound came from the table, but she could see them rocking back and forth with laughter, see them slapping each other's shoulders. Apparently their words, their happiness, was not hers to share this night.

That was fine. Miss Sarah needed the quiet. Jayhawk had worked invisibly beside her, but his movements were slow and distracted; bottles bounced unevenly in the air. Leftover drinks sloshed on the floor, as they floated to the counter. Finally, she'd shooed him off to join the other ghosts.

She took her time washing the glasses, then setting them on the plastic netting to dry. She scrubbed the length of the bar with a heavy detergent and extra elbow grease, as if she could scrub away the anger and sorrow and sadness that had built up in this club, like layers of dust and grime. Then she swept the floor, with long elegant movements, covering each inch of floorboard three and four times to capture the most minute particle of dust. She drew a dishtub of hot, soapy water and carried it table to table, washing not just the tops, but the support poles and the seats of the chairs.

"You scrub that damned table any longer, it gonna crumble to dust under your hand."

Miss Sarah looked up in surprise. She'd forgotten anyone was still in the club. A quick look around told her the other ghosts had left, or at least become invisible.

"Miss Minnie...I'm glad you could be at the party tonight. It meant a lot to my daughter." She couldn't look the ghost in the eye. She went back to her scrubbing.

Silence hovered between them.

"Ya know it ain't a good party lessun at least one fight breaks out," Memphis Minnie said at last.

Miss Sarah snorted, not caring it wasn't ladylike. "Maybe in your day. I admit I prefer things quieter."

Minnie picked up her guitar, strummed softly and began to sing.

I was born in Louisiana, I was raised in Algiers
And everywhere I been, the peoples all say
Ain't nothin' in rambling, either running around
Well, I believe I'll marry, oooh wooh, Lord, and settle down

The music faded away.

Memphis Minnie asked, "How old are you? How long's it been since you been with a man?"

Miss Sarah blushed and stammered, "That's none of your business."

The ghost waved her off. "I ain'ta talkin' sex. How long since yous had your breath took away so bad you plucked your heart out of your chest and gave it ta someone?"

Miss Sarah stood silent a long time. She surprised herself when she answered, "Not since before Sally was born. Her father. He died 'bout the time I gave it to him."

"It been eighteen years since you loved a man?" Memphis Minnie stuck her fingers in her ears and wiggled them, like she couldn't have heard right.

"I never stopped loving him."

"Somewhere along the line you fell in love with Billy Jay Hawkins."

Miss Sarah nodded. It was true. But those were cold arms to wrap around her at night.

The ghost sighed. "I got a heap of criticism for the men I loved and left. Some lef' me, but I never made a deal 'bout that. Weren't no use to complain. There was always 'nother one waitin' in the wings. I didn' keep 'em there, they just volunteered to stand in line. I was with Joe McCoy a good long time. Son Joe came along when I was older. Fiddlin' Joe Martin...I dated a lotta Joes. Guitar players, too. Jealous women usedta 'cuse me of tradin' husbands when I got tired of their guitar playin'." She grinned maliciously. "I won't say it weren't a factor. Sweet Willie Brown...you probably hearda him, on account of his pallin' around with Robert Johnson. There was a lot of talk 'bout me and Homesick James. He weren't sad when he was with me, I'll tell ya what..."

"You don't brag much, do you?"

Memphis Minnie cackled. Then her voice turned soft and serious. "It's a sad, mean old world out there, Miss Sarah, make no mistake. An' ain't nothin' gonna get ya through it but a man. I don't mean his money or his brains. You and I, we got that ourselves. I mean a strong shoulder to help bear the load, and a warm body to take the chill outta the night. Somebody that can touch ya just the right way and remind ya why the Lord Almighty put us here in the first place. You been wearin' a widow's shroud so long you got one foot and most of a hip in the grave, yourself. You better climb out before the undertaker come along and bury you."

"And Little Mustang?"

"That girl's eighteen. In my day, you weren't outta the house by fourteen, you better damned sure be payin' the rent."

"Things are different these days, and I'm glad of it. Eighteen is still young."

"And she's full of fire and piss and vinegar. Thinks she owns this club herself."

"She does."

"Glad you can see it. It don't take a spook to see where heart strings are attached. She belongs to this club, and you belong with that man. You got to take your love where you can find it, 'fore it's too late." The ghost leaned over her guitar again and began finger-picking a twelve-bar Blues. "Ever hear tell of Ida Cox? Blueswoman. She wrote a song puts me in mind of you."

Oh the Blues ain't nothin' but
a good woman wanting to see her man
Oh the Blues ain't nothin' but
a good woman wanting to see her man
She can't get when she want him,
gotta catch him when she can

Oh the Blues ain't nothin' but a slow achin' heart disease
Oh the Blues ain't nothin' but a slow achin' heart disease
Just like consumption, it kills you by degrees

Miss Sarah pushed open the front door of the apartment timidly and called out, "Little Mustang, you home yet?" She didn't know why she was creeping into her own home like a mouse afraid of its own shadow. But then, she didn't know why she was doing a lot of things these days. She crept down the hallway, checked the bathroom and bedrooms. Her daughter wasn't home, though bar-closing time had come and gone long ago. She suspected she wouldn't see Little Mustang again until the sun was well up in the sky.

She was too tired and too uneasy to sleep; there was no sense trying. By the dim glow of the nightlight, she went into the kitchen and started a pot of coffee. She sat down at the table and stared off into the darkness and began to think.

The sun had turned the sky a rosy pink, but had not yet made an appearance on the horizon when Miss Sarah shook herself out of her reverie. A heavy burnt odor hovered in the kitchen. Stiffly, she got up from the table to retrieve the coffee pot. She carried it to the sink and dumped it out, watching the black liquid swirl in eddies down the drain. She stared after it long after it was gone. Finally, she straightened, then shook herself to clear her head. She pulled the kitchen chair back from the table, then carefully climbed up on it. Reaching for the ceiling, she pulled the cover off the smoke alarm and removed the batteries.

From the kitchen cabinet she retrieved a pack of matches.

Then she left the room.

She stood in front of the bookshelves. One by one, she pulled the photo albums off the shelf and carried them to the kitchen.

She started with the 1967 album—the year she'd met Don at that singles dance. Tears fell on the plastic pages as she peeled the film back to remove the pictures. Soon the smiling faces of the young couple were obscured by the cherubic face of a baby in arms, then came the toddler, followed quickly by a two-year-old full of mischief. She took her time, pausing to look at each picture, as if memorizing the tiniest details. She raised the extra-special ones to her lips for a final kiss, before dropping them, one by one, into the sink.

The chore seemed to take hours, and yet the sun didn't appear to have moved when she finished. Both sides of the drain were heaped to overflowing with discarded memories. She stepped back, struck a match, and tossed the flame onto the photos. She watched her memories go up in smoke, and silently cried.

And now, here they all were, her handsome man sitting in that sleek, black Cadillac, with the engine revving; man and car eager to head off down the highway toward a bright shiny future.

Her daughter, Little Mustang Sally, brimming over with anger and betrayal, stood staring out the dusty frame window of the Lonesome Blues Pub. And she, Miss Sarah, stood, one foot in the gutter, one foot on the curb, and wondered if she could embrace love, if she had to abandon her daughter, everything she had lived for, at the same time?

She couldn't move. At the crossroads of her life, her arm could not reach for that shiny silver door handle, nor could her other foot step back up on the curb. To move in either direction was a betrayal of the one she loved most in all the world. Because she had realized last night, this morning, as she stared into the flames, that she truly did love this man. Love him with as much fear and passion and joy as she loved her daughter.

And so, there would be no happy ending. This man and this girl would never find common ground, would never declare a truce. She must kill off half of herself to let the other half live. She also knew that if she did not make the right choice, her soul would shrivel up and die. The problem was, she couldn't take the final step, in either direction.

She closed her eyes, turned her face toward Heaven. But God had stopped listening to her prayers long ago, and she'd stopped listening for His answers. Witnessing hellfire hadn't put her back on speaking terms with the Almighty.

An old man cleared his throat. She turned. Ratman stood near her morning glories, his face pushed into the middle of the flowers, as he inhaled their fragrance.

"Sarah," he said, turning to her. "Daylight's wasting. And your soul, just like these flowers, closes up when the sun goes down. It'd be best if you reached your destination before nightfall."

His words stole her breath away. They were full of truth, and some dark implications. He'd called her Sarah. Not Miss Sarah. She knew, in his wise old eyes, she had slipped from grace, fallen from his esteem. He had been first through her door when she opened the club. First to hold her baby in his arms. First to call her Miss Sarah. And last to leave her side each night. It was another badge of honor lost. Stripped from her. All that she had held dear, all that she had clung to was, in this moment, snatched away.

She had no pride, no dignity, and apparently no esteem–even from old friends–left. She realized she'd been burned and blistered by that ring of hellfire, so many years ago. And the wounds had infected her soul.

Her hope was all gone but one tiny spark, that spark she saw in the handsome man's eyes. Maybe that spark could grow, and she could once again become a woman who could stand tall, be sassy, and not shy away from the touch of the world.

She reached out, again. And this time, her hand grasped that shiny silver handle.

Mustang turned around before they pulled away from the curb. Didn't care to see their tail lights.

Even as the roar of the engine faded away, she didn't look back. She didn't figure Mama did, neither. Ratman, he waved 'em goodbye.

That was more than they deserved.

Miss Sarah looked back for a long time, though her daughter never turned around for a last look or wave.

Miss Sarah looked back for a long time, 'cause she knew she'd never see her little girl again.

The little girl who had called her Mama, the girl called Little Mustang, was dead. A woman stood in her place. A stranger, who would never call her "Mama" again.

The Blues ain't nothin' but a story that ain't been told Memories can keep you warm when you're feelin' cold

Little Mustang draped a black bed sheet over the front door, then moved silently into the club and draped one over the wall behind the bandstand. Ratman helped her, though neither said a word. When the last nail had been hammered into place, she turned to him, stiff and formal.

"I'd like some time alone."

He nodded and left without a word.

The door had barely closed behind the old man before Memphis Minnie appeared. She was dressed in a traveling coat—with a silver fox fur collar—and had a suitcase in her hand and her guitar slung over her back.

Mustang sank down on the steps of the stage, her chin propped up in her hand, her elbow on her knee. "You leavin', too?" Mustang asked, morosely.

The ghost set her suitcase down. "Got's to head back to Memphis. Check up on Son Joe. He was pesterin' a landlord what was raisin' the rent to try and evict a musician. Gots to go make sure he duhn't stir up so much trouble he gets hisself exorcised."

"But, you made a deal—"

"Made a deal with your mama," Minnie said.

"Now that she's gone, I need you more than ever." Mustang insisted. "The ghosts attacked me, too, you know!"

Minnie sat down on her suitcase. "Girl, now you know you didn't get more'n a bruise out of that. And you know they coulda seen to it ya landed on your head. They wasn't attackin' you. You was just another way to get at your ma. They preyed on her fear–and hers was so potent...ya know that bass player what was in here last Friday? The one so hopped up on cocaine he 'as playin' ev'rything in double time and was still pacin' the stage?"

Mustang nodded. Her mother had pulled him aside after the show, told him if he ever showed up that high again when he was scheduled to play, she'd ban him from the club.

"You mama's fear was like that to the ghosts."

Mustang's voice cracked. "But now I'm afraid."

Minnie said kindly, "Darlin', I sees that. But it ain't the ghosts you afraid of. What you's afraid of..." She shook her head sadly. "I can't help with that."

Mustang swallowed hard and squeezed her hands into tight fists, letting her nails bite into her palms, but she kept her voice steady as she said, "Think you'll come back and visit, sometime?"

"Hell, yes, girl. Chicago and Memphis, they's my homes. Can't stay put any place too long, but can't stay away forever, either. I'll be back by." She stood up, then stooped to pick up her suitcase. "They is one thing I can tell ya, and maybe it'll help. You's a wild woman–jus' like me. And you know what they say–"

"Wild women don't have the Blues," Mustang answered.

"That's right. You bemember that when ya starts gettin' down." Then she turned and walked away. Her image disappeared into nothing just as she reached the big oak door.

But Mustang wasn't feeling like a wild woman. She felt like a lost little girl. An orphan of life. And though she dug her nails deeper into her palms, the tears started falling down.

Ratman returned as the sun went down, returned with a couple of close friends–family now, he guessed–his partner in crime, Old George; the girl's mentor, Liz; and Liz's trusty guitar.

The three of them, Ratman, Old George and Liz, stared at the walls in shock. Stared at them a long time, but said nothing. They were stark and bare. The picture frames still hung there, but they were empty. Their own wide eyes were reflected back at them.

Finally, Liz carried her guitar case to the stage. She sat there on the edge, pulled out the ax, strummed it into tune. Then, with the voice of a woman older than any red-headed vixen ought to be, she began to sing. Ratman had heard this song before; Liz'd wrote it. A bouncy, lively little piece. But now, she'd turned it into a mournful dirge. 'Twas appropriate. Was a wake they were havin', sure enough.

> *My own mother, you believe she put me out*
> *Ohh, do you know what I'm talking about*
> *Lord how I've suffered by the family rules*
> *I'm serving a life sentence of the Blues*

Ratman pulled up a chair at the bar, sat across from the girl, who stood behind the counter staring at a shot glass full to the brim with whiskey.

He waited a while. Neither of them moved; neither of them said a greeting. They just sat there staring at the glass.

It came down to this moment, sure enough. They'd spent a heap a time thinkin' on the mother's destiny; but the fate of the girl, and all the temptation in the world, was sloshing around in that glass.

Finally, Old George lumbered over. He looked at the glass. Looked at Ratman. Looked at the girl. Looked back at the glass. And hurrumphed at the foolishness.

"You gonna drink that?" he demanded.

The silence stretched out. Finally, she shook her head no.

Old George picked it up, threw it back in a single gulp and slammed the glass down on the counter. Then he trundled off.

> *Ain't' nobody in this whole world care for me*
> *I'm moanin' just to easy my misery*
> *I've walked the soles off of my shoes*
> *I've serving a life sentence of the Blues*

When Ratman spoke, it was in a hoarse whisper. "*Miss* Mustang, might ya pour an old man a drink?"

She looked up, shocked. He'd called her...

She nodded, turned to the back wall and pulled down the best whiskey in the house. She picked up a glass, polished it, and poured a perfect shot with unwavering hands.

He sipped it as they shared a companionable silence, listening to Liz's song.

There was a faint knock on the door. The girl turned to answer it.

Her voice drifted back to Ratman. "I'm sorry. We're closed tonight; 's been a death in the family. Be back open tomorrow."

Lord how I've suffered by the family rules
I'm serving a life sentence of the Blues

The old man nodded to himself.

III.

1991
Tracks of a Hellhound

The sign on the outside of the door read:

> THIS CLUB IS HAUNTED.
> IF YOU'RE AFRAID OF GHOSTS,
> GO AWAY!

The sign on the inside of the door, after you paid the bouncer the four dollar cover charge said:

> 1. WHEN THE MUSIC'S PLAYING—DON'T TALK!
> (WE GOT 10 BEERS. YOU GOT 10 FINGERS.
> OUR WAITRESSES CAN COUNT.)
> 2. WHEN THE MUSIC STOPS—APPLAUD!
> 3. WHEN THE WAITRESS SERVES YOU—TIP!
> (THE EAGLE FLIES ON FRIDAY, BUT THE BILLS
> COME DUE THE FIRST OF THE MONTH!)

> WELCOME TO THE LONESOME BLUES PUB
> MUSTANG SALLY, PROPRIETOR

It was a Sunday afternoon and the music didn't start for hours yet—

Ratman took one more sniff at the morning glories that grew on the outside wall of the club—girl said she was gonna tear 'em down and put up an advert sign, but somehow, she never got 'round to doing it–before he rounded the corner of the building. He was relieved to see the big oak door open. He knew Mustang had already been at the club for hours, polishing tables, stocking the cooler, cleaning up the stage. But sometimes she didn't open the door right away, and his arthritis made it a chore to move it hisself.

He worried about the young girl, sometimes. She spent too much time at the bar. But with her mama run off and her left all alone, maybe it was better for her in here than out on the streets. She heard him shuffle in and greeted him with a smile. She had to be the only white girl on the North Side with a gold-capped tooth, but somehow, it looked right on her. Her mama hadn't approved, of course. But then, Miss Sarah wasn't here anymore. Hadn't been in a long, long time. It'd been hard on all of 'em when she left. But they got by.

"Hey Ratman, howya doin today?" She stood on her tiptoes and leaned across the bar to kiss his leathery cheek.

"Doin' a mite better now," he wheezed.

She laughed, and pulled out a bottle of Wild Turkey, filling his snifter up nearly to the rim.

Nope, the Lonesome Blues Pub wasn't a traditional bar. And Mustang wasn't a traditional bartender. She was too young legally, to enter the premises, but the woman was older than her age. She'd had a ghost for a nursemaid, had her diapers changed by some of the Blues greats, and even played guitar against a demon band from Hell–and won–but if Mustang had seen it, it'd walked in the doors of the Lonesome Blues Pub. He didn't reckon she'd been more than ten blocks away from the club in her whole life. Except maybe to ride the bus home, or go to Buddy Guy's annual birthday bash at his club in the South Loop.

"I've been waiting for you. We got a package from Dusty Joe at the Blues Historical Society. I didn't want to open it till you got here, but I did read the note."

"Well, girl, wha's it say?"

Dear Miss Mustang,
Here's a gift, one I think you'll appreciate, considering the club's history. A riddle which requires your special talents to solve.

Fondly,
Dusty Joe

She ripped the packing tape off the box and opened it, gently lifting a stack of lacquered disks out and setting them on the bar. She picked the top disk up, carefully cradling the edges.

"It's an old Bluebird label. But the rest is handwritten. Hard to read...October '35... Independent. Must be one of those demo records you could pay to have them make for you.

"RO JO... *Hellh*–I can't make out the rest of the word..." Her voice trailed off. Mustang connected the initials, date and half-scrawled title in her mind. Could it really be an unknown Robert Johnson record? Recorded thirteen months before his first San Antonio session?

It had to be a joke or a hoax, or some other artist.

There was one way to find out. "I'll get the record player out of the office."

She set the old portable player on the counter, then moved behind the bar to plug it in. The lights dimmed as the plug went into the socket. Wind began to howl through the room as Mustang picked up the top record and gently slid it out of the sleeve. A cold chill blasted across the bar as she carefully set the disk on the record player peg. The wind cried *"Noooooo"* as she turned the power on.

Mustang struggled against the buffeting wind, and shouted at no place in particular, "Jayhawk, *do* something!"

The bar's guardian ghost did something. It was as if he'd flicked the power switch in a virtual fuse box or slammed a spectral windowsill down. The lights came up, the wind died down, and the howl was reduced to a quiet moan, like a puppy whimpering in the dark.

"Thank you," Mustang said to the air.

"Now, play that thing," Ratman said.

And the eery, plaintive wail of a young Blues King cried out. "I've got to keep movin'..."

The loneliness and rejection, the evil thoughts and wanderlust that young Robert described, as much with his guitar as with his words, crept into her soul. Suddenly she understood how a body could want to run, even if it had no place to go and didn't know what it was running from.

It was as if the spirit of Robert Johnson had reached through the speaker and wrapped his cold dead hands around her heart. When the last despairing notes faded away, Mustang found herself crying. Her heart broke in two.

She turned away to grieve in private, and saw a man, or a specter of a man, sitting at the end of the bar. He wore a pinstripe suit, with padding that didn't quite hide his rounded shoulders, a felt hat, and a guitar hanging low down his back.

He nodded hello, then spoke soft. "I wish you hadn' gone an' done that. Ya let him loose again."

It was the spirit of Robert Johnson, Mustang knew, for he looked something like his famous "dime store" picture. Awed and honored by his presence, and remembering his fondness for whiskey, Mustang poured him a double shot of Wild Turkey, and one for herself.

This was Robert Johnson, King of all the Delta Blues Men, Father of the Chicago Blues sound, and an inspiration to countless rock and roll musicians. Mustang wondered suddenly if the spirit had ever heard Eric Clapton's version of *Crossroads* or the Rolling Stones' rendition of *Love in Vain*. She wondered if he'd like them.

She watched in fascination as he drank a ghostly image of his drink. The glass itself stayed on the counter, but when he set his drink back down, the whiskey levels matched.

When he had wiped his lips with a white handkerchief, he spoke again. "Them records weren't meant to be played. They was Bob's protection."

"Set who loose? Protection from what?" she asked.

"The hellhound, girl."

Somewhere out on Halsted Street, a hound bayed with a voice that was two parts hunger, one part frustration, and an equal measure of blamed meanness.

Ratman looked to the window. "I guess that'd be him, now." Mustang jumped when her friend spoke; she'd forgotten he was here. But that was Ratman's way, to drift into the shadows, and watch, unnoticed, seeing all. Dealing with hordes and hellfires with the same calm and maddeningly slow way.

He shuffled to the door and put his frail back to it, inching the massive wood frame closed.

"What are you doing? We open in an hour, and you're going to hurt yourself. Stop that!"

Ratman paused in his efforts to wheeze out an answer to her. "Mustang, you don't open your door to evil spirits. You done forgot what happened last time we had one of those in here?"

Mustang hadn't forgotten. She hurried around the counter and put her back to the door, then hung a Closed sign in the window and pulled the shade.

"Now what do we do?"

Robert answered, "We drinks whiskey and waits for him."

Ratman nodded at his wisdom.

Mustang said, "And then what?"

"Best way to deal with a recal'itrant hound is to face him down and show him who's master," Bob said.

Having never dealt with a hunting dog before, Mustang wondered just how one demonstrated this. But as she had no better ideas—now that all the doors and windows were locked—she hitched up a barstool and sipped her whiskey.

Unable to sit still, she left her perch, went around the bar and began polishing glasses. At least it kept her hands busy. Idle hands being a tool of the Devil, Mustang figured the Dark Lord had all the help he needed in the form of the hound.

Robert studied the girl as she washed the perfectly clean glass. She was just a sliver of a thing, with honey blond hair that fell round her shoulders, and a gold tooth that sparkled when she smiled. The girl looked more like a musician than a bartender, Robert thought, with her tight black pants, black silk shirt, and knee-high snakeskin boots. She even wore a mojo bag around her neck.

"You plannin' to hex someone, or you just wardin' away random spirits?"

Mustang fingered the beaded leather pouch. "It was a gift from Marvelous Marva Wright, Queen of Bourbon Street. Marva said it would ward off evil spirits and amorous musicians."

Robert chuckled evilly. "Spell musta wore out."

"Why's that?"

"I'm here, ain't I?"

Robert Johnson was known for three things in his unnaturally short life. His innovative style of playing the Blues, his womanizing ways (that likely got him murdered), and a persistent rumor he spread himself, that he'd sold his soul to the Devil in return for his musical gifts.

With that in mind, Mustang wondered which category he put himself into.

Outside, thunder crashed, and rain began drumming on

the roof.

The ludicrousness of their actions struck Mustang. They'd locked themselves up, and were going to turn away a band and business, just because some dog on Halsted Street had bayed at the moon. There were lots of dogs walked on Halsted. Mustang had thought about buying one herself, so she could join the evening parade.

"How do you know there's a hellhound after you?"

"Because you let it loose when you played the record."

"How and why, exactly, did you trap a hellhound on a record?"

Outside the hound howled again.

Robert looked at her as if to say, the howl was proof enough.

But Mustang stood her ground. She'd have her proof from the man's lips, rather than the hound's. Even if the man was a ghost.

It was only when Bob unslung his guitar and set it in his lap that Mustang realized it had been riding down his back the whole time. It hung there like a natural extension of his body. He picked at the strings softly before he spoke.

Mustang thought she recognized the melody of *Walking Blues*, but she couldn't be sure.

"It was October of '35, and we was playin' down in St. Louis. Me and Johnny Shines had been travelin' round together, you know. He was young an' still learnin', but he never tried to steal my licks, so I let him tag along. Anyways, we got the notion to hie on up to Chicago. Ain't never been, but a lot of our friends had made the trip, and cut some records. Came back speakin' highly of it. Some even stayed on a long spell.

"I was tired of St. Louis. I never could stay in one place for long. So we hitched our way north as far as we could, then caught the Illinois Central Rail and rode that into Chicago.

We pulled into town, neither of us even knowin' which neighborhoods allowed coloreds. We'd heard tell that a Bluesman could do worse than to look up Tampa Red down on the South Side. He lived above a pawn shop at 35th and State. Word was his wife would feed you a fried chicken dinner while Tampa helped you get situated musically. And that there was always a record producer hangin' around, scouting talent and hiring session men. At the worst, Tampa could tell you what corner of Maxwell Street you could set up and play at without hitchin' someone's territory."

The Maxwell Street Market had served for decades as an open air Blues audition center. Muddy Waters, Blind Lemon Jefferson and Big Bill Broonzy had all done their time playing impromptu street dances, the shoppers tossing their bags on the curb to jitterbug and Watusi. Many a Blues legend had been plucked off a Maxwell Street corner and whisked into a recording studio. Blues clubs—jook joints—in the city at that time were few and far between, but the studios churned out the "race records."

As Robert paused in his recital, their attention was drawn to the back of the bar. They heard a sound like a dog snuffling at the door; there was the crackle of fire in his breath and a tearing at the wood. The knob rattled. Mustang imagined a massive paw batting at it, the nails scratching across the brass knob. Snuffling at the keyhole. Three thumps at the door, but not a fist knocking. A tail wagging?

The noises moved away. Mustang let out her breath with a sigh. "Could it be that easy?"

"He'll be back," Ratman warned.

Mustang turned accusing eyes on Robert Johnson. He shifted uncomfortably under her gaze. "You know I sold my soul to the Devil?" he asked quietly.

"I'd heard that rumor," she said.

"It ain't a rumor. I told all about it in *Crossroad Blues*."

"I've heard the song," she said. "But do you really expect me to believe you went down to the crossroads at midnight, met the Devil and sold your soul, in return for learning how to play the Blues? Wouldn't it have been easier just to take lessons from Son House or Willie Brown?"

"Not just *play* 'em. I sold my soul to be the best. Ain't never been no one played like I do. Ain't never will be. 'Sides, Son and Willie laughed at me. Said I'd never 'mount to nothin'. But I showed 'em. People remember *me*. Only reason they recall Willie Brown's name is 'cause I wrote him into a song."

"And the hound?"

"The evil spirit come early, 'fore he were supposed to. I could see 'em comin', see his shadow prowlin' round the edges of the crowd, his red eyes burnin' in the taillights of auto*mo*biles that would pass by. Most times I could keep a town or two ahead, but sometimes he'd catch up and I'd have to walk offstage and leave my money behind. But the hound kept getting closer, trickier. He was near on to us by the time we boarded the train for Chicago. Johnny didn't want to spend the money for the fare. Said we could hitch and earn money at the towns we passed through. But I knew my only salvation was to board that train. I'd sit by the window at night, peering out. I could see him runnin' beside the tracks, just as easy as you please. I never did tell Johnny 'bout the trouble I was in. I couldn'ta beared it, if he'd quit me. I figured he was safe enough. The hound had no business with him."

Mustang wondered about that. Had Johnny Shines really been safe? Was she and Ratman? Robert Johnson was a talented musician, but he was an arrogant and selfish man, who thought nothing of manipulating others for his own benefit.

This was, after all, the same man who had told a musician friend that when he went to a new town, he always made a fuss over the ugliest woman he could find; because ugly women weren't likely to have a jealous man, and it only took a little attention before they'd do anything for you. Robert Johnson had lived off a series of such conquests.

'Course, if he had stuck to those methods, he might have lived a longer life. No one knew for sure who killed him, but the second most popular story said that a woman knifed him after he spent the night coming on to her, but left with another.

The most oft repeated story said he was carrying on with the barman's wife in a Three Forks jook joint where he was playing. The barman sent over a doctored drink. Robert was so arrogant that when Sonny Boy Williamson knocked the first bottle of whiskey out of his hand and warned him never to drink from an opened bottle, it was Sonny Boy who was victim to Bob's rage. When the second bottle arrived, already opened, Bob drank it down. He passed on three days later. Unkind folks said he crawled on his hands and knees and barked like a dog before he died.

"Storytellin' works up a powerful thirst," Robert said meaningfully.

Mustang refilled his glass, then turned to put the liquor away.

"You can leave the bottle." Women hadn't been Robert Johnson's only weakness.

"What happened next?" Mustang asked.

"When we got to Chicago, I pulled Tampa Red aside and told him my trouble."

"And he knew what to do?"

"Said he'd fix it right. Eli Oberstein–knowed as the man with a suitcase full of money–if he liked ya enough, he'd have you sign a contract and pay ya right there on the spot. Anyways, he was at Tampa's house that night. I played for him there in Tampa's living room, and Eli liked my sound, so he was willin' to arrange a test session for me on the Bluebird label. Eli wasn't too keen on the idea of a midnight recordin' session, but since it was a test, an independent recordin', I paid him for the privilege. And since they didn't have to hire any session men to accompany me, we finally talked Eli into it. Tampa just winked at me, when we got a handshake on the agreement. We wouldn't be tellin' Eli that none of his studio 'x'cutives was gonna hear the recordings. Cause those records weren't ever to be played."

He looked at Mustang resentfully.

"Why didn't you destroy them, then? You leave a record sitting around, somebody's gonna play it."

"I knows it," Robert said wearily. "But we couldn't destroy the records. That would break the spell."

"What happened at the session?"

He poured himself another drink before he continued. "Bluebird had their studio in the Webster Hotel at that time."

Mustang nodded. "The hotel's still in business. It's not far from here."

"This was a real rootsy tootsy part of town, back then. Some of Bluebird's bigger acts would record late into the night if things were going well. Eli said I could piggyback on the end of one of those sessions. Memphis Minnie and her husband Kansas Joe McCoy were recordin' that night. Memphis Minnie was a fine lookin' woman, and I never did know a gal to play guitar like that. It ain't really womanly, but Lord, she could play. She always recorded with her husband at the time. When she got tired of the way they played, she'd find herself a new husband. She was one cracker of a woman!"

Mustang grinned. "She still is."

"Anyways, Tampa told me how fix it with the recordin', but to be discreet-like, not to let on to the studio men that I was doing anything but cuttin' some demos. I said the things he wrote down for me to say, as they screwed the lacquered disk down to the turntable. Tuned my guitar special, played a certain way, with a special slide he'd doctored, you know. Tapped special rhythms with my foot as I played, and it worked, just like Tampa said."

Mustang looked skeptical.

Ratman spoke up. "No surprise that Tampa Red had the knowledge. There's people say you have to sell your soul to the Devil to play the Blues. It's the Devil's music and you can't play it otherwise. If'n that's true, then it only makes sense that they'd been workin' on ways to avoid timely payment of the debt."

Outside the storm seemed to howl in agreement. Thunder boomed and lightning struck nearby. In the flash of light, Mustang thought she saw the silhouette of a hound staring in the window.

"Ratman! Move away from the window!" she shouted, her voice cracking.

Ratman eased himself off the barstool, picked up his drink, and ambled toward the back of the room, with a slowness so deliberate Mustang wanted to rush over, pick the old man up and carry him to safety.

"No need to panic, Miss Mustang. We knew he'd be back," the old man said soothingly.

Mustang knew it was nights like this that had made her mother leave. And caused Mustang to stay. Spirits were drawn to the club, and Mustang was drawn to the spirits.

But that didn't mean she wasn't frightened, and that her fear didn't increase, when the hound howled *inside* the club, and an invisible hound's wet footprints started tracking across the floor. The size of an old seventy-eight record and just as heavily grooved, they started at the front door and stalked along the aisle toward the barstool where Robert Johnson sat.

The air seemed to shimmer above the footprints. If the illusion was any indication, the beast was huge. He'd be able to walk up to the bar and lay his chin on the counter. A growl rumbled through the room.

"Now would be a good time to show him who's master," Mustang said.

"Yes, I believe it would," Robert said. "Trouble is, I never owned a huntin' dog."

"Music's not been good to the dog. Maybe you could play

something," Ratman suggested.

Mustang noticed that his voice had just a hint of worriedness in it.

In a slow, smooth moment, Robert unslung his guitar and began to quietly tune it.

"I really don't think a sour note is going to matter at this moment," Mustang said, silently cursing her cracking voice.

Robert strummed a tentative chord, then began to pluck the bass line on the bottom string, while picking a simple melody on the strings above. Bending the string and shivering his hand, Robert Johnson didn't need a slide to make the strings talk back.

When the Blues knocked on my door, out the back I ran
When the Blues knocked on my door, out the back I ran
You know that he done caught me,
'Cause the Blues walk like a man

The beast set to whining by the end of the first line; and it didn't take much to imagine the dog tucking its tale between its legs and slinking out the door. No footprints marked its retreat, but the whining and jostling of barstools showed his path clear enough.

You can run, you can hide,
You can catch a Greyhound and ride
Well, you can run, you can hide,
You can catch a Greyhound and ride
But you know you can't outrun him,
Those Blues stay right at your side

The hound was gone by the end of the second verse, but Robert kept playing, whether to drive the hound farther away, or just to show off, Mustang wasn't sure. Either way, she was glad. She knew every song Robert Johnson ever recorded. This one wasn't among them. The mythical thirtieth song. In his short career, the man had only recorded twenty-nine. To Blues musicians, finding a thirtieth was like a quest for the Holy Grail.

You can offer him your money, your woman or your home
You can offer him your money, your woman or your home
But nothing you can do to make the Blues leave you alone

Mmmhmmmm, Well...

When the Blues come calling, walking like a man
So when the Blues come calling, walking like a man
Open up that door boy, put out your right hand

With a flourish, Robert plucked the last note, then slapped the palm of his hand across the strings to still their voice.

Mustang was breathless. And the pounding of her heart couldn't be blamed on a hellhound. "That's nice. *Real* nice."

Robert grinned at her, slyly. He knew the effect his music had on women. White or black, dead or alive, some things didn't change.

He pushed his hat back on his head, sidled up to the bar, and said, "Little girl, little girl, ya know I could write a song for you." Mustang blushed and tried to find a way to break the mood. She turned to Ratman for help, but Ratman was no longer there.

A quick search of the office, back hall and bathrooms turned up no one. To add to her worries, something was thumping on her front door. Storm, hellhound or customer? Mustang couldn't be sure. And she was in no mood to go to the window and find out.

She swore revenge on the spirit of Robert Johnson, if he'd been lying about just who the hellhound would hurt. She wasn't exactly sure how to hurt a ghost, but if anything happened to Ratman, well...she'd been around enough ghosts, that she knew she could find a way.

With the savage screaming of the storm and an evil spirit stalking 'round her door, who could blame her for jumping when the back door slammed open and Ratman staggered in?

"You nearly scared the life out of me! Where have you been?"

Ratman closed the door and bolted it, shrugged out of his overcoat and shook the rain from the drooping brim of his felt hat, then patted his pockets for a cigarette, coaxing the damp roll to a smoky life, before he answered her.

Mustang didn't repeat the question. It would do no good.

He answered, finally, "I went for suh-plies." He dug into his pants pocket and pulled out a square tin can and held it up for inspection.

Mustang read the label:

Doctor Pryor's Alleged Hot Foot Powder
for burning or sprinkling
manufactured by Japo Oriental Incense Company
Chicago, IL

"You've got to be kidding," she said.

Robert Johnson spoke up. "Old Bob can tell ya, it works, girl. I wrote about it in—"

"Yeah, I know," Mustang said wearily. "I've heard *all* your records, all right?"

Bob preened at the compliment, and Ratman started pulling cans of hot foot powder out of his other pockets. There were more than a dozen of them lined up on the bar when he finished.

"I take it you have a plan to go with these," Mustang said. He did.

The plan was simple. They'd sprinkle hot foot powder all along the floor, open the door and lure the hellhound in. Then play music at it. The idea was that between the powder burns and the beast's fear of Robert Johnson's music, they'd drive the dog away long enough for Bob to get a good head start on running.

Mustang didn't think much of the plan, but she didn't have a better one.

One thing bothered her though. From the lyrics of Bob's song, Mustang had never been sure whether the woman in question had sprinkled hot foot powder around his door to keep the wanderin' man from straying, or to drive out a no good man who'd been hanging 'round too long. She hoped it wasn't an important distinction.

With a final sip of Wild Turkey, for courage, she and Ratman began shaking a liberal coat of the powder along the floor.

"This stuff will be murder to sweep up," she grumbled, as she straightened up to replace her empty can.

"Juz hope it ain't mixed with somebody's blood 'for we're through," Ratman said darkly.

Mustang turned and looked at Robert Johnson, hunched over the bar, brooding deep in his drink. She wondered if ghosts could bleed.

They'd left a narrow border clear around the edges of the room, and Mustang tiptoed along this path. She threw the door open wide, then took up her post behind the bar. She knew the open door was all the invitation an evil spirit needed to come on in. Ready or not.

Still, the sudden appearance of the hellhound at the threshold shook her with surprise. They could see him this time. Four feet tall and seven feet long. And ugly as sin. His eyes burned with hellfire, as he turned his massive head to look around the room.

And then he leapt. Flying half way across the room, he landed on a tabletop. The barstools circling it clattered to the floor. The table rocked dangerously from side to side, but the hellhound was undisturbed.

His coat was coarse as steel wool, and black as the heart of Cain. He opened his massive jaws and growled, and the bottles rattled on the shelves. His breath was as foul as the Chicago stockyards. Sizzling strings of slather fell to the floor, mixing with the powder to form a lumpy paste.

Mustang judged the distance between the door and the table, and the table to the stage, and saw the fatal flaw in their plan. No one had realized the damned dog could fly.

Robert Johnson stood in the spotlight on the stage. His jacket and hat hung on a mike stand. His guitar down his back. Mustang thought it a damned silly way to hold a guitar.

Before she could catch her breath, the hound leapt again. But Jayhawk, the guardian ghost, or the simple dynamics of physics, interceded. The table toppled and the hound fell to the floor. He scrambled to his feet, shook himself, and lunged for the stage.

Still the powder had no effect.

A hare's breath before the dog reached him, Bob made a jump himself and took off down the aisle the way the hound had come.

The hound's long body didn't fit well on the stage, and equipment went flying as he turned around in pursuit. Mustang ducked behind the bar as Bob and the dog began a deadly game that was one part ring-around-the-rosy, and two parts keep away.

Ratman shouted, "Play, Bob! Play!"

Mustang realized she'd never heard Ratman shout before. She scrambled out of her hiding place and waved her hands wildly, shouting out something that was a cross between a banshee's cry and one of Ella Fitzgerald's scat phrases. She hoped to distract the hound long enough for Robert to get set up in a safe place.

He jumped into the bleachers, the section of the bar raised up a step. They were the best seats in the house. The wood railing and support beams also provided extra shelter for him. There wasn't a clear leap for the hound.

As Robert played the opening riff of *Hellhound on my Trail*, the dog charged. Robert backpedaled but kept playing, even when he rammed his back into a table. The hound continued to stalk him, the heat of his breath burning the musician's skin.

It was the same song that had locked the creature up sixty years ago, but it had lost its power over him.

They say that you can only summon a particular demon once. After that, you have no power over him. Perhaps that was true for locking one up, too.

The hellhound had the man cornered. It leapt, fangs bared, aimed for Bob's throat. But the musician slipped under the wooden rail, running for his life.

"Everybody to the stage!" Ratman hollered.

"Then what, old man?" Robert asked, panting, breathless from the chase.

"Dunno," Ratman said, shrugging. "Just seemed like it would be easier to defend the high ground. *You* got any ideas?"

"Done run out," Bob admitted.

While the hound was busy trying to untangle himself from a knot of barstools and table legs, Mustang charged the stage. This time Mustang wasn't waiting on the men to come up with another half-assed solution. She knew the answer. She had the plan.

There was magic in Robert Johnson's music. Mustang had seen it before, when she and Ratman drove off the Devil and his demon band by playing *Sweet Home Chicago*.

The Blues had changed since the musician first locked up the immortal creature. Robert Johnson's sound had given birth to Chicago Blues, but there were two important differences between the father and his child. Chicago Blues wasn't played by one wandering musician. To play Chicago Blues, it took a band, and that band had to plug in.

Mustang dashed up the stage stairs and grabbed the house guitar—the beatup, black and white Fender that was home to Jayhawk. Mustang knew she'd have his help as she played.

And she knew the magic song. It had come in to being as she

tried to learn Johnson's *Hellhound on my Trail* and *Crossroad Blues*, back when she was twelve years old, and had gotten the verses confused. Over the years, she'd added additional verses, until it evolved into a damned fine song. Ratman called it *An Homage to Bob*. Mustang called it *Hellhound Blues*.

Even though she was sharing the stage with the greatest Bluesman of all time, or at least the spirit of the greatest Bluesman of all time, Mustang was going to play lead. And she wasn't afraid at all.

She vamped on an opening riff and motioned to Ratman to pull out his harp. When Robert and Ratman had lined up behind her on the melody, she launched into the verse.

Babe, you sprinkled hot foot powder, all around my door
Babe, you sprinkled hot foot powder, all around my door
Then you wondered, what I was leavin' for

The hound stood still in his tracks.

When they reached the chorus, she let Robert Johnson fill in the riffs. He pulled out a switchblade, flicked it open and used the dull edge of the blade as a slide to make the strings whine.

Out of the corner of her eye, Mustang studied his technique. She was afraid if she was too obvious in her interest, Bob would leave the stage, hellhound or not. He'd done more to protect his unique style. Mustang knew of no other guitarist who could sound like two people playing when he was the only man in the room.

She launched into the second verse.

Goin' to the highway, Blues fallin' down like hail
Goin' to the highway, Blues fallin' down like hail
One road leads to my baby, the other to jail

The hound whimpered and fell to his haunches, then laid down on the floor, hiding his head between his paws.

When they came to the chorus, Bob whipped out the switchblade again. Two could play at that game. Mustang knew how to play slide guitar, too. She reached for a dead beer bottle, abandoned that afternoon by the rehearsing band. She grabbed it by the neck and smashed it against the side of the piano, then slipped her third finger into the neck and caressed the strings with the glass. The jagged edges flickered in the spotlight.

Gotta keep ramblin, Blues fallin' down like a storm of hail
Gotta keep ramblin, Blues, mmmmm fall like hail
Gotta keep movin, there's a hellhound on my trail

Now Robert was singing along, parroting back the second line to her first.

The hound began to howl, singing to the band, the world, and his Master, of his pain.

Mustang turned and gave a nod to Ratman. He stepped to the mike and poured all the suffering he'd seen in his seventy-some years into his rusty harmonica.

Water fell from Mustang's eyes.

The hound struggled to his feet and Mustang saw smoke rising from his pads. The powder had worked after all.

Standin' on the highway, Lord knows I can't be saved
Standin' on the highway, Lord knows I can't be saved
One road lead to the bright lights, the other down to my grave

The hound howled again, and Mustang's heart shattered for his pain. But it was a battle for the immortal soul of the greatest Bluesman who ever lived. He was arrogant and manipulative and sometimes downright mean. But his music was Redemption. Mustang thought she could hear the very souls in Hell sighing at their song.

That mean old wind's arising,
Leaves tremblin', fall right off the tree
Mean old wind's arisin', leaves tremblin' off the tree
As the Lord's my witness, the Devil's comin' after me

A mist formed around the hound, and Mustang thought she saw two arms tenderly lift the dog and carry him away.

Hear the hounds a bayin', but I can't go on
I hear the hounds a bayin', but I can't go on
'Cause every day been darkness, honey, since you been gone

They shared a victory toast of Wild Turkey, then Mustang watched her hero shrug into his coat.

"You don't have to leave, you could stay here, you know."

"I thank you kindly for that. But there's two reasons I can't take you up on a temptin' offer. First, Hell's got more than one hound, and they'd come lookin' for me here."

He smiled sadly.

"And the second reason?" Mustang asked softly.

He held up his foot. Black smoke curled from the sole of his shoe.

"Hot foot powder works on men as well as hounds," he said. "The spell done hit me. I got *Ramblin' On My Mind*." He set his hat more firmly on his head, and slung his rider low down on his back.

As he was about to step over the threshold, Mustang stopped him one more time. "Robert, how did you really die?"

"They was a woman involved." He stared long at her. "When Bob gets in trouble, they always is..."

And then he slipped into the night.

Rider=Guitar.

Oct. 31st, 1999
Chicago

You might have noticed, we skipped some stuff in there. It was two long years between my mama walking out and Robert Johnson walking in.

It wasn't easy after Mama left, though maybe I pretended it was. Me and Ratman and the club just about didn't make it. Lots of times. Cops shut us down four times in the first month, on account of my age. We finally figured out who we had to pay off to stay open. By the second time I missed payroll, half the staff had quit. The beer distributors and the bands all raised their prices the minute Mama was gone. The IRS nearly took the club 'cause I didn't know nothin' about filing quarterly taxes. And somewhere in there, I lost the apartment; couldn't meet the bills on both places. I put a cot in the office, but more often than not, I slept on the bar.

Don't get me wrong; I ain't whining and I'm not making excuses. I brought more than a few problems down on myself. I had a chip on my shoulder and a coal in my heart. And wax built up in my ears; I couldn't hear nobody's advice.

But somehow, we got by.

And maybe someday I'll tell you some of those tales; like the time I got into a cat fight with one of the musician's girlfriends at a South Side club, or the time the ghosts strung a thief up in the rafters, or the time Old George died and came back. Came back alive, I mean, after his dying was my fault. But see, they weren't my proudest moments. I did some awful things, and had some awful things done to me. But this here's my story, and I don't much want those tales told.

Did I mention that once the protective eye of Mama hawk was gone, the men – musicians, patrons, cops and kids, tourists, regulars, didn't make no matter – they figured this sweet young thing was fair romantic game.

Come to think of it, maybe I will tell you that tale...

Sincerely,
Mustang Sally

IV.

1996
Damned Fool Man

Jimmy "That's *Mr. Blues* to You" Jones had just kicked off the second set with a Detroit-tinged version of his song, *Dreamy Eyed Girl*, when the trouble started. I shoulda known it was coming; there'd been signs all night long.

You're a dreamy eyed girl, baby,
Don't do nothing fast
You're a dreamy eyed girl, baby,
Don't do nothing fast
When you bend the mattress springs,
Ya know how to make it last

For one thing, Jayhawk had been jumpy all night.

The regulars were used to the ghost bussing tables; the dirty glasses and empty bottles floating slowly through the air, just above their heads. And the first-time visitors? The sign on the front door said, "This Club is Haunted. If You're Afraid of Ghosts, Go Away!" So they'd been warned.

You're a dreamy eyed girl, baby,
Looks like you asleep all the time
You're a dreamy eyed girl, baby,
Looks like you asleep all the time
When you close those peepers tight,
Hope it's me you got in mind

If the first-time visitors were scared 'cause most places that claimed to be haunted didn't have such *visible* manifestations, or real ones even, well, that was their problem. My problem was tonight the place was packed, my second bartender had called in sick, I had a jumpy ghost, and trouble was brewing in the air.

Mr. Blues sneezed during a guitar solo. Just what I needed, a band with a cold, to pass it to everybody, staff and patrons alike. He quickly wiped his nose on his pocket handkerchief, then stepped back up to the mike.

> *You're a dreamy eyed girl, baby,*
> *Drive men crazy on the street*
> *You're a dreamy eyed girl, baby,*
> *Drive men crazy on the street*
> *But nobody will love you like me,*
> *No man you meet*

Normally, bartending alone wasn't a problem. Jayhawk would pour shots when it got busy, and shots made up about half our business. But tonight, he didn't have the control to handle the bottles; he was even dropping empty glasses—some on people's heads. I heard a yelp and a "Watch it!" followed by the crash of another glass. We'd go through a case of crystal tonight if Jayhawk kept up at this rate.

"Mustang! What the hell's wrong with your ghost tonight?" I sighed and turned to the old man. He was one of the felt-hat, gold-toothed regulars. He had the look and manner of one of the itinerant Bluesmen, but to my knowledge, he'd never picked up an instrument. "Junior, you know damn well he isn't *my* ghost. And you been hangin' 'round here long enough to know that when Jayhawk's jumpy, trouble's steppin' in the door. So, drink up and get out, or order down and stick around."

"Hit me," the old man said, nodding at his snifter with the tip of his battered felt hat.

I knew Junior wasn't goin' anywhere—he'd stayed through many a night when the specters overshadowed the show on the bandstand.

> *You're a dreamy eyed girl, baby,*
> *Men's hearts littered at your feet*

You're a dreamy eyed girl, baby,
Men's hearts littered at your feet
My heart's all shriveled up,
Since you kicked me out in the street

Truth be told, I didn't really mind if there was a little trouble while this band was on the stand. It'd serve him right; at thirty-two, Jimmy "That's Mr. Blues to You" Jones was a baby by Blues standards, good-looking, smooth-talking, dressed with flash, flashed the cash, and had about eight hands that never stopped moving, especially when they were close to a woman. In his vocabulary, "No!" meant "Talk sweet to me, sugar...and I might."

As owner of the club, I could decide who was in and who was out of the scheduling rotation, but Mr. Blues had a new release out getting national airplay, and his father, a legend in Chicago, used to play here at the club for drinks, back in the days when Mama had first opened the place up and was struggling to make ends meet. I figured my family owed the Jones family some time on stage when it could do the family name–and family coffers–some good.

Love to pluck those eyes out, baby,
Let 'em dream away in an alkyhol jar
Love to pluck those eyes out, baby,
Let 'em dream away in an alkyhol jar
Your dreamy eyes on my dresser,
You know your heart wouldn't be far

Family debt or not, what Mr. Blues was singing was not a traditional Blues lyric, and was in poor taste, even by Blues club standards. I knew for damned sure this wasn't on the new album. I stepped to the end of the bar, which brought me just two table lengths from the front of the stage. That didn't mean I had a clear view, though. The floor was packed with dancers, who'd all lost their groove after the last lyric. The white kids were still bouncing, trying to get back in the rhythm. I say white kids, 'cause that's all there was out there. It was way too early for the black folks to start dancing. But white kids? They'll dance to anything. I should know, being one of 'em.

Got your eyes on my dresser,
Your heart on my bathroom sink
Got your eyes on my dresser,
Your heart on my bathroom sink
Your kidneys in my crisper drawer,
What would the neighbors think?

The Blues can be violent sometimes, but it's usually just shooting a lover that's done you wrong. A shotgun, a pistol, a quick knife fight, or a hangin', once in a while a little poison, maybe, but the Blues isn't graphically violent–that's left to Rap. I'd been listening to the Blues every night for all twenty-five years of my life, and I'd never heard a dismemberment song before. Can't say I was glad to be enlightened.

I motioned to Ratman to spell me behind the bar. I wanted the booze covered, in case I had to go talk to the boys on the bandstand. Ratman was getting older, though he'd seemed old for as long as I could remember. Still, he was there waiting on the step every afternoon when I opened, and he walked me home every night when I closed. He wheezed when he tried to talk, 'bout choked when he tried to laugh, and walked with a limp after he'd been sitting too long. But he'd saved my hide a couple hundred times; from demon bands, roving hands, angry drunks, kids on junk, and from the slavering jaws of a hellhound or two–'course in both cases the hellhounds had been after someone else. But Ratman, he got rid of 'em, just the same.

Got your liver in a pickle brine,
Your toes all mixed up with cream
Got your liver in a pickle brine,
Your toes all mixed up with cream
If my mother ever saw this,
Ya know that she would scream

"He's playin' a mighty peculiar song, Miss Mustang," Ratman wheezed.

"Ever heard anything like it?" I asked.

He shook his head, dislodging his hat. "Nope, nope...now wait a minute."

He crooked a finger at his buddy, who was lurking at the end of the bar trying to eavesdrop on what we were saying. I should have known to call him into the conference to begin with. Ratman and Old George were closer than two peas in a pod. They were black and withered with age, too tough to chew and too bitter for most folks' tastes, but they were all I had on my plate.

"Old George, that song there remember you of anything?" Ratman wheezed.

Old George perked up, a gold tooth shining through his grin. "Yessir." He took his sweet time taking a sip of whiskey before he said more. He was enjoying his audience. Like we don't let him talk to his heart's content most every night. Finally, he swallowed, gurgled and said, "'Course it do. Don't you bemember Old Bloody Fingers McKrackin? Called him that 'cause his hands 'uz always tinted red. Police broke in to a South Side club and 'rested him. Said they found the decapacitated bodies of a hundred wimmins in his crawl space."

"De-ca–what?" I asked.

"They 'uz all cut up," Old George snapped. "Anyways, as I was sayin', afore I was so rudely interrupted by girl-childs who don't know their vocabulary, he used to sing them dark lyrics–they didn't call him 'Bloody' jez for his dirty hands. He 'uz known to sing about drippin' body parts and all sorts of bodily goos. I only heard him play the one time. He opened up with *The Burned-Up Body Autopsy Blues*. Song went on for twenty minutes, walkin' ya right through ever step of the cuttin', and the texture of the crispy skin, and how it felt peeling it back, and how the body fat had all melted and run into little pools. By th' time the song was over, half the audience had lost their supper or fainted dead away. 'Tweren't a pretty sight–nor smell. He 'nounced his next number was ta be *Girl, Your Liver Tastes So Fine (In a Sauce of Red Wine)*, but I didn't stay for no more." The old man shivered.

For once his ghost stories were creeping his ownself out, instead of my patrons. I felt smug about that. Then I saw him grin. Damned fool was enjoying this.

Those pretty little finger tips
Are resting on sponge cake in a custard goo
Those pretty little finger tips

Are resting on sponge cake in a custard goo
But when you got a hungry heart,
What's a poor man to do?

"That 'bout sounds like one of hisns lyrics–ya reckin Mr. Bones be channeling the spirit of Old Bloody Fingers?" Ratman asked.

"'Spose it's possible. Lord knows he couldn't come back in his own body, after what his mama had done to it. Paid that mortician half her life savings to do it–it bein' a special order and all. She alwus said it was worth every cent, jez for the peace of mind."

His words were loaded, he was waiting for us to drag the story out of him. Normally, I'd go along for the ride. But something–I don't know what–told me I'd better pay close attention to the next verse of the song. Maybe it was the shit-eating grin on Mr. Blues's face. Maybe it was just the general direction the song had been heading. Or maybe it was the spirits in the club shouting a psychic warning in a pitch only my sixth sense could hear. Whatever it was, I turned to face the band, and stared Mr. Blues right in the eyes. Those eyes, that were normally coffee-brown and full of arrogance, were shot full of red sparks and glowing like hellfire. A deep growl came out of his throat and he sang...

Squeezed your brain into a Jello mold,
Ya know the temporal lobe took the brunt
Squeezed your brain into a Jello mold,
Ya know the temporal lobe took the brunt
But that ain't nothin, compared,
To what I did to your–

"That's enough!" I shouted. I pulled the plug, blacking out the stage sound system, and quickly turned up the stereo. The break was coming early, but the band wasn't going on again until we got a few things straightened out.

"Blue," raunchy songs, filled with double entendres, sly sexual references and naughty innuendo were a staple on the Blues scene, and a lot of times the euphemisms weren't very euphemistic. I'd seen sailors blush at some the more creative verses of *They Call Me Dirty May* and *Meet Me With Your Black*

Drawers On. But Jimmy "That's Mr. Blues to You" had crossed the line. It weren't from Hell, but there was fire shooting out of my eyes, too, as I marched toward the stage.

"Miss Mustang!" Ratman shouted.

I whirled around, ready to vent some of that steam on him.

"You might need this," he said, and tossed me my mojo bag. I flipped the leather lace over my head, letting the pouch hang down on my chest, and swung back toward the band. I'd seen enough strange and awful things to ever scorn a little magical protection. I plowed through the kids still cluttering up the dance floor and climbed the steps to the stage. Fists on hips and fire in my eyes, I shouted, "What the HELL do you think you're doing? Your pa and my ma may have been friends, but I won't allow that sort of shit in here! You got that, MISTER Blues?"

He wolf-whistled, licked his lips and hissed, "Baby you're so hot, you'd evaporate the WET spot!"

"Get out. Now. You'll never play here again." I wasn't shouting anymore. I didn't have to. I'd gone way past that shouting, all hot and fiery mad stage; I was at cold fury now. Without another word, I turned and marched back down the steps, pausing only long enough to pull the plug on the nearest amp–to make sure the band got the message–and went back to my bar.

Mr. Blues sneezed, and a harsh wind howled through the club. That was some powerful sneeze! A coincidence–but it amused me to think it wasn't. The lights flickered, and I thought I saw shadows and awful shapes scrabble across the walls. When the lights came back up, they had a rose-colored cast.

"Aw c'mon, honey, we was just makin' love to ya," Mr. Blues whined from the stage.

The drummer, known only as Butterknife, nodded eagerly. "We didn't mean no disrespect, Miss Mustang," he whimpered. I could have sworn he was panting–and not from the heat of the club.

Just then the stereo started playing Muddy Waters's *I Just Want to Make Love to You.* I turned around to hit the eject button, only to find Jayhawk had rearranged the sound-level indicator lights to form a heart shape. I wasn't surprised he was messing with the lights on the stereo; he'd done that as long as I could remember; playing ghostly baby-sitter, keeping me amused with the trick. But he'd never done the heart thing before, not even on Valentine's Day, or the night I brought in my first date. This new trick had me worried.

By the time I'd turned back around, the drummer had almost climbed over the bar, to get close to me. Laying halfway across the wooden slab, like some snake trying to escape his cage, he hissed—okay, maybe he was trying for a sultry growl, but it sounded like a hiss to me.

"Baby, they call me the Butterknife, 'cause I'll cover you with my creamy goodness and slip it in so smooth—"

"I don't have time for this!" I yelped and nearly ran for the other end of the bar.

Out of the frying pan...

At the corner of the bar was Yoshi, a Japanese college kid who'd been hanging around the club ever since the semester started. He drank hot tea spiced with gin, and usually did his homework before the first set started. I let him spread his books out until the crowd got thick.

He'd never hit on me before—and most of the college boys try it at least once. But now he had a weird look in his eyes; like embarrassment and passion were warring for control. His lips were moving in a silent sort of blubbering. He sneezed, then all of the sudden he dropped down on one knee—so hard he might have cracked his kneecap—and started singing, *"I got the my baby's gone, got to be strong, but you look so fine, can't get you off my mind, lovesick Blues."* 'Course, since he was on the other side of the bar, I couldn't see nothing but the one hand flung up in the air. His voice floated up to me, though, and that was bad enough.

I heard a sneeze behind me, and found Old George had come behind the bar. He was doing this knee-bend, bouncy walk, hiking his elbows up with each bounce. It took me a moment to realize this was meant to be a sexy, prowling kind of dance. And then he sang. Old George shouldn't sing, either.

"Got the lovesick Blues, feel it down in my shoes—Right down to the bunions, baby!—'Cause I can't have you!" He reached his arms toward me and puckered his lips up.

I was backed all the way up against the booze, so there was no escape that way. I hoisted myself up on the cooler, and swung myself over the bar. That might have been a mistake. Behind the bar I only had to fend off the amorous attentions of Old George. His lips may be wrinkled, his breath may be foul, and his stories are invariably dirty. But he was harmless, compared to the flock of men out on the floor. Half of them were down on their knees serenading me–and they were the half that shouldn't never sing–and the other half were lurching toward me like zombies, arms outstretched, lips puckered up and love on their mind.

It was no comfort that the women in the club weren't sneezing, and didn't seem to have suddenly come over all hot and bothered in love with me. They were hot and bothered *at* me, but it was the mad kind. The *Girl, I ought to claw your eyes out* kind. Like I'd done this.

So far, the women were only getting physical with their men, but the pulled arms, face slaps, curses and kicks weren't dampening the ardor of my club full of drippy-nosed suitors. I heard half a dozen sneezes behind me, and I took off running; looking for the cavalry, sanctuary, or a man with a strong immune system and a good idea. I found Ratman bent double, crouching so low he was standing under a table, instead of beside it.

"Ratman!" I gasped. "What's goin' down here, and how do we stop it?"

He gave me an apologetic smile and wheezed. "Honey, I'm not gonna be much good to you this time. Got to confess, I've got some unnatural thoughts clouding up my brain, you being a youngun I nearly raised, and all. It ain't right, but there you go."

I felt myself fly backward.

A handsome, young business exec who'd been coming in regular every Tuesday, and for whom I'd been indulging a few naughty fantasies of my own, had pulled me into his arms and was now pouring his heart out in a song. *"Nighttime is the right time, to be with the one you love, ba-by..."*

I struggled out of his grasp and clawed my way back to Ratman. "You've got to have some idea why every man in the bar has suddenly been overcome with lust with me," I pleaded.

His eyes apologized, and his lips sang,
Got a fever baby, ragin' in my brain
I look at you and I feel a pain
Want you so bad you know it hurts (deep down inside, baby!)
When you talk to me, make me feel like dirt
Don't know what I'll do
I got the lovesick Blues

His eyes brightened, liked he'd suddenly had a good idea. He nodded and sang, "*You know what to do.*"

And I did. They all had the Lovesick Blues. And the only way to cure the Blues is to sing; sing till they slip right out your soul. I knew just the song that'd do it. A song of my own creation, one I'd been working on to vent my frustration about my lack of a social life that didn't involve me taking money after the transaction. One that vented my frustration that even though I'd been running this club for seven years, and my mama had run it for eighteen before me, I was still treated like a circus freak for being the wrong gender. Women in the Blues are supposed to be cocktail waitresses or singers, not club owners or musicians. Least that's what way too many men who'd walked through my life had told me.

The band followed me up as I climbed the stage, showing their appreciation of my various attributes with an improvised vamp.

> *Meet me in those red satin, crotchless,*
> *Little white lace, in just the right place*
> *Black see-through nothings*
> *Cause baby, your body does things, to me*

> *I'm the one above you*
> *Can't WAIT to love you*
> *Baby, your body does things to me*

I blushed. I'm not much good at being coy, so the blush was real. I never had the time or the teacher in the ways of feminine wiles, though I'd watched some of the neighborhood prostitutes and college coeds ply their trade. I smiled prettily, having learned that much, picked up Jayhawk's guitar, kicked the amp up to eleven to drown out the boys, and laid down the basic Chicago beat—made famous by Muddy Waters's *I'm a Man*—and began to sing...

> *There's too many men in my kitchen, (bah-Bahhh-ba BUMP)*
> *Waitin' for coffee and eggs (bah-Bahhh-ba BUMP)*
> *I can't get to the stove,*

Around last night's empty kegs
Too many men in my house, boy—
What's a poor girl to do?

I saw a woman in the crowd stand up and shout, "Tell 'em, girlfriend!" She was waving one fist in the air, and hanging on to her man with the other. He was trying to crawl his way to the stage.

I got men lined up in the hallway,
Complainin' the hot water's all gone
I got men lined up in the hallway,
Sharin' two to a towel, and then some
Too many men in this house, boy—
What's a poor girl to do?

Butterknife started laying down the beat for me on the drums. Mr. Blues shot him a dirty look, but not even the Lovesick Blues can overcome that basic, primal, Blues beat.

Too many men for comfort in my parlor,
Waitin' to court with me
Too many men in my parlor, girl
All wanting time alone with me
Too many men in this house, boy—
What's a poor girl to do?

Jimmy "That's Mr. Blues to You" Jones thought he could shut my song down with a little musical voodoo. He grabbed a mike and whanged away on his guitar.

You're a Black Magic woman
Want to love you day and night
You're a Black Magic woman
Lick ever' inch of yo' skin, make you feel all right

He was wrong; his voodoo couldn't shut me down. 'Cause I was singing from the heart. This club was my proverbial house, and the problem was real enough; too many men, and ain't none of them the right kind.

There's too many men in my living room,
Drinking beer and watching TV
There's too many men in my living room,
Bettin' on every game they see
Too many men in this house, boy—
But what's a poor girl to do?

I saw the neighborhood bookie and a couple of husbands shake their heads, like they were shaking off a bad hangover, then slink out the door after that verse. The women were all grinning and shouting out encouragement. The men were all looking hangdog.

There's a whole band of men in the basement,
Trying to serenade me
I've got a rock and roll band in the basement
Playing their instruments all out of key!
There's too many men in this house—
What's a poor girl to do?

At that, the bassman and harp player slunk off the stage. Butterknife was still pounding the drums and grinning like a fool. I guess he figured he'd gotten in good with the woman he was after. Mr. Blues was glaring daggers into me. The rose-colored light was sort of wavering about the room, hovering, floating like a cloud. Where it hung, the men were all moony. Where it had cleared, there were only sheepish grins, embarrassed mugs, or red faces—whether from a slap or a blush, I didn't know. But I knew how to sweep that love-dust cloud out.

But don't you just know my bedroom's empty,
Not a single man in sight
Not a single man has crossed the door of my bedroom
To near on a fortnight
There's too many men in this house, now!
And not a ONE knows how to treat a girl right!

Butterknife and me, we finished with a flourish, and the room was clean. No rose-colored lights. No sneezes. No smoochy, grabbing, octopus-armed, lovey-dovey men. Not toward me, anyway. And the rest of the women in the club weren't having none of it neither, when their men turned on the let's kiss and make up routine.

Finishing a song that's been well-received by the audience–be they demons from Hell, spell-struck zombies, or a plain, old regular-folks audience–is a rush more powerful than any drug I know. It 'bout lifts you off your feet, makes your head float in the air, and gives your body the shakes. It's more addicting than cocaine and dulls the senses to anything that's happening around you; ain't nothing can compare to what's going on inside your head. I don't know how long it was before the laughter penetrated my buzz. It was a belly laugh that'd been goin' on for sometime.

I focused my eyes and saw Junior sittin' at a table just to the left of the bandstand, slapping his knee and roaring so loud he might spit out a lung.

"Hot damn! Miss Mustang, I do believe that's the best show you OR your mama ever done put on!"

I grinned at the old man. "Glad you liked it...I'll see if we can't get the ghost to sneeze your way next time. Let 'em all chase you."

His eyes twinkled. "Believe that'd be all right–if'n it was the women chasin' me, ya understand." He cackled.

Ghostly trouble made for a good show–if you were a spectator. It wasn't so fun if you were responsible for exorcising the spirits and keeping your patrons safe. Just 'cause they were fun to watch, didn't mean ghosts 'n' spirits were always safe to be around. But this night hadn't turned out too bad. We'd get another write-up in the *Spooky Spectator* and maybe even *Blues Scene* and *Living Blues*. So, all's well that ends well. Or so I thought...

...until I heard Mr. Blues snarl in a dark and deep and demon-filled voice, "Surely you didn't think that little piece of musical fluff would drive me away? It might work on the tourists, but little girl, I'm Bloody Fingers McKrackin. I was playin' the Blues when they was red-hot, dirty, and ain't no white folks allowed. I've EATEN better wimmins than you–usually in a curry sauce. Helps tenderize the tough parts."

He sniggered and leered and took two menacing steps

toward me. I thought he was gonna grab me, but instead, he snatched up his guitar.

The band slipped into their places, shakin' like they felt the Devil's claws scrapin' down their backs, and maybe they did. Mr. Blues to You/Bloody Fingers McKrackin windmilled his arm and struck a dark and minor and chill-filled chord that seemed to bounce across the room and turn everything it touched to ice. And then he sang...

I'll tell you a tale—it isn't very nice
It'll turn your blood as cold as ice
Freeze your veins, and stop your heart
So cold CPR can't give it a start
It's a tale you'll always remember
The ballad of Bloody Fingers

The nightmare started on a wintery night
A pretty young girl had just put out the light
Climbed into bed, her covers so warm
Folded her hands and prayed to the Lord
But no Heavenly hand could reach as quick
As Old Bloody Fingers gave his knife a flick

This girl wasn't as pure as snow
She did some things that her mother didn't know
By day Bloody Fingers was a music man
She'd go to hear him play in the band
She'd giv'n him, then taken back, her heart
Now Bloody Fingers was gonna cut it apart

The knife sank deep and she gave a scream
He twisted it to see it gleam
Light slowly dimmed in her big brown eyes
She gave one final mewling cry
Warm and red running down his hands
Mr. Bloody Fingers felt like a new man

He loved this girl, no matter what you think
To keep their love alive, he needed a link
Someway to bind her, keep her soul

They'd be together forever more
Her spirit was quickly fading away
So, he said, "I guess I'll have to eat her today."

He started with that pretty nose
Planned to work his way down to her toes
After just a few bites he said, "It's kind of bland
I'll take her to the kitchen for a helping hand."
Added a little macaroni and some tomato sauce
That's what he served for the very first course

Her liver he tied up in twine
Marinated it in a little red wine
Let it roast for a couple hours
While he rolled her fingers and toes in flour
Baked them in to a proper pie
Topped it with ice cream, my, oh my

"I'll saute her ovaries with onions and cream
Lungs I'll put in the crock pot to steam
Her stomach will make a fine sausage sack
For her rump ground up with body fat."
He wasn't really a very good cook
But what he didn't know, he found in cookbooks

He cried a tear with every bite
But some of the dishes were quite a delight
I'll tell you some of his favorite recipes
You can try them yourself, if you please
For Kidneys Au Gratin chop them up fine
And saute them first in a cup of red wine...

I grabbed a mike and yelled over the music, "How *long* is this damned song?"

That kind of threw him, and for just a moment, he spoke in Mr. Blues's voice, "There were one hundred and seven verses, last time I counted."

"I think we get the idea." Okay, so maybe it's not a good idea to be sarcastic to the ghost of a mass murdering cannibal, but I'd rather die by the kitchen knife than be bludgeoned to death through the ears by a song that long.

Mr. Bloody Fingers flung his guitar away. That wasn't a good sign. He seemed to grow another three or four feet taller and his arms seemed to stretch like they could reach across the room.

"I've learned some things since I cooked my first wimmin. Not only do I have some lovely new recipes to try, I've learned a few surgical techniques that'll let me keep you alive as we work our way through the courses. We're gonna spend an eternity together–at least, it'll feel that way!"

I squeezed my eyes shut as I felt his claws curl around my arms. I opened them back up after I heard a sizzling sound and a yelp. Bloody was standing there shaking his hands, trying to cool the burning flesh of his palms that was still sending little tendrils of smoke into the air.

I looked down at my arms, they were as honky-girl lily-white as ever.

He snarled and lunged at me. His arms wrapped around me in a bear hug, and then they burst into flame.

I was untouched, except for the smell of his burning flesh.

He hopped around the stage, pounding his arms against his sides to smother the flames out.

I heard Ratman crow, "Lookit your mojo bag!"

I looked down and saw the leather pouch was doing a shimmy, twisting back and forth on its leather twine. God bless Marvelous Marva Wright. The Queen of Bourbon Street had given me this mojo bag; told me it warded off evil spirits and amorous musicians, and Old Bloody Fingers fell into both categories. I'd have to find out which voodoo priestess she'd used and send in a *big* order.

So I figured it was all over–I'd cured all the other guys in the club, and I had powerful gris-gris that protected me from Bloody–but ya know, my timing had been off all night.

First thing that happened was all the doors in the club slammed shut. In fact, I heard about six doors slam shut, and the club only has two. Dunno what that meant; maybe it was the psychic passages the ghosts came through slamming shut, too, so nobody, spook or spectator, was getting out tonight. Whatever it was, I didn't take it as a good sign.

"Maybe I can't have you, but, there's a whole bevy of tasty, tender morsels in here. And I mean to eat them, one by one. You're welcome to join me, of course. A good meal should never be eaten alone."

He jumped off the stage and began prowling through the aisles, stopping before each woman to poke her ribs and pinch her biceps. Amidst the screams of terror and protest, I heard him muttering to himself, "Too much muscle–she'll be stringy...Too much fat, won't do for anything but bacon...A bit on the old side–meat will need a lot of tenderizing..."

I hurried down the steps after him. "The club doesn't have a kitchen, and you said yourself, without some special preparation, flesh tastes pretty bland. So why don't you just give it up as a lost cause?" I was trying to reason with him. All right, it's never worked on a ghost before, but there has to be a first time. Unfortunately, this wasn't it.

"With candles, a few papers–your monthly schedules will do–and a metal sink, I think we can improvise a grill. The booze will serve as seasonings, and I can always send one of the boys out to the convenience store just down the block for a bit of flour, egg, and what not. I'll take the limited amenities as a challenge–you'll be amazed at the tastes we can whip up on a barbeque."

He selected Doreen, one of my brand-new waitresses. She'd just finished training on Tuesday. She was working full-time nights and going to school by day, and somehow raising a baby girl at the same time.

He dragged her toward the stage, pulled a power cord out of the amp and used it to truss her up like a turkey. At least, he was trying to. She was putting up a good fight. A couple guys at the nearest table rushed him. He whiplashed his head around to face them, and flames shot out of his eyes. Out of nowhere, the howling wind came back again, picked the men up and slammed them against the far wall. Smart folks were cowering under their tables, hoping not to be noticed. Panicked ones were crushed up against the doors, trying to pound them down or break the locks. With no success.

I know I should have been scared. But as I watched Old Bloody Fingers hogtie Doreen, something in me snapped. You see, I was responsible. I was the one who ran this club, who put up with the ghosts, who didn't have 'em all exorcised or burn down the place. It was my fault a young, single mom was about to be eaten by the channeled spirit of a cannibalistic, serial-killer Bluesman. I don't take shit from the customers: tourists, drunks or college kids. I don't take shit from hotshot bands. And I wasn't about to take this shit from a ghost. Eating my customers was out of line.

Mojo bags are good, but music's the most powerful magic I know. And to cast Chicago Blues magic, I needed help. 'Cause Chicago Blues has to be played by an electric band.

We usually have some musicians lurking around the club, hoping they'd be invited to sit in for a number or two. I scanned the crowd, but it was early, and as luck would have it, the gang hadn't shown up yet. I couldn't use Mr. Blues's band–they were under Bloody Fingers's spell...

Well, the old men might be rusty, but they knew how to play. "Ratman, Junior, Old George, to the stage, please."

Ratman had already pulled out his rusty harp and was blowing some warm-up riffs. He waited at the foot of the stairs till I could come down and help him up. Old George followed close behind, and shook his fist at the bass player till the kid handed his instrument over. I knew it'd been years since Old George had played–a nerve problem had crippled his hands so bad he couldn't hardly feel the strings. But he still knew where all the notes were.

Junior just stood there protesting. "But Miss Mustang, I don't play!"

"Junior, you been hangin' out in this club every night for the last ten years. In all that time, you had to pick up something. Drums ain't hard. Just hit 'em on the beat. You *can* keep a beat, can't you?"

He just nodded. He looked like he wanted to say more, but my face was tellin' him I wasn't in a mind to hear excuses. He picked up the drumsticks. Butterknife was giving me a kicked-puppy look. I shoved him off the stage.

I pointed to three girls hiding under one of the front tables. "You, you, and you. Come sing backup."

The girl closest stuck her head out. "I don't really feel like singing."

"Feel like dying?"

She shook her head no.

"Then come sing."

Without another word, the three crawled out and climbed the stage. It was two black women and a white one, all in short black dresses. Classic. And precisely what we needed. We'd be invoking the gods of voodoo and Blues–the same thing, really–and the rituals, the makeup of the band, had to be perfect.

I jumped back down off the stage and grabbed my guitar from behind the bar. There were several already on stage, but I didn't want to use them, for a variety of reasons.

Bloody Fingers was still fussing with the knots on Doreen. I kicked his guitar off the stage. I didn't dare touch it with anything other than my boot. Too much black and evil magic in there. Bloody looked up and snarled, but went back to his work. Guess he figured we couldn't hurt him. We'd see about that.

There was another guitar on stage–the house guitar. The ghost's guitar. I spoke to the air. "Jayhawk, you gotta play with me. If you want a place to live after tonight." I held my breath and waited. Jayhawk had never taken on physical form in all the twenty-five years of my life. He'd pour drinks, bus tables, throw some wind around, make the lights flash; do all the things a poltergeist might think of in a Blues club. But he'd never materialized before. I wasn't sure he could. But I needed a rhythm guitarist, and he was the only one in the house. Besides, you need a specter to fight an evil spirit.

I held my breath, and slowly a silver-blue image wavered into view. The edges were fuzzy. The legs weren't there at all. And there was a gaping hole in his gut where he'd impaled himself on a mike stand; that had caused his death. But there was a head, a chest and arms; all the body parts you needed to play a guitar. With uncertain, see-through fingers, he picked up his ax and slung the strap around his neck. For a brief moment, we looked into each other's eyes. There was so much I wanted to say to him. So much I wanted to ask. But now wasn't the time. Maybe it never would be.

He grinned. He'd been a handsome man. A cocky, arrogant, lady's man. I could tell from his smile. I let that cocky smile tap open my own deep keg of anger at *that* kind of man. You know the kind I mean. God's gift to women. Slick as grease. Polished white teeth. A mouth full of lies. A man like Jayhawk. A man like "That's *Mr. Blues* to You." A man like Old Bloody Fingers. They were all different degrees of the same kind of dude; the kind that won't take *No* for an answer.

I called out, "Key of E, and make it bounce," then jammed out the first chord. I set the pace, letting the band fall in behind me, pick up the rhythms, get a feel for their instruments, again. And while they warmed up, I vamped. Just a little talk with the girls in the club. "Girls, are you as *sick* as I am of *that* kind of man? The kind that won't take *No* for an answer, no matter how loud, hard and long you say it?"

"YOU KNOW IT!" I heard a woman shout from a corner table.

"I'm gonna tell you a tale about *that* kind of man, 'bout how he treated me, and how polite I was—I didn't want to make a scene."

"I *heard* that." The comment came from one of the backup singers. I glanced back. The girls had already figured out a few steps of choreography and were groovin' along.

"But ya know, you can grow old and spinster-gray waitin' for these fellas to take the hint."

"HELL, YOU CAN'T BUY 'EM A CLUE AT K-MART!" It came from under a table, but the woman followed the comment out.

"That's right," I said. "They're clueless in Chicago...Detroit, St. Louis. Hell, anywhere you find men, you'll find this kind. They think their shit don't stink. And they think women can't think. They think they can turn their X-ray lust eyes on us, and we'll just turn to jelly and quiver 'cause *they chose* us, and ain't we just so damned lucky?"

And then I sang...

> *I got the damned fool man won't take No for an answer Blues*
> *You know the type—dressed in a sharkskin suit*
> *Waltz right in like he owns the place*
> *Hit on all the women, now it's a disgrace*
> *I got the damned fool man won't take No for an answer Blues*

The backup singers yelled in unison, "TELL IT, SISTER!"

> *I was sitting in a club, just minding my own biz*
> *I'd come out to hear some music by my good friend Liz*

A shark came in—you know the kind I mean
Looked so fine, and one thing on his mind
Sat down beside me, and I got the Blues
I got the damned fool man won't take No for an answer Blues

I snuck a look at Ratman, and saw his eyes twinkling brighter than spotlights. He'd probably been one of those damned fool men, back when he was a young stud. But he was old enough to laugh at 'em now. I nodded for him to take a solo. He brought that harp up to his lips and blew a tune all full of laughter and mockery.

He ordered a bottle of champagne and an extra glass
Turned so all the bar could see; flashed a big wad of cash
Said, "Hey pretty baby, come home with me tonight
I know how to treat a woman right."
He smiled at me, and then I knew
I got the damned fool man won't take No for an answer Blues

I signaled a chord change and mouthed the word "vamp." When the band settled into the chord, I stepped aside and let the girls step up.

I got the damn fool man
(damn fool man!)
I got the damn fool man
(damn fool man!)
Got the damned fool man won't take No for an answer Blues

I was having so much fun I'd almost forgotten why we were performing. I turned to look at Bloody Fingers. And somehow, just at that moment, a spotlight seemed to turn itself, and pinpoint him in a bright circle of light. Ain't no kind of evil likes the light. He kinda squirmed there, like a bug stuck on a pin. And I grinned.

This man thought he was God's gift to womankind
And I was his lucky pick—at least for tonight
His hands started roamin'—you know where they were goin'
Said, "I'll make you feel, honey, I'll make you SQUEAL!"

Some man's treated me worse, but I don't know who
I got the damned fool man won't take No for an answer Blues

And then Jayhawk stepped forward...well, more like floated forward. He thrust that guitar neck out like a machine gun, and his hands blistered over the strings like a fire raging out of control. A whine of feedback poured out of the speaker—but it was controlled, in tune, it ebbed and flowed, then roared, with his guitar solo. He wasn't playing one instrument, he was playing two. And his music seemed to coalesce in the air, take on form, thin and sharp and silver, with a wicked point. That sword lunged forward and seemed to pierce Bloody Fingers right in the heart. Old Bloody Fingers clutched at the wound, and a redness seeped over his hands.

He said, "When you've had me
You won't want another man in sight
All it'll take, pretty baby, is just one night."
One arm went around my waist
The other went to a more PRIVATE place
I knew right then, what I had to do,
I had the damned fool man won't take No for an answer Blues

As I sang, my words curled out like tendrils of smoke and wrapped themselves around that evil musician's body, and when they'd trussed him up tighter than a turkey, the wisps turned into hands that grabbed the hilt of that sword, and drove it in deeper. Then twisted it.

I tried to run, but I couldn't in these high heel shoes
I slapped his face and wished he get a clue
He laughed and said, "I LIKE 'em feisty!"
I said, "How's this?" And gave him the knee-hee

Right on cue, Doreen kicked out at Bloody Fingers and connected with the Package, The Family Jewels, Big Jim and the Twins, Willie and the Poor Boys, The Meat with a Beat, His Wang, Dang and Doodle. That dangling piece of fleshy anatomy that convinces a man he's superior, that there just ain't nothing on God's green Earth that is as fine and wonderful as that flapping slab of flesh, and therefore he is completely and utterly *justified* in treating the rest of God's creatures—and most especially unmarried women—like shit. But I'm not bitter.

In short, she'd kicked his prick. And hot damn! If that didn't feel good to me! He bent double—that's what a man's gotta do, when one of Eve's descendants attacks Heaven's Gate.

When me and the rest of the girls in the club had stopped giggling, I finished the verse...

> *It wasn't nice, but he had to rue*
> *Day he gave me*
> *Th' damned fool man*
> *won't take No for an answer Blues*

The Sisters, as I'd just named the backup singers, stepped up, did a fancy little two-step, kick, twirl, and kick again, giggle, then chimed in...

> *I got the damn fool man*
> *(damn fool man!)*
> *I got the damn fool man*
> *(damn fool man!)*
> *I got the damned fool man won't take No for an answer Blues*

It was the giggling that did it. Drove Old Bloody Fingers out of Mr. Blues to You's body. 'Cause *that* kinda man, he don't like giggling—not unless it's his fingers doing the tickling. His only weak spot, other than the Package, is his ego. And it's a strong wall, but giggling will crumble it every time. I kinda felt sorry for Mr. Blues—it wasn't the most comfortable moment for him to repossess his mortal shell. But hell, Mr. Octopus-arms "'No!' means Maybe" kinda deserved it, too. A bit of cosmic justice for all the times he'd come on too strong.

And in a take back the night, take back our life, celebration of womanhood, we sang another verse, even after the evil was gone.

> *I got the damned fool man won't take No for an answer Blues*
> *You know the type—dressed in sharkskin suit*
> *Waltz right in like he owns the place*

Hit on all the women, now it's a disgrace
I got the damned fool man won't take No for an answer Blues

I know, all the menfolks out there are gonna say I'm a man-basher, or you know, *funny that way*. 'Cause that's what they 'bout always say when a woman says no to a man. Somethin' musta got programmed into their genes that tells them they are absolutely irresistible, and if a woman says no to them, it must mean she just don't like men at all. Just never 'curs to them that you just might not like him. If you need some proof I like men, well, just remember the fact there were four men up on that bandstand with me. Okay, one was a ghost, and three were knockin' on the door that's between Senior Citizen and Heaven—but that don't mean they aren't each and ev'ry one of 'em ALL MAN. And they're good men. (And yeah, if you was wondering, all four cringed when Doreen's kick connected, even the ghost.)

Problem is, all men are, at one time or another, a *damned fool man*. And damned fool mans got to be dealt with, or they get out of hand. Otherwise, they don't just go through life breaking hearts—they start cutting them out and eating them, too.

I'll tell you another thing. It's powerful hard sifting through the mashers and the Just-Friends, and the Mr.-He-Ain't-Rights to find one man that'll keep you satisfied at night.

There's only one thing I know that'll ease an aching heart when you're lying there alone and lonely in bed, all through a long, dark night, and you think he ain't never comin', Mr. Right—it's a song.

And you know, it's got to be a blues song.

V.

2000
Stranger Ev'rywhere

Ain't it hard to stumble when you've got no place to fall?
Ain't it hard to stumble when you've got no place to fall?
In this whole wide world I've got no place, no place at all
I'm a stranger here
I'm a stranger ev'ry where
I would go home but, honey, I'm a stranger there

–Traditional

I was downstairs in the cellar taking inventory on the booze when I heard the massive oak door of the club slam open. I thought I heard the plaster crack on the wall where the front door hit, but that was probably just my imagination. I sighed, set my clipboard down and headed for the stairs.

There were only three people I knew who were strong enough to slam that door open on their own. The first was Preacherman, a demon from Hell, but he hadn't visited the club in over a dozen years, and he generally made his entrance at midnight during a wild thunderstorm. The second was Doctor Damage, a WWF pro wrestler from Chicago, but he and a couple other mock-bruisers were on a goodwill envoy to Japan, doing a joint exhibition with some sumo wrestlers.

The third was Harpsicrazy. He got the moniker from the late, great, Lefty Dizz, who supposedly said after one jam session, "That boy play harp so crazy he like to burst a lung! And wouldn' that a been a mess to clean up!" Some folks just called him Harpo, like the Marx Brother, on account of him actin' crazy, whether he was playing his harmonica or not.

Harpsicrazy scared the waitresses, which meant I had to handle him. Sure enough, when I got to the top of the stairs, Harpsicrazy was alone in the bar. Jennifer had probably locked herself in the women's bathroom. Well, I couldn't really blame her.

Harpsicrazy was spinning in a quarter-circle on the barstool at the back end of the bar. Back and forth, like he was caught in a loop, or like a record stuck in a scratched groove. "I needs my bottle." The barstool squeaked as it turned. "I needs my bottle." *Squeak!* "I needs my bottle." *Squeak!* He spotted me then, but that didn't stop the repetitious movement. It did add a few words to his broken-record spiel though, and that was generally a good sign. "I needs my bottle *quick*, Miss Mustang."

I spoke as gently and nonthreateningly as I could. "Why don't you tell me what's wrong, first."

"I NEEDS my BOTTLE, Miss Mustang!"

Harpsicrazy wasn't a big man, but he had unnatural strength; he could toss any of the solid-oak, double-thick, warped-to-the-point-they'd-hardly-move doors in the club open with one hand. He was only five and a half feet tall when he stood up straight–which he didn't often–but he was all leg, and they seemed to bend in the oddest places. Harpsicrazy bobbed his head as he walked and flung out his knees. He brought to mind a pink flamingo, whose feathers had been battered and torn in a hurricane, and whose color had all faded away because he wasn't eating proper. But as often as not, he had half a hopeful grin on his face as he tried to fight through the gale-force storm that'd been his life. It was impossible to say how old he was; might have been twenty, might have been forty. He was old in spirit, and far too young in the head.

"I NEEDS my BOTTLE, Miss Mustang! I NEEDS it."

I could see the fear in his eyes, the fear that lurked just below the jagged scar above his right eye. The scar just below the eyebrow–I often wondered what kind of wound could leave a scar that nasty, yet leave the eye unhurt. The fear in his eyes was growing bigger, and there was a wildness flaring up just behind the fear.

As it does on anybody, a little alcohol relaxes Harpsicrazy. And too much makes him aggressive and crazy, like it does most folks. Only most folks' crazy can't compare to Harp's.

"All right, Harp," I said. "But you're starting early, and we have a deal. Just three drinks a night, right? You can't give me a hard-luck story later tonight and wheedle more out of me. And I don't want a scene, either. You got that?"

"I needs...I *got* it...my bottle. I needs...I *gotcha, sure*...my bottle NOW, Miss Mustang."

I set a shot glass in front of him. He cradled it in his hands, rolling it around from palm to palm, like a set of worry beads. I caught a whiff of Lysol in the air, as I turned to unlock the wooden cabinet behind the bar and pull out his private bottle. We had our ritual, even when he needed a drink at the worst moments. Especially at the worst moments. He set the glass down carefully on the bar, adjusting the positioning minutely to place it at a particular location only he knew. Then he took the bottle in both hands and slowly spun it around, peering suspiciously at the seal. He leaned forward to do this, so close that his nose almost touched the neck of the bottle and his eyes had to cross to focus.

He was peering at the black wax seal he'd put on there last time he'd been in. The black wax seal he put on every time he was in, 'cause he was afraid someone was going to poison him.

They say paranoid schizophrenics tend to have bizarre delusions, usually on a specific idea or theme. Poison was his. He thought someone was going to put arsenic in his whiskey and cyanide in his tea. He only ate cold, canned vegetables–he had to open the cans himself–and he never cooked them, for fear someone had coated his Teflon with strychnine. He even carried a bottle of Lysol with him in his coat pocket along with a rag, to meticulously clean the seat of every chair he sat on. Sometimes he cleaned every surface in sight. Hell, I'd even seen him spray Lysol on the tree out front. I counted it as a mark of trust that he hadn't poured it all over the counter in front of him. The faint odor in the air told me he'd wiped down the barstool, though.

He gave a fierce nod when he'd finished inspecting the bottle then shoved it across the counter to me. I grabbed a clean bar towel, wrapped it around the neck and twisted. I felt the wax seal break apart in my hand. I pulled the stopper out and poured an even measure into his glass. He sniffed it; then, quick as a snake, his hand darted out, he gulped the shot down and slammed the glass back down so hard I heard it crack.

"You okay, now?"

"Yup."

I heard the bathroom door creak open and I waved my hand behind my back, signaling Jennifer to stay put. This wasn't the time to introduce a new party into the conversation. "Wanna tell me what's wrong?"

"Know that cartoon where the kids play 'kick the baby'?" He didn't wait for my answer.

"It ain't funny. That's all I'll say...And another thing, they oughtna...And you know my daddy kicked me in the head—but he always did like to play football—reckon he's God's quarterback, now? He was a mean man...But momma always said sometimes God needed meanness, and that the angels could be mean when they had to...So maybe it's true...Maybe he's up there kicking things still...But they oughtna laugh about it... Kick the baby's not a fun game...No sir..." Then he stared off into space.

I stood there quietly, not wanting to startle him or set him off again. I had no idea what he was talking about. But then, I didn't watch cartoons, I hadn't known his dad, and he talked crazy at least half the time. Leastways, I always assumed it was crazy.

Harpsicrazy looked around the joint carefully—he thought he knew where he was, but sometimes that got confused in his head—he'd see places from his memory, people too, that weren't really there in front of him, and he wasn't very good at telling the difference between the real and the memories...He looked around suspiciously, 'cause it was always possible that someone was trying to trick him, trap him. But it sure seemed to be the Lonesome Blues Pub, where sometimes other folks saw people that weren't really there either, so it was okay then. And Miss Mustang, Little Miss Mustang, Mustang Sally—that song—she was named for that song that Lefty used to play. Lefty said it was a toorist song—no good Blues anymore—the Whiteys had taken all the color out of it. But then Harpsicrazy didn't see much color in anything, except when he'd "gone and gotten all excitable," as his mother used to say. Lefty didn't like playing the song–'cept here–in Lonesome Blues, on account of Miss Mustang, her being a baby and all; it calmed her when she cried. Harp wondered if he'd seen her cry, or if it was just a memory of what Lefty had told him. He never could be sure what was true and what was just hazy stuff his brain whipped up–like whip cream! "My brain's whip cream. Frothy, sweet. I'm so sweet!" he cackled to himself.

Miss Mustang–she had a gold tooth that glittered when she smiled–and that was a Black thing. And, because his color-vision was off, on account of the lobotomy, he wasn't sure if she was Black or White. She had long straight hair, that sometimes maybe glittered like the sun used to–and that was a White thing. But she had that gold tooth and those snakeskin boots and a true love of the Blues–and that was a Black thing...And yet, if he remembered right, and he was never sure that he did, Whiteys loved the Blues more than Blacks these days. Blacks on the stage–and sometimes Whites and Yellows–but Whites in the audience. Almost never Blacks. At least at the North Side clubs. No Blacks unless they were other performers, hoping to sit in, or come to see a friend, or audition maybe for the band. Harpsicrazy only went to the North Side clubs 'cause the buses ran more often there, and the bands were more likely to let him sit in and play harp, and sometimes they introduced him like he was someone special–was he one time? Maybe he was, one time–and then all the people, all the White people–maybe they were White–applauded and he felt like someone special, whether he was before or not. Whether he was before or not, the applause felt good. He felt special, for that brief moment before the applause died away. And special? Special meant normal. *Special meant normal.*

I watched Harpsicrazy slowly slip into a funk, his lips moving in a rush of silent conversation, as he cradled the whiskey bottle against his chest like a misshapen teddy bear. The bottle was his security blanket and I could trust him with it. He'd hold it all night long, but only I could pour from it. He might beg and plead for another drink after he'd had his limit, but in all the time he'd been coming in, he'd never once tried to pour his own drink. I trusted him—that far at least. Besides, I had a club to run.

I left Harpsicrazy sitting at a prime spot at the bar. It was where the high-tipping regulars sat. But I knew he'd move when the first set started, lured by the music to the seats closest to the stage.

Business in the club was two parts regulars and one part a mix of tourists and college kids from DePaul. I coddled the regulars more than most clubs would. But the tourist business was spotty and unreliable. And because half the world didn't tip in their own country, they didn't tip in the bar, either. That made for surly waitresses and hard times. Like me, and my mama before me, I only hired women who were on their own, trying to make a mostly-honest living in a tough old world. The cops called the place Miss Mustang's Home for Wayward Girls. Me, being Miss Mustang, called it the Lonesome Blues Pub.

Mama, still wearing funeral-black, had bought the fire-gutted club, remodeled it and opened it up and tragedy drawing tragedy, ghosts had flocked to it over the years. The regulars were used to it, but the tourists usually left pretty quick when they found out the sign on the front door wasn't just an advertising gimmick. I didn't blame the tourists for leaving. The ghosts had driven Mama away too. But the Lonesome Blues was my home, and the ghosts and the regulars were enough world for me.

So if you're wondering why I tolerated, maybe even indulged Harpsicrazy...well, it's not like he's the only misfit to pass through the doors of the club.

I heard the band banging on the back door, wanting to unload their equipment. At that moment I was on my knees with my hands plunged into a steaming hot bucket of Lysol and water. With suds dripping down my elbows, I didn't much care to answer the door. I hollered down the bar, "Harpsicrazy, you gonna hang out early, you gonna help. Get the door and tote for the band, okay?"

"Yes ma'am. You bet. I can carry good," Harpsicrazy assured me, with that eager-puppy bark in his voice that said he just wanted to be tolerated. It didn't take much to make Harpsicrazy happy—not yelling at him or tossing him out of the club was about all it took. I hated the world for lowering his expectations so far down he'd have to look up to see the gutter.

As he flopped by, I ducked so his legs didn't flap out and kick me. I watched to make sure he got all the locks on the door figured out right, then I gave the band a shout and went back to my scrubbing.

The boys in the band were friendly with Harpsicrazy, they razzed him the whole time he was helping them load their gear in.

"Hey Harp! You gonna blow with us tonight?" I heard Mr. Bones Jones, the keyboard player, say.

"Hell, he'll play whether we want him to or not!" Skinhead Murphy, the drummer, chortled.

"Yeah...and maybe you'll let me have a mike tonight!" Harpsicrazy said hopefully. The band laughed good-naturedly, and Harpsicrazy cackled, pleased with himself.

I had just finished mopping and was climbing to my feet when I saw a seizure start in on Harp. It was a mild one, as these things go. He shook like a willow tree in a windstorm, his arms flapping wildly, like a pelican trying to lift off. He dropped the drum case he was carrying. Skinhead gave a yell–then he realized what was going on.

In a few seconds, it was over; Harpsicrazy muttered an apology, picked up the case and, wobbly but determined, climbed the steps to the stage. All was back to normal...for now.

See, Harpsicrazy gets thunderstorms in his head. Then his brain dumps these electrical discharges that send adrenaline and fear coursing through his system. And nobody, especially not him, knew what he'd do when the fit was on him. Sometimes he just stood and shook, other times he went wild, got violent, got crazy. Those fits, combined with his tremendous strength, made him a dangerous customer. But he wasn't the most dangerous, or the most unpredictable, customer we'd ever had. And so, as long as he followed the house rules–took it easy on the alcohol, ate at least one meal a day, and went home when I told him to–I let him hang around the club. That was probably bad for business. But Lonesome Blues seemed to be the only place he really felt safe. And I knew the feeling.

> **Hitch up my buggy, saddle up my old black mare**
> **Hitch up my buggy, saddle up my black mare**
> **Goin' to find me a fair deal in this world somewhere**
> **I'm a stranger here**
> **I'm a stranger ev'ry where**
> **I would go home but honey, I'm a stranger there**

—Traditional

Mr. Bones Jones had kicked off a storming first set with *Hoochie Coochie Man*. I knew it was a sign of good things to come—'cause most bands kinda coast through that first set. Place was packed, the shots were poppin', we were servin' beer so fast I couldn't keep it cold, and there didn't seem to be any ghosts lurking around tonight. Or so I thought...until I spotted Willie Dixon floating in a sitting position just above a barstool. The woman to his left had put her purse on his lap, thinking the seat was empty.

Dixon popped in occasionally to catch a set. He'd been a talent scout, producer, arranger and standup bass player for Chess Records throughout the fifties and sixties. He might be dead, but that didn't mean he couldn't keep up with the scene. Who knows? Maybe he still scouts for one of the local labels. A whisper in a sleeping ear, a cold chill on the producer's spine...

He'd written dozens of Blues classics: *Little Red Rooster, Hoochie Coochie Man, Seventh Son, Spoonful, Back Door Man* and *Wang Dang Doodle.* He'd played with and produced all the great Chicago musicians: Muddy Waters, Howling Wolf, Koko Taylor, Little Walter, Bo Diddley, Otis Rush, Buddy Guy, even Chuck Berry. The Chicago sound had the name *Willie Dixon* stamped on it.

And Dixon had a smile stamped on his face. He oughta, the band on the stand was kicking ass with one of his tunes.

I soon realized Dixon wasn't the only ghost in the club tonight. Scrunched into a corner, hanging around with the high-tipping regulars, was Big Maceo Merriweather. Big Maceo was from an earlier generation of Bluesmen; his heyday had spanned the twenties, thirties and forties. Born in Georgia, burnished in Detroit, hit the big time in Chicago; Big Maceo was a piano player, but no one had ever accused him of "tickling" the ivories.

He played classic barrelhouse, double-fisted style. The man favored an eight-to-the-bar bassline and didn't need no amplification. He'd pound those keys so hard he'd break about three ivories a night. For post-war Blues, he'd done for piano what B.B. King had done for guitar: created a sound so new and striking it left its mark on every player who pulled the bench out after him.

I was pleased we had such auspicious guests in the club, and even more pleased they weren't causing a ruckus. From the way the folks around them were acting, I was fairly certain no one else saw them. And that was fine by me. Ever seen a tourist try to get an autograph from a ghost? It's not a pretty sight.

I was pouring a dozen-draft round, but paused to give Mr. Bones a nod of appreciation when he called Harpsicrazy up to play the last number of the set, a bouncy rendition of *Down Home Blues*. The song was always a crowd-pleaser, 'cause even if you'd never listened to the Blues in your life, you could sing off-key right along with the next person; song only had maybe fifteen words total, and the band made sure to repeat the two whole verses about six times each. So no matter how you walked in, you walked out of there knowing one whole, gen-*u*-ine Blues song by heart. (And good luck getting the repetitious tune out of your head.)

To break the words up a bit, Mr. Bones gave each of the instruments a solo. I watched Harpsicrazy shift back and forth from one foot to the other, now shuffling, now almost hopping, in his eagerness for that moment when he got to step into the spotlight.

And when that moment came, he shone brighter than any light aimed at the stage. He took the song into double-time, sluicing out a blistering run up the scales, followed by one of those long-winded vibrato slides that resembled a train whistle and made you worry he might pass out from lack of air. He bent the melody around, upside down, backward, then brought it round in a twist, right again. He mimicked each of those movements with fierce jerks of his body. His foot didn't just tap in time, it pounded on the wooden stage, the bass drum just an echo to his thumping boot. He jerked back and forth in time to the beat, bending nearly double, so fast and fierce I was afraid he'd kneecap himself and end up with a bloody nose.

"What's with him?" I heard a frat boy at the bar holler to his girlfriend.

I could relate. Harpsicrazy was having a fit–the other kind of fit–when the music took hold of him and transported him out of this miserable, mean, old world. Only the Blues did it. Fact was, we had to be careful not to put the radio on when Harp was around, 'cause any music other than the Blues would upset him. Jazz made him nervous, rock made him loud, and country made him aggressive. Classical put him to sleep–out like a light, and I didn't let anyone, drunk or otherwise, sleep on my bar. But the Blues calmed him when he was upset, soothed him when he was afraid, and transported him into another realm entirely when he was happy.

And when he was playing the Blues, in the spotlight–not just skulking around the base of the stage whispering notes into his harp and hoping neither the band nor the waitresses would make him stop–he was ecstatic. It was as close as I'd ever come to seeing someone experience a religious ecstacy. But revelations are always too good to last.

My heart felt heavy for him when the song ended; he took about five bows and climbed down off the stage. He was grinning from ear to ear from the applause and the rush and the compliments of the band, but you could see in his eyes the sadness that the moment was over too soon. Folks like Harpsicrazy ought to have more *moments* in their life.

Harpsicrazy could feel his whole body *tingle*. He was so hot the sweat seemed to sizzle as it ran down his body. He snagged his bottle off the corner of the stage, where he'd stashed it for safekeeping, then let it hang loosely by his side, swinging slightly as he walked toward the bar.

He was bouncing, adding a beat to every step as he walked, he knew it made people look at him funny–maybe they looked at him funny–but maybe they wouldn't, nah, not after he'd *played*, not after he'd burned that song up! They couldn't look at him funny now. "Don't care if they do."

Nope, this was his "happy" walk, his "Ain't I some hot shit" walk. Lefty had always said he looked like a funky stork when he walked this way. "You a funky-ass stork, man," Lefty would say, then laugh—a friendly laugh—friendly, so Harpsicrazy knew it was all right and he didn't mean no harm.

"Funky-ass me," he said, swinging his bottle up to plop on the counter. He started to slip into an empty barstool, then checked himself. "What I thinking? Ain't thinkin'. Can't forget jus' cause I feel funky." He pulled the can of Lysol out of his pocket, sprayed the seat of the barstool down, coated it till it glistened with the wet, then whipped his rag out and swabbed the leather down. "Make it shine, mama always said, 'baby boy, baby boy, make it shine, shine like the sunshine, uh-huh.'" There was a boy watching him, bright eyes staring through the gloom, a White boy—he thought he was White—dressed like they do... The room seemed to tilt, and Harpsicrazy stumbled, trying to catch his balance.

"Dude, what's your damage? They make you play and clean house, too? Hope they pay you double."

There was a smile—a smirk—a maybe-not-friendly smile on the boy's face...College boy, shouldn't talk to college boys...but that was just paranoid—his mama said so. "They ain't all out to kill you," she'd say. College boy, just want to talk to the musician. They liked talking to the musicians...Then the bar seemed to tilt back to the way it'd been before, and he was the Funky Stork again. "We jez gonna have a conversation is all," Harpsicrazy told himself, out loud, probably shouldnta said it out loud, but they'd have themselves a talk, he and this college boy—after a drink. It was time for his drink. He pulled out the barstool so he could stand right close to the bar, wrapped his arms around his bottle and grinned expectantly at Miss Mustang. But she was serving another patron. "Didn't see me," he said. "She'll look this way in a minute."

College boy looked at his bottle, too close, no reason, no good reason, to be looking at Harp's own bottle, and said:

"Gotcha own bottle there man? They allow that?"

But Harp was gonna be funky. So—funky—he say, "I've had a bottle in front of me and a frontal lobotomy—and the bottle's better, I know." And then the boy, and now his friends, laughed again, but not a friendly laugh—not like Lefty's—a laugh that made him worry...Made the voices in his head start chittering.

"Poison! He's got poison on his hand, don't let him touch you, he

*touch you it'll sink into your skin, have you crawling on the floor
and howling at the moon, then you roll over and die, maybe. Poison!
He got poison in his eyes, he stare at you too long and it'll sink into
your head like a laser beam, fry your brains to mush, leave you
dribbling on yourself and walking like a zombie who ain't got no
home. Poison! He's got poison..."*

"NO!" he shouted at the voice.

Miss Mustang was rushing over now, he musta screamed out
loud, hadn't meant to—he'd been talking to the voices, and they
could hear him inside his head without him moving his mouth,
but sometimes he forgot that when he got scared and they came
'round pestering him.

*"Miss Mustang, she's no different, she's got that deadly, South
American curare in a little bottle back there, she's gonna pour just a
drop—it only takes a drop—into your shot glass and then she won't
have to fool with you—"*

Harpsicrazy could feel the sweat pouring down his face, a
cold sweat, clammy and sticky, smelled like fear. Not like the
good sweat he'd worked up on stage, the sweat that said he'd
played hard under the lights for all the people.

*"She's no different. She's no different. SHE'S NO
DIFFERENT!"*

Finally Miss Mustang came, looking worried, looking like
she was afraid he was going to have one of his fits. Harpsicrazy
wanted to reassure Miss Mustang, but he didn't like lying to her,
and he didn't know if he was going to have a fit or what. "I
NEEDS a drink and my COINS, Miss Mustang."

He watched as she hit the no-sale button on the cash register,
heard the ching of the bell, and saw the drawer slide out. She
reached into one of the change trays and pulled out two Susan B.
Anthony dollar coins. She kept them there for him. For times
like this.

"Thank you, Miss Mustang," he said. He bent his head
sideways, then slotted a coin into each ear...Mama said he wore
the coins so much they'd stretched his ears out...He listened,
then breathed easy. He couldn't hear the voices no more. No
more. And now a drink, to calm him down, the voices always
worried him. And a drink because he'd played well, and worked
up a thirst, and he was most of the way through the night, and
this was just his second drink. It was just his second drink, wasn't

it? Yes, Miss Mustang would tell him if it'd been more. She wouldn't let him have no more. No more. And that was good, though sometimes it hurt him so. His thirst so powerful and she wouldn't let him have no more. But that was a good thing. Tough love, Mama called it. Tough love, when Daddy called it, was something else. But Miss Mustang, tough love was not too many drinks, 'cause when he'd had too many, he got crazy-like. Sometimes got violent, that's why Daddy'd given him the lobotomy. And he didn't want another one of those procedures. No sir!

"Second drink, Miss Mustang. Pour the second one now, okay?"

Miss Mustang nodded, she still looked worried, so Harpsicrazy thanked her as politely as could be, and smiled friendly at her, then sat down on the barstool next to the college boy, not even drinking the drink before he sat down. To show Miss Mustang that he was all right. Not nervous. Not fit-like. The boy that maybe still wanted to talk to him. Maybe? He did, sure enough, 'cause he was talking right now...

"So what's with the coins, man?"

"They keeps the voices away."

"Voices? You crazy, or what?"

"Nah, I'm not crazy no more. Not since the lobotomy. Not crazy no more, just HARPsicrazy." He cackled to himself. It was a good line. A line that made people laugh...But not these people.

The boy reached across Harpsicrazy's drink. No reason for him to be reaching over a man's drink. Unless he was putting poison in. Could be putting poison in! But he was just getting a bar napkin...Leaning back with a bar napkin in his hand...But was that a ripple in his drink? Boy could have dropped something in the drink. Could have...He lifted the glass up to his eyes, peering through the amber liquid, looking for a pill—sometimes Daddy used to drop pills in his drink—looking for a funny swirl of color, something that might show poison in his drink. But it was dark in the bar, too dark to see anything in there. And probably he was being paranoid. Probably. That's what Mama would say...And Miss Mustang was busy. She wouldn't want to fuss with pouring his drink out and getting another. And he didn't want to dump it out and waste his second drink...Not with just one more tonight. And a whole 'nother set, a whole 'nother hour, maybe more, before he went home.

The college boy was raising his own glass, saying "Cheers" and "Drink up" and "Aren't you thirsty?" And Harpsicrazy was thirsty, yes he was. So he raised his glass and clinked it with the college boy and said "Cheers" and "Here's to ya–and me, too," like Lefty used to say. And then he gulped down his drink, trying not to think about the poison what might be in there. Trying not to think at all.

Trying not to think about what the college boy meant when he whispered to his friends, "Let's see what voices he hears *now!*"

I saw the college kid lean over Harpsicrazy's drink. Saw something plop in the liquid.

I tried to get to him, to stop him from drinking it, but Jennifer and the bouncer had just brought up a couple dozen cases of beer from the cellar, and they were stacked in a mountain behind the bar, waiting to be put in the cooler. There was no quick and easy way over or around them. And the band was playing too loud for my yell to be heard at the other end of the bar. I prayed Harpsicrazy's natural, and maybe legitimate, paranoia would kick in and protect him. That he'd ask me to pour it out and pour him another drink. But he didn't. And all I could do was watch, as I tried to climb over those damn beer cases, as he drank the drink with shaking hands.

I saw the shimmering outline of Valerie Wellington sitting on top of the stack of beer cases, legs crossed and shaking her head. I heard that "Million Dollar" voice say, "He done got himself poisoned, again. That drug gonna mess him up." And I thought, well she should know. Her death certificate said brain aneurysm, but folks knew what caused that in a woman just thirty-one. Then her image faded away, and all hell broke loose.

It's hard to trust when the whole world treats you mean
It's hard to trust when the whole world treats you mean
I been done in by a man I never seen
I'm a stranger here
I'm a stranger ev'ry where
I would go home but, honey, I'm a stranger there

–Mustang Sally

Harpsicrazy knew he'd been poisoned when the colors came flooding back.

"Oh no! Not the rainbow! Not the rainbow!" The reds slashed across his vision like a tidal wave, and the greens oozed over his eyes, the yellows creeped in at the corners, and the purples blew in on an ill wind, with swirling fingers of silver reaching tendrils all through his sight. He looked quick at Miss Mustang, 'cause he had colors now, and he'd forgot to look last time, and sure enough, she was White, with hair the color of sunshine, and a gold tooth gleaming in her mouth–and wasn't that just the oddest mix of Black and White you ever did see! He saw Valerie Wellington sitting on top of some beer cases, and he waved at her, 'cause it'd been a long time since he'd seen her, on account of her being dead. And he figured that was about all he was gonna be able to do before the fit hit him, and he hoped he'd remember what Miss Mustang and Miss Valerie had looked like, when it was all over.

And then the thunderstorm crashed in his mind, and he felt his muscles seize up and burn like fire, then orange flames licked across his vision. He saw a face in the flames, an evil face, face that looked like his daddy's, in a white doctor's coat, all dripping with blood. But that wasn't right, Daddy hadn't given him the lobotomy. Daddy'd been in jail at the time, jailed for killing a man with his bare hands...he hadn't been in Reno when he done it, but they'd jailed him just the same...That was when Mama had read about the lobotomies, and how they'd take the violence out of a man. And she'd looked and looked for a doctor to do it for him– "'Cause we can't afford those fancy drugs." and "If we don't do something, you're gonna end up in jail or the electric chair for sure." –Finally she'd found one that'd do it, though the other doctors had said they didn't do that sort of thing no more...He said he could do it with an icepick, clean and easy, that way they wouldn't have to saw off the top of Harpsicrazy's head—he didn't want them to saw off the top of his head, 'cause then his brains would fall out, wouldn't they? Well wouldn't they?...The doctor had wrapped his fingers like a claw around the eyeball, pushed it down low in the socket, and it hurt, hurt so Harpsicrazy had moaned, but it didn't hurt like nothing compared to what came next...when that doctor had hauled back his arm with that shiny silver icepick in his hand, drove that metal spike through the top of the eye socket, right through Harpsicrazy's brain. Blood had spurted all down the doctor's coat, and was dripping down Harpsicrazy's eye, and he thought he was blind, and he thought the pain would never go away, and he felt that silver pick, slivering around *inside* his head... "Cutting the connections to the frontal lobe," the doctor said... But something had gone wrong, maybe the pick had gone crooked, or his frontal lobe had been wired differently, or something, 'cause it hadn't taken all the violence away—just pushed it down deep, in a pit, where all the colors were. And the anger and the colors all stirred about, until like a volcano, they'd get all hot and explode.

Harpsicrazy could see the fire of colors, and the doctor with his daddy's face, and that shiny silver icepick reared back in his hand, and that evil-spirit doctor laughed a hideous, wicked laugh, and swung that pick at Harpsicrazy, and he fell to his knees, howling in pain as he felt that silver hammer strike deep into his brain...

At the exact same moment Harpsicrazy screamed, all the club lights flickered off. The music played on. I scrambled for the breaker box. There was a babble of frightened voices and a high-pitched cackle. Then the lights blazed on at twice their regular strength. And Harpsicrazy was up on the bandstand.

He lifted one of the old, oversize Peavey speakers over his head; suddenly my storm-battered flamingo looked more like King Kong. He howled in a voice more beast than man, then launched the speaker into the thickest knot of the crowd, and howled again in ghastly glee as it slammed into a man's head.

People scrambled, and fell in a domino heap. Harp put his back up against the tower of speakers and sent them toppling to the floor, crushing a table and a man's leg beneath.

There was a crush of bodies at the front door. People were screaming, punching and clawing to get out. Harpsicrazy bounced the bass drum down the stage steps and laughed as it bowled folks over like walking, wobbly nine-pins. My bouncer and one of his biker buddies took advantage of the narrow aisle created by the runaway drum. They rushed the stage.

Harpsicrazy picked up a hollow-bodied Gibson guitar and swung it like Hank Aaron swinging a Louisville Slugger, aiming for the cheap seats. Bouncer took the blow full to the head. It didn't knock his noggin off, but it spun his body completely around, flinging blood and most of his teeth in a wide arc across the barroom. That was the last of the heroics.

When Harpsicrazy ran out of drums, speakers and guitars, he went after the mike stands, hurtling them like javelins through the air.

The beer cases were still in my way, and I was never going to fight my way through the crowd on the other side of the bar. So I started using the cases like stepping stones, climbing the tower of cardboard and cans, to get to the other side.

All of the sudden, Valerie's ghost appeared again, sitting on the top peak, hands on hips, and clicking her tongue. "Now girl, you been good to Harpsicrazy, and he like you. But you don't really think you gonna handle the condition his condition is in, all by your lonesome white ass, do you?"

"What do you suggest?" I asked the ghost. "I got a stampeding crowd, a bunch of injured folk and a berserker on the stage. I can't hide back here forever."

She clucked again. "Hold on to your britches. Let me get some help." Then she vanished. Again.

I ducked as a cymbal went whizzing through the air, a deadly Frisbee that could decapitate a man or cut off a hand, if you were foolish enough to try and stop it. Luckily, it hit a wooden support post, imbedding itself so deep it nearly sheered through the pole.

I didn't have time to wait for Valerie's cavalry. As far as I knew, no one was dead yet—or at least no one was dead that had been killed tonight—but that wouldn't be true for long. I climbed on top of the bar and walked the wooden plank toward the stage, wondering all the while what I could say to Harpsicrazy to keep him from killing me.

The crowd was still thick on the other side of the bar, pushing and screaming, as if that'd get 'em out quicker. I heard wood splinter, and saw one side of the doorframe rip away from the sheer force of a hundred bodies pushing on it. The back door was standing wide open, no waiting. But you had to pass by the stage, and the madman, to get to it. So it was empty. Until Lefty Dizz walked in.

Well, he more floated than walked. He took a look at Harpsicrazy, still throwing lethal projectiles–though the stage was starting to look pretty bare–then crooked a finger at me and mouthed the word "C'mere." Least that's what I thought he mouthed. He was see-through and the shadows behind him made it kinda hard to tell.

The rage and the wrongs of the world hung like a cloud of blue smoke around Harpsicrazy, clouding his thoughts and blurring his vision. But that evil doctor was out there, yes sir, out there with that shiny silver icepick. Just waiting for a chance to sneak up on Harpsicrazy, sneak up on him and finish the job, drive that silver pick into his brain–not again, no sir, not again–fix that job he'd botched the first time. "Not gonna get my other eye, no sir, other eye's why I can think at all, can't do that more'n half the time. Not gonna put that pick in my eye again." That doctor, that back-alley doctor, was out there beyond the smoke, in the shadows waiting, for a chance to rush the stage, and the orderlies would hold him down and the evil doc would grab Harp's eyeball and...NO SIR. Doctor's goons had already tried once, but Harp knew how to handle hospital orderlies on account of all the practice he'd had at the clinics. Clinic had learned never to send less than five men after Harp, all of them with tranquilizers, but back-alley goon doctor with Daddy's face didn't know, he'd only sent two and with no tranquilizers even, and Harp could handle two, handle two while slipping out of a straitjacket.

All the folk were leavin', visitin' hour must be done, they

know I escaped again so security checkin' everyone at the gate, that why they all lined up and waitin' so–Harpsicrazy didn't remember being checked back into the ward, Mama didn't like takin' him there 'cause of the money it cost, money she didn't have on account of Daddy being in jail and they still payin' the lawyers off. But sometimes the cops would take him in, into the ward–was he in the ward? He didn't remember going...and this didn't look like County–but the icepick doctor was out there, and the orderly goons had come after him...

He saw Miss Mustang walking down the hospital corridor–Miss Mustang come to see me, she ain't never done that before!–He wave at her, "Hi Miss Mustang!" She waved back, but looked all hesitant. Hospital must make her all nervous. Can't blame her, don't like 'em much myself. Don't like 'em one bit.

"OUT! WANT OUT! OUT!" He pounded on the locked and padded door of his cell, knowing he'd have to scream loud and pound hard for anybody to hear.

I had jumped down off the bar and was easing my way across the open space in front of the stage, when Harpsicrazy waved at me. For a moment I thought maybe his fit was coming to an end, but then he started attacking the back wall of the stage, the wood already splintering. While his back was turned, I rushed past, into the foyer behind the stage, where Lefty Dizz was waiting.

Lefty looked pretty good for a guy who'd been dead seven years. His sharkskin suit was creased, there was a crisp red satin handkerchief in his lapel pocket and his black felt fedora sat on his head at a jaunty angle. His Stratocaster was as beat up as ever; paint peeling, wood dented and chipped. It'd had some hard use from his upside-down, left-handed playing. And from the fact that he often played it one-handed, guitar dangling down over the edge of the stage, or hanging in front of him as he walked through the crowd, turking it up, bumping his guitar on people's heads, tabletops and doorjambs along the way. Lefty Dizz had been known as Scarecrow, and Mister Showmanship; renowned for his wild antics on and off the stage. The shit-eating grin on his face suggested things hadn't changed much in death.

"How-do, Miss Mustang," he said, bopping his hat at me.

"Been a while, Lefty," I said, trying to match him note for note for cool and nonchalance. It was a losing game, but then, it wasn't his club or life at stake.

He grinned again then ducked his head. "I know you already got a band booked, but you got Lefty Dizz in the house! Suppose me and the boys get up for a number or two?"

I stared at him. Speechless. Flabbergasted. Piss-mad and blue in the face. When the steam from my gut had boiled up to my ears and was threatening to explode out like twin whistles blaring a construction-site break-time, I opened my trap and let loose, "Harpsicrazy's gone psychotic, my club's in shambles, I got at least nine injured customers, they're probably gonna sue my ass for every dollar me and my descendants ever earn, and YOU WANNA KNOW IF IT'S A CONVENIENT TIME FOR YOU TO CUT IN ON THE BAND? YOU'RE DEAD, DAMMIT! WHY DON'T YOU GO BACK TO THE CEMETERY AND ACT LIKE A RESPECTABLE GHOST?"

He just shrugged and said, "Might calm the crazy outta Harp."

"Boys? You said 'BOYS'." I was trying to convince myself I hadn't heard right.

He gestured behind him to the four ghostly guys standing just outside the door.

They tipped their felt hats and said in unison, "Ma'am."

That damned voice, that voice that told him that everybody wanted to poison him, that voice that knew all about arsenic, and cyanide, strychnine, and deadly African fungus, that voice that said even Miss Mustang be out to get him, that voice, was still screeching in Harp's ear, goading him on. Telling him to kill the orderlies before they injected him with a lethal dose of morphine, telling him to break out of the ward before the icepick doc came back, with the tip of the pick having been dipped in Mienie-Mienie Indian bean extract from Africa—doctors traveled a lot and it wouldn't be no hardship to get that evil stuff.

"I needs my coins! Gots to have Susan save me!" Harp was digging deep in his pockets, but his Susan B. Anthony's weren't there. And then he remembered; he'd gone to the store to buy Lysol and cigarettes, but he hadn't had enough money with him, so he'd used his Susan coins. He'd had to ask Miss Mustang for the spare set–the spare set!–he reached up and felt his ears. The coins were there. "I shouldn't be hearing voices, I gots my coins in!"

They want to kill you, poison you, yes, they've got Nitrous Oxide they spray in the air, they've hidden it in their little perfume bottles. The girls, yes. And cyanide tablets. They've got them glued to the spokes of the ceiling fan, fan spread that poison with every whirly-twirl. And they've got wolfbane, the roots of wolfbane in their threads, woven into their clothes, their shirts, pants, and socks, that causes a burning and tingling, a numbness of the tongue, a dimness of vision, and a feeling so cold, like ice water running through your veins, yes... So many poisons! Creeping through the air, brushing up against you, swirling into you drink, crawling on your skin, ain't no place safe, ain't no place!

"Susan? Susan B?" Harp called, his voice quivering in his own ears. "Maybe she on vacation. Or maybe this one too loud and hurts her ears, too!" He dug into his pockets again and came up with three quarters and a nickel; his change from the drugstore. With shaking hands he slotted two quarters into his right ear, on top of the Susan dollar. That was the ear where he heard the voices the loudest. In his left ear he put the other quarter and nickel. He could hear the nickel sliding around as he moved his head.

Your daddy, dear old dad, Daddy arranged all this, he never did like you, never did, wants you dead boy, DEAD! He'll poison you, yes. Drop pellets in your soup. He'll drop pills in your drink. He'll drop rat poison in your pudding, he's done it before. He don't like you, son. Never did.

As I looked at the faces of the Bluesmen standing there, I realized this was no slouch of a backup band. Even though the neon light of half a dozen beer signs was flickering through their images, I could still make out who they were. Legends, every one. Up front was Willie Dixon carrying his standup bass–I hadn't seen him leave his table–standing side by side with Big Maceo Merriweather, cracking his knuckles, warming up his fingers to play.

Behind them was the infamous Little Walter, with a full belt of harmonicas around his waist. Little Walter had toured and recorded with Muddy Waters and Willie Dixon–so I guess I shouldn't have been surprised to see him there. He'd had as profound an influence on the Chicago harp as Muddy had on guitar, Big Maceo on piano, and Dixon on the package-deal. He was the best of the blowers. He was also an alcoholic and a high-spirited, mean-tempered man. He'd pulled a pistol on at least one of his band members when a rehearsal was going badly, he'd gotten into a knife fight on stage with Sonny Boy Williamson II, and he'd been found dead, beaten to death, in a Chicago alley in '68. I wasn't exactly delighted to have another violent psychopath in the house.

Behind him was a face I didn't know. No mystery, he was carrying drumsticks and the kit was stacked up just outside.

"Who's the skin player?" No disrespect intended, nobody remembers the Blues drummers.

He stepped forward and put out his hand. "Freddy Be-low, ma'am. Played with Little Walter, Muddy Waters, Junior Wells, Chuck Berry. I was house drummer at Chess under Dixon. Nice club you got here."

"Thank you." I suppressed a shudder and shook his hand. I shuddered 'cause I don't much care to touch ghosts; it's a weird feeling, like someone's tugging on your soul, trying to pull it out.

It was an all-star lineup, a dead-guys revival tour. I knew folks who'd give their right arm to have seen any one of these guys play–too bad Harp was in the midst of clearing the house. But then again, if Harp weren't going crazy, the All-Stars wouldn't be playing. Gotta take the good with the bad.

I looked around for Mr. Bones; professional courtesy said you checked with the bandleader before turning the stage over to another band. I didn't figure you had to let down your manners just 'cause all hell had broken loose. If we did that around here, the club would have turned into a biker bar long before now–Hell and its minions came visiting that often to the Lonesome Blues Pub.

The live band had cleared out, so I waved the dead guys to the stage and ducked as Harpsicrazy flung a drumstick like a knife. Freddy Below shouldered me out of the way and lofted a cymbal up in front of us, like some gladiator's shield. The drumstick pierced it, impaled itself two inches through the metal, and came to rest about two millimeters from Freddy's eye. From the look on his face, I guessed Freddy wasn't into the boozing, brawling and downright-deadly behavior the others had gone in for.

"Relax, son," Little Walter said. "He's out of weapons, and besides," he drew a pistol from his belt, "ain't no drumstick can hold up against a Colt .45." The man may have been a ghost, but the gun looked real.

"Put that thing away," Lefty told him, as he walked by with his guitar.

"All's I'm saying-" Little Walter started to say.

"We ain't gonna need it," Lefty insisted. Without a hint of fear, he climbed the steps of the stage, his wingtips making a clomping sound as he went. It didn't seem right that ghosts could clomp, but there you were.

I heard a *ka-CHUNNNNNNNG* come from the stage. Harpsicrazy had climbed on top of the upright piano and was crouching in the back corner.

"Miss Mustang, how 'bout getting that boy his bottle of whiskey? And mebbe a drink or two for the fellas in the band, while you at it," Lefty said.

"His whiskey bottle's what started this," I said.

"Then mebbe you better break open a new one."

I started to protest, but Lefty cut me off. "Boy done gone around the bend. Booze ain't gonna make him worse, and mebbe it'll help put him to sleep."

"I see what you mean," I said, and headed for the bar.

Ain't it hard to be living, when you got no friend alive?
Ain't it hard to be living, when you got no friend alive?
I'm going down to the river, cross o'er to the other side
I'm a stranger here
I'm a stranger ev'ry where
I would go home but, honey, I'm a stranger there

–The ghost of Lefty Dizz

The nickel had slipped out of his ear when he'd climb up the stairs and broke into the nurses' office, and now Harp could hear the voices in his left ear as loud as his right, and the shriekin' and the hollerin' and the carryin' on was 'bout to drive him out of his skull. "I'd give it up and let you have it, my skull, sure enough I would, if I knew where I could go. I'd give up my head—but you'd take my body with it, then where would old Harpsicrazy be?" The voices wouldn't be still and let a man think—a man's got to think—and he'd gotten himself in a pickle without a paddle this time, sure enough again. He'd been here before, in the nurses' office, locked himself in here before, why hadn't he remembered that, run the other way? He wasn't ever gonna find the door out of County! Mebbe it was like Hell, all a maze and no way out, just halls running on forever. But he'd been here before, locked himself in here for several hours, maybe a day. He'd found the medicines, the ones that made a body feel good. And wasn't that some of that medicine now, sitting out on the desk, pretty as you please, not under lock and key, not locked up like a bottle ought to be, and he read the label careful, didn't want none of that poison, or that drowsy medicine, or that medicine that made him feel like he was floating above his body, could look out over the clinic and see all there was to see, but couldn't move his feet to run from a fire, but this wasn't that floaty medicine, or poison or knock-out drops. This was the good stuff. The feel-good stuff. And the bottle was full. No worry that somebody might have mixed the labels, might have dumped something in there that didn't belong. He broke open the seal and upended the bottle to take a long, deep slug. Wasn't right, wasn't proper to drink out of a bottle, lessen it was a beer—that's what Mama said—but there weren't no glasses in the nurses' station, and he wasn't sure one had to mind one's table manners in County. Most folks didn't even eat at the table, got fed through a tube in their arm, and there wasn't nothin' mannerly in that.

He took another slug from the bottle, and sat down on the desk cross-legged...found he was swaying gently to the music. There wasn't music at County, not this kind, not the Blues. But there had been once, in the nurses' station...maybe the nurses liked the Blues...or had that been Mama, who'd brought her phonograph along to the clinic, the doctors had called 'cause "Old Harp had locked himself in the nurses' office and where were they gonna drink their coffee and put their purses?" But he didn't mess with no purses, he wassna thief. He just drank the medicine and danced to the music...danced to the Blues...till they coaxed him into openin' the door, 'cause Mama, and that pretty ward nurse, had promised they'd dance with him, just dance with him...he wasn't in any trouble, nah, and they wouldn't strap him down again...can't blame a man for wanting to dance just a little, hear just a little music...

There was only one amp set up, but Lefty Dizz started playing, softly picking out a haunting tune on his guitar. The stage seemed to rebuild itself around him. The few patrons who hadn't yet made it out the door drifted back in, just a step or two—within bolting distance if Harp's pitching arm got stronger—to hear the music.

The musicians were hauling their own gear, but Jayhawk was handling setup—'bout time the house ghost did something to help out tonight—floating the speakers and mike stands overhead, bumping them down gently in the proper places, electric cords snaking through the air to plug themselves in and only once getting crossed up and tangled.

Then Willie Dixon joined in, plucking a lazy bass line, like a rolling river on a Sunday afternoon. And then the snares were there, Freddy Below, with soft jazzy swirls from the brushes, so soft you didn't notice their entrance, just as if they'd always been there. Then Little Walter was *wah-wahing* on his harp, like a lonesome train whistle at midnight, long and low and blue. There wasn't no way you could fight the lull of the music.

It was working on Harpsicrazy. He wasn't throwing, or pounding, or beating, or smashing things anymore. His eyes were closed, a pensive look on his face, his body swaying oh so gently to the music. I smiled a little myself, when I realized I was swaying, too.

Big Maceo Merriweather was last to climb the stairs. Last to take his place on stage. One had to wonder what Harpsicrazy would do when his seat erupted with music. Big Maceo carefully lifted the bench out, rather than scraping it along the floor; he didn't sit at first, just sort of squatted arm's-length away from the keyboard, stretching so his fingertips could barely curl and touch the keys. He came in whisper-soft, a little trill on the high notes, a slow stroll down the bass line, and Harpsicrazy set to rocking harder–no, not harder, with more confidence, more focus, somehow.

They played soft like that for some time, before Valerie Wellington picked up a mike and sang a Blues lullaby, *Willow Weep for Me*, a Billie Holiday classic, a dreamy little number, lapping gently at the banks of the mind, lulling us all back from the cliffs of madness–at least those who hadn't stampeded out of the club, taking the door, the frame, and half the front wall with them.

Big Maceo had just hooked the leg of the piano bench with one foot, slid it toward himself and taken a seat, confident now he could play without danger (what a madman could do to a ghost, I didn't know) when Harpsicrazy lobbed both legs over the top of the piano, kicked his heels against the soundboard where the sheet music would sit and swung his legs wide, passing them through Maceo's torso with each swing. Maceo turned a little greener with each swing–I had to grin to myself–it was 'bout time a ghost got the taste of that sort of medicine. Bodies and spirits weren't meant to pass through each other like some sort of swinging door.

Harpsicrazy didn't seem to mind, he kept kicking, faster and harder, insistent now, his heels pounding a beat twice as fast as that the band was laying down.

Lefty Dizz nodded at the band. "Believe he'd like us to pick up the tempo." Then he launched into a rocking rendition of *Got My Mojo Working.*

Got my mojo workin' but it just don't work on you!

I approved wholeheartedly of the Muddy Waters tune. Blues is full of magic, both the lyrics and the music, and this song was chock full of potent hoodoo. Dixon was slapping the bass, thumping it so hard it sounded like the bass drum. Little Walter had a harp in each hand, switching keys between the chorus and the verse to deliver an indescribably complex harmony. Maceo was pounding the keyboard in a double-fisted jump that had the piano rocking back and forth. I held my breath and waited for

Harpsicrazy to slide off.

As the band chimed in on the chorus.

I got my Mojo working but it, just don't work on you!

Lefty Dizz went to work. He was gonna grandstand to a near-empty house. The band fell into a simple groove that would let him solo and soar, dance and prance, move and groove any which way he choose.

He dipped his hat to a jaunty angle, then let that guitar swing down like the pendulum of a clock just before it strikes midnight, like an ax sinking into a cord of wood, like a cleaver falling to take off a chicken's head. It was a deliberate and deadly stroke that would have cold-cocked one of my customers if there'd been any in the joint sitting near the stage. Guitar swung down, wrist jerked up, neck of that guitar started sliding sweet and wailing loud, as Lefty peacocked down the stairs, balanced on a rung of a barstool then stepped nimbly up on top the bar and pranced down the length of it–playing all the time, just that one hand, jerking that wrist up and down, the fingers forming chords, and somehow hanging on at the same time, the feedback and pressure on the strings ringing out the sound. And it was sassy and mean and full of the hottest shit in town.

Lefty danced then, a quick sort of tap dance two-step, heel and toe of those snakeskin boots clicking like castanets on the bar. Freddy Below picked up the rhythm and tossed out a new one and Lefty matched it with guitar and boot heels.

Then Harpsicrazy climbed to his feet, right there on top of the piano, his head brushing the wooden beam of the ceiling, and he crowed, he kicked his feet and flapped his elbows and crowed, a big "Cock-a-doodle-doo!"

And the music was burning fast as fire and hot as Hades and Lefty tossed the solo over to Little Walter. Little Walter was more lethal with a harmonica than he'd ever been with a Colt .45. He climbed right up on the piano with Harpsicrazy, nearly stepping on Big Maceo's fingers to do it, and Maceo, he didn't stop his double-fisted playing, and they'd better both hang on if they were gonna be prancin' on top of *his* boneyard. He made those white ivories shout, like a Sunday morning, You-KNOW-You-Sinned-the-Night-Before Revival Meeting choir.

Little Walter wailed on his harp, like a banshee calling the Illinois Central Rail into the station– "You're late and we got menfolks on that train!" He wailed and he whistled and he *wah-wahed*, and he said, "Boy, why don't you blow some!"

And out came Harpsicrazy's harmonica, he raised it to his lips to blow, and matched note for note, tone for tone, attitude for bad-ass attitude everything that Little Walter done, then he switched over and done his own. And the band followed him down, 'cause Harp's song wasn't full of the hope of new love, and all-consuming power, and sexual stallion prance that made up *Muddy's Mojo*.

Harpsicrazy's song was deep and dark and filled with terrors that'd keep you up nights, praying for salvation and thanking God for the nightlight. Filled with all those demons in the dark that'd driven man to come up with fire in the first place, and taught him to pile that kindling high, to drive 'em as deep in the forest as they could go. Filled with sharp teeth, and long claws, and red flame eyes, and silver hammers, and evil brews, and a daddy mean as the devil. His harp told a tale of heartbreak, but a spirit, a spirit there, wandering lost through the woods and nightmares and evil visions. Spirit of a good man. Spirit of redemption! Spirit of the Blues!

And Harpsicrazy was filled with the Blues, you could see it pouring into him, starting at the toes, his body quivering, shivering, glowing somehow, a golden light climbing up his legs, his body, swirling around his neck, climbing into his head through his ears, to shine like beacons out his eyes.

It's a hard old world, the road lead always down
It's a hard old world, the road lead always down
But onest in a while, a friend may come around
I'm a stranger, ev'ry where I go
When I'm feelin' strange, I pull my harp and blow
'Cause I'm a stranger here
I'm a stranger ev'ry where
I would go home but, honey, I'm a stranger there

–Harpsicrazy

I wish I could say we cured him. But truth is, life doesn't work like that. The band played nonstop for three hours–ghosts don't have to take union breaks–and they kept Harpsicrazy dancing and playing and wrapped in the music he loved, until the drug–the poison–slowly leached its way out of his system.

The cops came, long after the danger and madness had died down. The only charges I pressed were against that college boy. He was dragged out in handcuffs, hollering it wasn't fair. "The psychopath done it."

I put the word out that any patron that pressed charges against Harp would have me and the ghosts to mess with. But, if they neglected to file a complaint with the police and brought their doctor or hospital bills around, the club would pay 'em. I didn't know how that would set with my insurance agent, but I'd honor the promise somehow.

The cops wanted to arrest Harpsicrazy, or at least take him in for questioning. But the senior officer on the scene had been our neighborhood beat cop when I was growing up. He'd looked the other way when, as a girl, I'd helped Mama out in the bar. He'd always approved of Miss Mustang's Home for Wayward Girls. At Christmastime, when he was supposed to be collecting donations for the Policemen's Widows and Orphans Fund, his collection tin was usually lighter going out than it was coming in. More than a few of our waitresses over the years had come to us with desperation in their eyes but his name on their lips. Many of "his girls" worked here still. He agreed to release Harpsicrazy to my recognizance, without us having to go through the formality of seeing a judge, so long as I promised Harp would come in willingly, and in a semisane mind, if someone actually filed a complaint.

When I'd run all the officials out, Lefty Dizz, Willie Dixon, Little Walter, Freddy Below, Big Maceo Merriweather and Valerie Wellington played me a lazy, after-hours, all-worn-out-and-too-tired-to-sleep set, while Harpsicrazy snored on the bar.

He'd greeted them all, though, when the madness had trickled away. Made me cry, the way he hugged Lefty, hugged the air and his own arms, wasn't much of Lefty really there. Both Harp and Lefty were misty-eyed, missing friends too long gone–one off of the earth, the other out of his mind.

As the sun started to peek through the east of what had once been my front wall, the ghosts just faded away.

I sipped a double shot of whiskey, and dabbed at my eyes, and thought about how I'd always felt sorry for the ghosts; how hard it must be to move through the world, but not be of it. I felt a hollowness in my heart when I realized it was worse for Harp. He moved through the world, he moved among ghosts, he moved among his memories; but not in his life, his memories, or his delusions, was there any comfort. Any place he could call home.

I was left with a club broken down to its timbers, the certainty that even if I could find the money to rebuild–the club's *reputation* might not make it through this night, and a psychotic snoring on my bar.

And I was left with one more thing...

...the certainty that for Harpsicrazy, tomorrow would be just as hard as today.

EPILOGUE

When the light had crawled on shaky hands and knees halfway into the shadows that filled the bar, I picked up my whiskey bottle, my glass, and moved. I found a barstool so deep in the shadows that the light from the gaping hole in the wall wouldn't never reach, and I sat there.

A flock of pigeons flew in, all flapping wings and coos. The leader landed on the bar and strutted down the length of it to greet me. I wasn't feeling very hospitable, but I tilted my glass and splashed a little of the whiskey on the counter, in case the pigeon got thirsty. He fluttered backward with a startled look. Who knew a pigeon could make faces? But he cautiously goose-stepped closer to investigate the puddle, once I'd gone back to hunching over my drink.

The sun had risen, and dipped down behind the building across the street again, before the old man stumbled into the bar. His hands were gnarled, his suit was wrinkled, and arthritis had shrunk him smaller than a man ought to be. He tipped his felt hat back on his head, scratched his jaw and said, "Musta had a good crowd on Sat'day." His snakeskin boots clicked on the wooden boards. He shooed the pigeon away and wheezed as he climbed onto the barstool beside me. He hooked a hand around the bottle and slid it closer to him, then upended it to take a slug. He swallowed audibly, exhaled a sigh, then clomped the bottle down on the counter.

"Club alwa's did need a bigger door ta haul gear in, but iz gonna get cold come winter."

Our eyes were drawn to the tree out front. The leaves were already tinged with amber.

"Ratman, the club hasn't got any insurance, 'cept for liability. And mosta my savings went into updating the sound system last year. And new barstools. Shouldn'ta bought the barstools."

"You c'n only patch 'em up with duct tape so long," he said reasonably.

I nodded, and we sunk into a long silence.

"Where ya been?"

"Was visitin' ma sister in Clarksville. I tole ya 'fore I went."

I shrugged. "Musta forgot. Got a few things on my mind."

It was his turn for a question. I wondered which one he'd pick.

"Old George outa the hospital yet?"

"Haven't seen him. Meant to go visit yesterday." I waved a hand toward the debris.

"He gonna be put out."

"Grumpy as hell."

"Missed all the 'citement."

"Yeah, you too."

He stood up on the rungs of his barstool and stretched down the counter to grab a dirty rocks glass. He dumped the remains into a half-full pint glass, then sat back down. He pulled out the tail of his red dress shirt and polished the glass.

"There's clean ones back there. I think there's a couple that ain't broken."

"Don' wanna get up. The alkehol'll kill the germs." He poured himself a double, then topped off my drink.

"I ain't got no savin's to give ya, child," he said after a while.

"Wouldn't take it if you did, old man."

I took a slug of my whiskey, coughed when it went down wrong, then started to take another. I looked at the glass, set it back down. There's nothin' worse than a sad drunk.

The old man reached out and took my hand. We didn't look at each other, just sat there, me clinging tight to his hand.

"This is the only home I've ever known," I said at last.

The question hung in the air between us.

Ratman cleared his throat and shifted uncomfortably on his seat. I wondered if it was his arthritis or what he was about to say that made him antsy.

He took a breath so deep I thought it'd pop his lung. Then

he let it out with a whoosh.

"Ya know, I gets a card ever' Christmas from your mama."

He pulled a cell phone out of his coat pocket and put it on the bar between us.

I'd given him that cell phone, paid the bill each month. I was worried about a frail old man walking home alone from his bus stop each night. He didn't live in a very good neighborhood and couldn't afford to move. I couldn't afford to pay those phone bills now.

I nudged the phone away with my elbow. Didn't want to touch it with my hand, lest my fingers betray me.

"I get a card, too. Don't open mine, though." I tried to keep the accusation out of my voice. Didn't do a very good job, though. Drunks have a tendency to be honest.

"They're doin' right good. He's climbed up the comp'ny ranks. Got a nice house in the suburbs, a little g–." He stopped that thought. Tried again, "Got a goodly amount set aside. Yore mama asks 'bout you, first thing, ev'r year. Talks about ya. Speculates on what ya might be up to."

I didn't answer.

"She'd help you out."

"Don't reckon I want a baby sister at this point in my life. And I don't reckon I can ask for money without being friendly to him. That ain't gonna happen."

I turned my head so he wouldn't see the tears. I wanted so desperately to call my mama. I'd picked up the phone behind the bar a dozen times just today, even started to dial. Finally, I yanked the cord from the wall. That stopped the temptation, and the pesky phone calls from bands, patrons and city officials who'd heard the word.

I wanted to hear my mama's voice so much it hurt. But I couldn't call her now. Not like this. Not after I'd destroyed her club. I'd be fulfilling that man's lowest expectation of me. When I got back with Mama, it wasn't gonna be like this.

I pounded my fist on the bar, smiled grimly as I heard glasses tinkling as they bumped together. The pain that rushed up my arm felt good. Felt solid and strong, when everything else inside me felt weak.

I said, "She started with nothin' and a baby. At least I ain't got no kid."

"Got any plans?"

"Ain't got none of those, either." I reached for the bottle. "'Cept me and Mr. Beam. I guess we got us a date tonight. Reckon we'll just hang around till the landlord comes to evict us."

"He been by yet?"

"Yep. Yellin' 'bout structural damage and broken leases."

Ratman turned on his stool to face me, pulled on my elbow till I swung around to face him. His jaw was set tight and his eyebrows were hunkered down till they nearly touched his nose.

He demanded, "Ya got 'nough savin's to pay a couple months rent on the place, throw a few dollars in toward repairs?"

I shrugged. I'd been over this ground in my own head. I was resigned to my fate. "Not enough. Not enough to put this place back into any kind of shape that the inspectors would allow. I can make the rent for a few months–if I move out of my apartment and sleep here again–but then what? Get a job bartending at the Kingston Mines? Tips ain't gonna pay to rebuild this place, and I ain't got any other marketable skills."

He said gruffly, "Seems to me you got yourself a guitar."

I sighed. "You know I haven't played a full gig in years."

"I reckon your fingers still remember where the strings are, and if you studied a bit, you might even pick up a song or two."

"So I practice a bit. Then what? The band scattered years ago. It'd take weeks of rehearsal, if I could find anybody who ain't already hooked up, then where would we get gigs? Some of the local club owners might take pity on me, squeeze me into their lineup. Between 'em, maybe get a gig or two a week. At the end of the night, you split the money between the band. What are ya left with?" I sighed. "I could make more money bartending." I turned back to the bar and looked at my reflection in the dusty mirror.

The voice beside me was quiet, but insistent. "Robert Johnson didn't have no band. Neither 'id Memphis Minnie."

"Oh what?" I said. "I strike out on the road, an itinerant Bluesman, wanderin' from town to town, playing for drinks and dimes?"

"Musicians don't get paid for shit, but I reckon they make more than that."

"Nobody hires solo guitarists. Those days are gone."

"These coffee shops where the kids go, do. Some clubs'll

have a warm-up act. They'll go in for a country Blues, Delta kinda sound for that. Travel light, live cheap."

His voice got funny. "Maybe find yourself a partner. Duo is easier to pitch to a club. Cuts your money in half, but not as bad as a band."

I challenged him right back, "You volunteering to go on the road with me, old man? You and your harmonica?"

"Child, I got too old for that years ago."

"B.B. King still tours. He's older'n you...isn't he?"

"He's got himself some money. Can afford some luxuries to ease an old man's aches and pains."

I couldn't tell if he wanted to be persuaded, or if he was just yearning for something he knew he couldn't have. Me? Well, I'd never been on the road. And just now, it didn't sound romantic. Didn't sound exciting. Just sounded scary.

I'd have to give up my apartment. 'Bout everything I owned. Have to hope the club's landlord would stand by me and not rent the place out while I was gone. Have to hope the customers would come back after the club was closed so long. And what about the ghosts? Would they wait for me? Would Jayhawk?

I had nothing but shattered dreams and a club in shambles. And no faith to go on. I looked at the stage. Two guitars sat in the corner; my beat-up old acoustic next to an equally banged up electric Fender. Most clubs had their own amps. Jayhawk might enjoy the road.

I wondered if I could carry two guitars and a suitcase.

Biography

Tina Jens is a blues fanatic, frequently visiting many of the legendary Chicago clubs, including the Checkerboard Lounge, Rosa's, Kingston Mines, Buddy Guy's Legends, and Blue Chicago. But her favorite haunt is a neighborhood club right around the corner, called B.L.U.E.S., which is suspiciously similar to the Lonesome Blues Pub. She can be found loitering at the back of the bar several nights a week.

She is a two-time Bram Stoker Award nominee, and the producer of the long-running live fiction series Twilight Tales. She also edits the Twilight Tales line of anthologies. Her short stories have appeared in dozens of publications. Prior to writing fiction, she worked as a report for several Midwestern newspapers and magazines.

Born in Iowa City, and raised along the banks of the Mississippi River in Ft. Madison, IA, she has a degree in mass communication from the University of Wisconsin–Milwaukee. She moved to Chicago in 1989, where she lives with her husband, Barry; her guinea pig, Mocha; and her Japanese fighting fish, Not Dead Yet. Their condo is filled with gargoyles, teddy bears and herb plants, in approximately equal numbers.

You can visit her web page at http://www.TinaJens.com.

Recommended Listening List

The real musicians mentioned in the book are listed here, with my favorite album by each artist. I hope you'll enjoy their music, too.

Freddy Below	No solo work, but appears on many of Little Walter & Muddy Waters' records.
Barkin' Bill	Gotcha!
Big Bill Broonzy	Good Time Tonight
Jimmy Burns	Leaving Here Walking
Big Time Sarah	Blues in the Year One - D - One
Willie Dixon	I Am the Blues
Lefty Dizz	Ain't It Nice to Be Loved
Liz Mandville Greeson	Look at Me
Buddy Guy	Damn Right I Got the Blues
Jimi Hendrix	:Blues
Earl Hooker	Blue Guitar
John Lee Hooker	Mr. Lucky
Lightnin' Sam Hopkins	Texas Blues
Alberta Hunter	Amtrak Blues
Blind Lemon Jefferson	Blind Lemon Jefferson
Robert Johnson	King of the Delta Blues (remastered edition)
B.B. King	Live at Cook County Jail

Big Maceo Merriweather	The King of Chicago Blues Piano
Charley Patton	King of the Delta Blues: The Music of Charley Patton
Tampa Red	The Guitar Wizard
Koko Taylor	Two Fisted Mama
Little Walter	The Best of Little Walter
Muddy Waters	The Best of Muddy Waters
Junior Wells	Hoodoo Man Blues
Sonny Boy Williamson I (John Lee Williamson)	Sugar Mama
Sonny Boy Williamson II (Alek "Rice" Miller)	His Best
Howlin' Wolf	Rides Again
Marvelous Marva Wright	Born with the Blues
Memphis Minnie	Hoodoo Lady
Valerie Wellington	Million Dollar Baby

Selected Bibliography

The following works were invaluable in the writing of this book.

Chicago Blues: The City & the Music by Mike Rowe,
    Da Capo Press

Chicago Blues as Seen from the Inside, The Photographs of
    Raeburn Flerlage, ECW Press

Down at Theresa's...Chicago Blues, The Photographs of Marc
    PoKempner, Prestel

Beale Black & Blue: Life and Music on Black America's Main Street
    by Margaret McKee and Fed Chisenhall, Louisiana State
    University Press

Searching for Robert Johnson by Peter Guralnick, Obelisk Books

Woman with Guitar: Memphis Minnie's Blues by Paul and Beth
    Garon, Da Capo Press

*The History of the Blues: The Roots, The Music, The People from
    Charley Patton to Robert Cray* by Francis Davis,
    Hyperion Books

Nothing But the Blues: The Music and the Musicians by Lawrence
    Cohn, Abbeville Press

The Blues Makers by Samuel Charters, Da Capo Press

Encyclopedia of the Blues by Gerard Herzhaft, The University of
    Arkansas Press

Love in Vain: A Vision of Robert Johnson by Alan Greenberg,
    Da Capo Press

The following videos

Blues Masters: The Essential History of the Blues,
   Rhino Home Video Series

Legends of Bottleneck Blues Guitar, Rounder Records

*Can't you Hear the Wind Howl? The Life & Music of
   Robert Johnson*, a Peter Meyer film from Winstar

And the speakers at:

"Hellhounds on my Trail: The Afterlife of Robert Johnson" a
   conference sponsored by The Rock & Roll Hall of Fame &
   Museum's American Masters Series (Excerpts of this
   excellent conference and series of blues concerts are captured
   on the video *Hellhounds on my Trail: The Afterlife of Robert
   Johnson,* a film by Robert Mugge from Winstar)

THE BEST IN ALL-NEW NEO-NOIR, HARD-BOILED AND RETRO-PULP MYSTERY AND CRIME FICTION.

THE BIG SWITCH — A Brian Kane Mystery   Jack Bludis

Hollywood, 1951. Millionaires, moguls and movie stars dazzle in the land of dreams. Money talks, when desperate glamour girls are a dime a dozen. There's a seamy underbelly beneath the glossy veneer. Scandals lurk in every closet, sins too dark for the silver screen. It's all a sham, everything's a scam, everyone's on the make, no one's who they seem.

This is Kane's turf. Brian Kane, Hollywood P.I.

It's a standard case, as un-glamorous as they come: Hired by a mega-star's wife to catch her cheating husband with another casting-couch hopeful. Till one starlet winds up dead. Then another. When Kane's client turns out to be an imposter, and thugs are trying to scare him off, he's suddenly suspect #1 in his own case. And the body count keeps growing…

But it's personal now, and not even a vicious murderer can keep Kane from getting to the bottom of the big switch.

1-891946-10-2

AND FLESH AND BLOOD SO CHEAP — A Joe Hannibal Mystery   Wayne D. Dundee

The hero of the popular St. Martins hardcover and Dell paperbacks series is back! Hard-boiled Rockford, Illinois P.I. Joe Hannibal is at it again, this time swept up in a murderous mystery in a Wisconsin summer resort town. Deception and death lurk behind the town's idyllic façade, when a grisly murder is discovered and Hannibal knows for a fact that the confessed killer couldn't have done the deed!

It'll take two fists and a lot of guts to navigate through the tacky tourist traps, gambling dens and gin mills to get to the truth, while dangerous dames seem determined to steer Hannibal clear of the town's darkest secrets. In the end, Hannibal himself, and everyone he cares for, may be in jeopardy as he learns that murder may be the smallest crime of all in this lakeside getaway!

1-891946-16-1

> *"Mike Hammer is alive and well and operating out of Rockford, Illinois."*
> **Andrew Vachs**

WAITING FOR THE 400 — A Northwoods Noir   Kyle Marffin

Autumn 2002 Release

They found the first girl in the Chicago train station, a dime-a-dance and a quarter-for-more chippy. Suicide. A train ticket still clutched in her hand: Watersmeet, Michigan, the end of line…

400 miles north, Watersmeet station master Jess Burton wastes away in his tiny northwoods depot with big dreams of big city life, watching the high-rollers and their glamour gals hop off the train for their lakeside mansions and highbrow resorts. Till the night Nina appeared on the depot platform.

Nina…Big city beautiful and clearly marked 'property of'. The kind of dame that can turn a man's head, turn him inside out and upside down till danger doesn't matter anymore, till desire can only lead to death. Because folks are dying now, and Jess is in over his head, waiting for the 400 and the red-headed beauty to step off the train with his ticket out of town.

1-891946-14-5

NOW TRY THE FINEST IN TRADITIONAL SUPERNATURAL HORROR!

NIGHT PLAYERS   P.D. Cacek

Welcome to Las Vegas, home to glittering casinos, to high stakes, high-rollers, high priced call girls. 'Round the clock vice, where the nightlife never ends. It's the perfect place for a new-born vampire to make her home.

Meet Allison Garrett, the unluckiest gal who ever became a vampire, with an irreverently sharp tongue to go along with her sharp teeth. Meet her sidekick, Mica, a Bible-thumping street corner preacher. Both of them are on the run from the catty coven of L.A. strip-club vampire vixens they narrowly escaped from in P.D. Cacek's Stoker Award nominated debut novel Night Prayers. Hiding out in Las Vegas, Allison's now a night-shift showgirl, while Mica tries in vain to bring the good book to gamblers, crooks and hookers. And everything's as idyllic as it can be for a preacher and a vampire setting up house in sin city. Till the evil vampire that cruelly turned Allison shows up along with his bloodthirsty minions, and it'll take more than a gambler's luck to save Allison and Mica this time!

1-891946-11-0

BELL, BOOK & BEYOND — An Anthology Of Witchy Tales   Edited by P.D. Cacek

The Horror Writers Association

Stoker Award winner P.D. Cacek brings you 21 bewitching stories about wiccans, warlocks and witches, all written by the newest voices in terror: the Affiliate Members of the Horror Writers Association. From fearsome and frightening to starkly sensual and darkly humorous, each tale will cast its own sorcerous spell, leaving you anxiously looking for more from these new talents!

1-891946-09-9

"If these authors are indeed the future of horror, the genre is in good hands...If you care about where horror is headed and who's going to take us there, this fine, spooky volume is a must read."
Garret Peck, Sinister Element

"Genre fans will obtain a taste of the destined in this witchcraft anthology."
Harriet Klausner

A FACE WITHOUT A HEART —   Rick R. Reed
A Modern-Day Version Of Oscar Wilde's The Picture Of Dorian Gray

Nominated for the 2001 Spectrum Award for "Best Novel": A stunning retake on the timeless themes of guilt, forgiveness and despair in Oscar Wilde's fin de siecle classic, The Picture Of Dorian Gray. Amidst a gritty background of nihilistic urban decadence, a young man's soul is bargained away to embrace the nightmarish depths of depravity–and cold blooded murder–as his painfully beautiful holographic portrait reflects the ugly horror of each and every sin.

1-891946-08-0

"A rarity: a really well-done update that's as good as its source material."
Thomas Deja, Fangoria Magazine

"Depicting modern angst with unerring accuracy."
Reviewer's Bookwatch

MARTYRS
Edo van Belkom

250 years ago, French Jesuits erected a mission deep in the uncharted Canadian wilderness, till they were brutally murdered by a band of Mohawks. Or so the legends say.

Today St. Clair College stands near the legendary massacre site, the mission's memory now more folklore than fact. Then St. Clair professor Father Karl Desbiens and his band of eager grad students set off to locate the mission ruins. The site's discovered, artifacts are found, the mystery of the Mohawk massacre may be solved…

…Till the archeological dig accidentally unearths an old world evil. There was no 'Mohawk massacre'. A malevolent demonic power was imprisoned in the remote Canadian wilderness by the original missionaries. But now it's been unleashed. Now the nightmare will commence. Father Desbiens has his own inner demons to struggle with, his own crisis of faith to overcome. He's an unlikely martyr to the faith he already questions, but the demonic presence has invaded St. Clair college, leaving a bloody trail of horror among his students.

1-891946-13-7

WHISPERED FROM THE GRAVE
An Anthology Of Ghostly Tales

Quietly echoing in a cold graveyard's breeze, the moaning wails of the dead, whispered from the grave to mortal ears with tales of desires unfulfilled, of dark vengeance, of sorrow and forgiveness and love beyond the grave. Includes tales by Edo van Belkom, Tippi Blevins, Sue Burke, P.D. Cacek, Dominick Cancilla, Margaret L. Carter, Don D'Ammassa, D.G.K. Goldberg, Barry Hoffman, Tina Jens, Nancy Kilpatrick, Kyle Marffin, Julie Anne Parks, Rick R. Reed and David Silva.

1-891946-07-2

"A chilling collection of ghost stories…each with a unique approach to ghosts, spirits, spectres and other worldly apparitions…Pleasant nightmares."
Michael McCarty, Indigenous Fiction

"A landmark collection…I loved this anthology."
A. Andrews, True Review

"This timely work refutes the current charge that ghost stories have lost their appeal… buy this book. Read it. Rediscover what is means to be a child cowering in the dark, listening for shuffling feet…and whispers."
William P. Simmons, Folk-Tales Review

Gothique — A Vampire Novel
Kyle Marffin

International Horror Guild Award nominee Kyle Marffin takes you on a tour of the dark side of the darkwave, when a city embraces the grand opening of a new 'nightclub extraordinaire', Gothique, mecca for the disaffected Goth kids and decadent scene-makers. But a darker secret lurks behind its blacked-out doors and the true horror of the undead reaches out to ensnare the soul of a city in a nightmare of bloodshed, and something much worse than death.

1-891946-06-4

"An awfully good writer…this is a novel with wit and edge, engaging characters and sleazy ones for balance, a keen sense of melodramatic movement and a few nasty chills."
Ed Bryant, Locus Magazine

"Bloody brilliant! A white-knuckle adventure filled with plenty of chills and thrills…this book just never lets up."
M. McCarty, The IF Bookworm

Storytellers   Julie Anne Parks

A writer who once ruled the bestseller list with novels of calculating horror flees to the backwoods of North Carolina. A woman desperately fights to salvage a loveless marriage. A storyteller emerges — the keeper of the legends — to ignite passions in a dormant heart. But an ancient evil lurks in the dark woods, a malevolent spirit from a storyteller's darkest tale, possessing one weaver of tales and threatening another in a sinister and bloody battle for a desperate woman's life and for everyone's soul.

1-891946-04-8

"A macabre novel of supernatural terror, a book to be read with the lights on and the radio playing!"
Bookwatch

"A page-turner, for sure, and a remarkable debut."
Triad Style

"Genuine horror and the beauty of the Carolina wilds. It's an intoxicating blend."
Lisa DuMond, SF Site

Carmilla: The Return   Kyle Marffin

Marffin's provocative debut — nominated for a 1998 International Horror Guild Award for First Novel — is a modern day retelling of J. S. LeFanu's classic novella, Carmilla. Gothic literature's most notorious female vampire, the seductive Countess Carmilla Karnstein, stalks an unsuspecting victim through the glittery streets of Chicago to the desolate northwoods and ultimately back to her haunted Styrian homeland, glimpsing her unwritten history while replaying the events of the original with a contemporary, frightening and erotic flair.

1-891946-02-1

"A superbly written novel that honors a timeless classic and will engage the reader's imagination long after it has been finished."
The Midwest Book Review

"If you think you've read enough vampire books to last a lifetime, think again. This one's got restrained and skillful writing, a complex and believable story, gorgeous scenery, sudden jolts of violence and a thought provoking final sequence that will keep you reading until the sun comes up."
Fiona Webster, Amazon

"Marffin's clearly a talented new writer with a solid grip on the romance of blood and doomed love."
Ed Bryant, Locus Magazine

The Darkest Thirst   A Vampire Anthology

Sixteen disturbing tales of the undead's darkest thirsts for power, redemption, lust...and blood. Includes stories by Michael Arruda, Sue Burke, Edo van Belkom, Margaret L. Carter, Stirling Davenport, Robert Devereaux, D.G.K. Goldberg, Scott Goudsward, Barb Hendee, Kyle Marffin, Deborah Markus, Paul McMahon, Julie Anne Parks, Rick R. Reed, Thomas J. Strauch, and William Trotter.

1-891946-00-5

"Fans of vampire stories will relish this collection."
Bookwatch

"If solid, straight ahead vampire fiction is what you like to read, then The Darkest Thirst is your prescription."
Ed Bryant, Locus Magazine

"Definitely seek out this book."
Mehitobel Wilson, Carpe Noctem Magazine

The Kiss Of Death
An Anthology Of Vampire Stories

Sixteen writers invite you to welcome their own dark embrace with these tales of the undead, both frightening and funny, provocative and disturbing, each it's own delightfully dangerous kiss of death. Includes stories by Sandra Black, Tippi Blevins, Dominick Cancilla, Margaret L. Carter, Sukie de la Croix, Don D'Ammassa, Mia Fields, D.G.K. Goldberg, Barb Hendee, C.W. Johnson, Lynda Licina, Kyle Marffin, Deborah Markus, Christine DeLong Miller, Rick R. Reed and Kiel Stuart.

1-891946-05-6

"Whether you're looking for horror, romance or just something that will stretch your notion of 'vampire' a little bit, you can probably find it here."
Cathy Krusberg, The Vampire's Crypt

"Readable and entertaining."
Hank Wagner, Hellnotes

"The best stories add something to the literature, whether actually pushing the envelope or at least doing what all good fiction does, touching the reader's soul."
Ed Bryant, Locus

Shadow Of The Beast
Margaret L. Carter

Carter has thrilled fans of classic horror for nearly thirty years with anthologies, scholarly non-fiction and her own long running small press magazine. Here's her exciting novel debut, in which a nightmare legacy arises from a young woman's past. A vicious werewolf rampages through the dark streets of Annapolis, and the only way she can combat the monster is to surrender to the dark, violent power surging within herself. Everyone she loves is in mortal danger, her own humanity is at stake, and much more than death may await her under the shadow of the beast.

1-891946-03-X

"Suspenseful, well crafted adventures in the supernatural."
Don D'Ammassa, Science Fiction Chronicle

"Tightly written...a lot of fun to read. Recommended."
Merrimack Books

"A short, tightly-woven novel...a lot of fun to read...recommended."
Wayne Edwards, Cemetery Dance Magazine

Night Prayers
P.D. Cacek

Nominated for the prestigious Horror Writers Association Stoker Award for First Novel. A wryly witty romp introduces perpetually unlucky thirtysomething Allison, who wakes up in a seedy motel room — as a vampire without a clue about how to survive! Now reluctantly teamed up with a Bible-thumping streetcorner preacher, Allison must combat a catty coven of strip club vampire vixens, in a rollicking tour of the seamy underbelly of Los Angeles.

1-891946-01-3

"Further proof that Cacek is certainly one of horror's most important up-and-comers."
Matt Schwartz

"A gorgeous confection, a blood pudding whipped to a tasty froth."
Ed Bryant, Locus Magazine

*"A wild ride into the seamy world of the undead...
a perfect mix of helter-skelter horror and humor."*
Michael McCarty, Dark Regions/Horror Magazine